D1527262

The Whispering Sentinel

By Ruth Kyser

Scripture quotations are taken from the King James Version of the Bible.

Photo of young woman on front cover used with the permission of Anita Peppers, photographer.

Cover design by Mary C. Findley.

ISBN 9781493792795

DEDICATION

This book is in memory of my Grandma W;

A woman who instilled in me her faith in God,
her love for all growing things, and some really good recipes!

Love and miss you, Grandma!

<u>OTHER BOOKS BY RUTH KYSER:</u>

The Dove & The Raven –
A Christian Historical Romance"

"Endless Season"
A Christian Contemporary Romance

"True Cover" (Book 1 in the "True Cover" series)

"Bluecreek Ranch" (Book 2 in the "True Cover" series)

"Second Chances" (Book 3 in the "True Cover" series)

"Mattie's Heart"

"Clara's Heart"

"Laurie's Heart"

"The Healing Hills"

"Without Regrets

"A Place Called Hart's Desire"

"One Last Christmas"

Train up a child in the way he should go:
And when he is old, he will not depart from it. –
Proverbs 22:6

PROLOGUE

1856

The young woman brushed tears from her eyes and tried to concentrate on the words she painstakingly wrote. The lady of the house had been gracious enough to provide her with a quill pen and ink so she could write a few words in her diary. It might have seemed strange to the older woman when she asked for such items, but she was determined to chronicle everything that was happening.

She scratched out a few more words and sniffed as a few tears fell onto the page where she had just written. Closing the worn leather diary, she capped the ink and pulled the blanket over her and reclined on the pallet on the floor. The people here had been kind, but she was so terrified. What if they found her? What would she do then? They would make her go back—and she couldn't...wouldn't return.

The diary was still on the floor beside her. She grabbed it and quickly got up in a panic. If this was found by the wrong people, what would they do to her? She had been foolish to write it all down on paper.

Her eyes swept around the little room in dismay. There was no place to hide anything here; it was much too small. Then she saw a little opening in the wall just above the doorway and pushed her diary into the crevice. She would have to remember to retrieve it before she left this place, but at least she would be able to sleep a little better tonight knowing if they did find her and capture her, her secrets would be safe.

Curling up under the borrowed wool blanket, she prayed for the fear to go away. She was so alone and so scared. The only person she still had anymore was her Heavenly Father, and Mama had always told her He would protect her. She prayed her mama was right.

CHAPTER 1

"You did what?"

Sandy looked across the desk at her friend, Rachel Foster, and tried not to laugh at the expression on Rachel's face.

"I bought a house."

The other young woman pulled her desk chair closer. "Really? That's so exciting! Where is it—in the 'burbs of Sylvania? Or did you actually find something here in Toledo you could afford?"

Sandy didn't say anything for a moment. Rachel was going to be even more shocked by her answer to that question than to her initial news. She was having a difficult time believing where the house was located too. Sandy had never done anything this unpredictable before.

"I bought my grandmother's old house."

The seconds ticked by and Sandy could almost hear the wheels turning as she waited for her friend to process what she had just told her.

"I know what you're going to say…." Sandy began before Rachel interrupted.

"Your Grandma Baker's old house? Didn't you tell me she lived somewhere on a farm up in Michigan?"

Instead of responding, Sandy sat quietly and watched Rachel's face.

"You didn't!"

Sandy finally gave a little nod, but knew by the look on the other woman's face, she wasn't happy with her.

"When I was back in Bradford Mills settling my dad's estate, I drove by Grandma's old place and noticed a realtors' sign in the yard. I called their office and made an appointment to go see it, and once I did…."

"Are you crazy, Sandy? What are you going to do with an old farmhouse in the middle of nowhere?"

Sandy didn't have an answer—at least not one Rachel was going like. She tried to keep her voice composed.

"As a matter of fact, I'm going to live there. I've given notice on my apartment, and I'm moving to the house in two weeks, right after I sign the paperwork. It was a bank repossession, so I got it at a great price and will get immediate possession."

It was silent in the room for a moment as Rachel continued to stare at her, a glazed look frozen on her face. Sandy almost jumped out of her chair when the phone on her friend's desk rang. Rachel turned to answer it, and Sandy almost felt guilty at how thankful she was for the interruption. She had known her best friend wasn't going to be happy with this move, but she had hoped Rachel would understand her need for a significant change in her life.

As she waited for Rachel to wrap up the phone call, Sandy glanced down at her wrist-watch. She needed to get going. She'd already stayed longer than she'd planned. It was supposed to be a brief stop by Rachel's office to share her news, and the last thing she wanted to do was jeopardize her friend's job. Sandy had recently lost her own job as a marketing executive, and she didn't want anyone else to share the same fate.

She watched the other woman handle the party on the other end of the phone call with her typical panache. Rachel never failed to amaze her. She could handle the toughest client with kid gloves, and when all was said and done, they usually decided to go with whatever she suggested.

She and Rachel met right out of college and had even shared an apartment for a short time. Rachel was Sandy's opposite in coloring. Whereas Sandy had red curly, out-of-control hair, and freckles sprinkled across her nose, Rachel had flawless skin with straight blond hair, cut into layers at the chin. Her blue eyes sparkled as she looked out on the world around her, and Sandy loved the fact that Rachel could usually make her laugh no matter how bad things were in her life. And for the past month or so, things had been bad—really bad.

Rachel finished her phone conversation and hung up the phone, then turned to face Sandy again.

"Aren't you being a little irrational about all this?"

Sandy laughed a little at the look of dismay on Rachel's face, and then sobered as she realized how much this had shaken her friend. She had known all along Rachel would be upset with her moving away, and she didn't want to make light of her feelings.

"Why do you think I'm irrational?"

Even though they sat in a small private office where no one could overhear, Rachel moved closer and lowered her voice. "I mean, first your fiancé breaks off your engagement right before you send out the wedding invitations. Then you lose your job, right after your dad dies. I guess you acting this way shouldn't be surprising. It sounds as if you're trying to recapture the safety and innocence of your childhood by 'running away to Grandma's house.'"

Sandy chuckled, although she wondered how close Rachel actually was to the truth of what was going on in her head.

"Since when did you hang out a shingle, Miss Psychiatrist?" She shook her head firmly. "Rachel, it has nothing to do with any of that. I just…." Sandy struggled as she tried to clarify her thoughts. There was no way she could adequately explain her need for something different at this juncture of her life—a change, a fresh beginning. The recent happenings in her life had left her feeling overwhelmingly crushed. Hopefully, this move would give her a fresh start.

"It's not difficult to understand. The house was for sale at the right price; I need to find a new job anyway, so why not move and start over?"

"I still think you're making a terrible mistake, Sandy." Rachel shook her head again firmly and then reached out to pull Sandy into a hug. "Besides, I'll miss you something awful! I can't believe you're doing this!"

✞✞✞✞

Two weeks later Sandy's thoughts returned to her conversation with Rachel as she watched the two men from the moving company she'd hired unload the last of her furniture and boxes. She surveyed the disorder around her and wondered if perhaps her friend had been right. Maybe she was crazy to make this move. But after everything she'd been through recently, the first time she'd walked through the big old oak door of the house with the realtor, she had felt like she was coming home. And she had been honest with her friend when she had told her she needed a new start for her life.

True—it wasn't the fresh beginning she'd envisioned a month and a half earlier. Back then she'd been busy addressing wedding invitations and looking for a good caterer. Then her fiancé, Mitch, had halted all the wedding plans with the simple words:

I'm not sure we're ready for a step this serious, Sandy.

Maybe he hadn't been, but she had. She'd been ready since their first date. Mitchell Wright was what she'd always fantasized her husband would be—a top executive in a large corporation; tall and athletic, with brilliant blue eyes and blond hair; a graduate of Ohio State University, and currently working on his Master's degree. Socially, he was involved in a number of non-profit foundations and, even though he liked to let everyone know how good a person he was because of it, Sandy had thought he was a great guy—until her eyes had been opened and she had seen him for the man he was.

She'd been in shock when he expressed his desire to call off the wedding. 'Postpone,' was the word he'd used, but Sandy had clearly heard what he wasn't saying. After three years together, Mitch had changed his mind and didn't want to marry her after all.

So, she'd put the stack of partially addressed invitations in a cardboard box, sealed the top firmly with packaging tape, and marked it 'Wedding Invites,' then wedged it in the back of her bedroom closet, and desperately tried to forget it had ever existed. She had discovered the box when she had been packing for her move and had brought it with her, although she didn't know why. She should have thrown the box in the nearest trash bin. It didn't matter anymore though. That part of her life was behind her, and she was starting a new life—or maybe a new old life. She had come full circle and returned to the place of her childhood.

When Sandy had made the trip back to Bradford Mills to pack up her dad's old house and settle his estate, it had seemed natural to drive past all her old haunts. She'd gone past the high school where she had graduated; the small white frame church where the family had attended weekly worship services; the house where she and her parents had lived; the bank where her Dad had been branch manager for years until his retirement. And she'd also driven past her mom's parents' two-story farmhouse—although to Sandy it had always been referred to as 'Grandma's house' since her grandfather had passed away many years before she was born.

The newer version of the old Victorian style farmhouse looked somewhat different from the house in her memories though. Old painted clapboard siding had been replaced with bright white vinyl siding. The wide covered front porch, with its white rails, turned posts, and little spots of gingerbread trim in the upper corners near the eaves had been freshly painted. And the white wooden porch swing, where Sandy had spent hours reading the old classics and watching the world go by, was no longer there. The pink old-fashioned roses climbing up the trellis at the end of the porch were also gone. Some of the old trees around the place were vanished as well, along with the old red hip-roofed barn, the silo, and the chicken coop.

It hadn't surprised Sandy to discover how much the house had changed over the past eight years. She was different, so why wouldn't the house have changed too? But thankfully, Sandy's favorite old pine tree still remained—standing straight and tall in the yard, not far from the house's front porch steps. And the place still looked familiar enough there had been a tug on her heart to see it again, especially when she had driven by and seen the 'for sale' sign in the front yard. She had pulled the car over to the side of the road and quickly scribbled down the name and phone number of the realtor on a piece of paper she dug out of the bottom of her purse. Still parked out front, she'd called the realtor's office from her cell phone and the next thing she knew she was doing a walk-through with the real estate agent and standing in the kitchen of the old house.

It wasn't the same outdated kitchen of her childhood, by any means. The old pale-blue painted wooden cupboards filled with her grandma's Blue Willow dishes were gone, and the cast iron wood-burning cook stove had been replaced with a state-of-the-art stainless steel gas stove. The countertops were granite, and beautiful oak cupboards now covered the walls. But Sandy still felt the familiarity of the place when she stood at the kitchen sink and looked out the window toward the backyard. She could almost hear Grandma reminding her to get busy and wash those dishes before the soapy water in the sink got cold.

Sandy and the real estate agency had worked out a deal with the bank—the same one her father had been employed by for all those years ago. The bank agreed to sell her parents' house in town, and she'd take over this house and make the small monthly payments required by the bank. Her dad's house was worth much more than this one, so when it sold she would be able to pay off this house's mortgage and still have money left over to do some of the work needed. She was optimistic her parents' house would sell quickly since it was a newer style ranch home in a favorite neighborhood in town. The realtor had assured her, even in a tough housing market, it wouldn't take long to sell. Whether it was true or not, Sandy was banking on it.

So, here she was.

Sandy stood at the front bay window and watched the moving van pull out of the driveway, then glanced behind her to see all her earthly possessions scattered throughout the house. She felt her gray striped cat, Boots, rub against her legs as he walked circles around her. Sandy leaned down and scooped up the old cat and snuggled him against her chest, gaining comfort as she heard his gentle purr. She'd had Boots for four and a half years, and he had already been an old cat when she had found him at the humane society and fell in love. The name fit him perfectly because of his four white paws.

Mitch had barely tolerated the cat, and the feeling from Boots toward her former fiancé had been similar. Now it was just her and the cat, and that was all right with her. As Sandy put the cat back on the floor, she watched him saunter from the room, sure he was about to do some investigating of his own in this new place.

Likewise, she turned and slowly strolled through the rooms of the old house, one by one. It soon became evident to her what had more than comfortably filled an apartment was not going to fill a house. There were going to be some empty spots in several of the rooms until she found the time and the money to get additional furniture. Maybe she'd have to hit some garage and estate sales this summer.

She took a deep breath and started to dig into boxes in the kitchen, unpacking most of them first so at least she'd be able to find food and dishes for eating meals. When she was interrupted in her work by the growling of her stomach, she made an evening meal out of a bowl of soup and some crackers. She cleaned up the dirty dishes and made a mental note to make time the next day to go into town for groceries as the refrigerator was pretty bare.

After her brief meal, she returned to unpacking boxes and tried to decide what piece of furniture should go where. The house wasn't huge but had more than enough room for her.

There was a good sized living room and another room downstairs off the living room she planned to use for her office. It needed repainting and some other work done on it first so she decided in the meantime, a corner of the living room would have to do for her computer desk and tall wooden bookshelves. Upstairs were four bedrooms. Once she had the money to do so, she had plans to convert the smallest one into an upstairs bathroom.

In the middle of unpacking a box of books, Sandy glanced out the window and noticed it was getting dark. She groaned as she remembered her bed frame lay in pieces on the floor in the bedroom at the top of the open stairway. She looked around and realized she didn't have a clue which box held her bed sheets and blankets.

She found Boots and put him in the laundry room off the kitchen with his food and water, and he quickly curled up on his blanket in the corner of the room and appeared to be quite content with his new surroundings. Eventually, the cat would have the run of the house, but for the first few nights, until Sandy knew all her stuff was unpacked and put away, Boots was going to have to stay someplace where she knew he was safe. Closing the laundry room door behind her, Sandy heaved a weary sigh and decided the living room sofa would have to do for her bed tonight. Still wearing her grubby sweats, she found her pillow, pulled an old quilt over her, and curled up on the sofa.

Within minutes, and for the first time in many months, she slept the sleep of a small child.

CHAPTER 2

The sounds of a bell ringing slowly sank into Sandy's brain. She heard it and at first was confused and wondered why she had set her alarm the night before when she didn't have to go to work. Even when she understood what it was, getting her eyes open and her body to respond was a struggle. The sound echoed through her head again.

The doorbell!

She rolled off the couch and into a standing position, pulled her curly red shoulder-length hair out of her eyes, yawned and tried to stretch the kinks out of her neck. Then she remembered whoever was ringing the doorbell was more than likely the plumber/handyman the realtor had promised to send over, so she hurried to answer the door, stubbing her stocking-footed toe on a table leg in the process. Hopping on her one good foot, she glanced down at the watch on her wrist. It was after 8:30 a.m.! She couldn't believe she'd slept so late.

Sandy reached for the front doorknob and peered through the tall narrow sidelight window out of habit before opening it. A tall man with dark brown wavy hair stood with his back to the door, gazing out over her front yard.

Hmmm.

The hesitation she felt before opening the door to a stranger—especially a man—was born of having lived in the city for the last eight years. She finally twisted and unlocked the deadbolt, tugged the door open, and spoke to the stranger's back through the wooden screened door.

"Can I help you?"

At the sound of her voice, the man turned around to face her.

It can't be him.

"Hi," his deep bass voice spoke with the familiar soothing sound she remembered so well.

Even though years had passed, she'd never been able to forget the sound of his voice. She'd always thought he should have been in radio with that deep, sultry voice.

"I'm from Victory Construction. Pam at Hasting's Realty called and said you wanted some estimates done."

Sandy nodded and then realized she hadn't opened the door.

"Yes, that's right. Please come in, Tom."

The man paused halfway across the threshold at the sound of his name, squinting until little lines appeared around his eyes. Then a smile lit up his face, and those darling dimples appeared in his cheeks. He looked just as good now as he had back in high school. No. Better.

"Sandy, it that you?"

She gave him a nervous nod, then ran her hands down her sweatpants as if doing so would make them appear less rumpled. Her face grew warm from embarrassment as she thought about how dreadful her uncombed hair must look.

"Sorry I'm such a mess. I slept on the couch last night." Sandy moved aside so he could come into the entryway area further. "You know what it's like—first night in a new house and all, with nothing unpacked…."

She closed her mouth with a snap as she realized she was nervously prattling.

It was really him. Tom Brannigan.

Sandy couldn't believe it—after all these years. So, he was still living here in the same small town where he'd been born. What had he said the name of the company was where he worked—Victory Construction?

She felt Tom's eyes resting on her and then he turned to give the room a cursory glance.

"I knew the old house had sold, but I had no idea you'd bought it. Wasn't this your grandparent's house?"

Sandy nodded and folded her arms across her chest in a failed attempt to steady her nerves. It was too early in the morning to face all the feelings rushing over her at the appearance of Tom Brannigan at her front door. She headed toward the kitchen.

What she needed was a cup of coffee; a strong cup.

"Yes, it was," she answered as she turned to leave the room. "Come out to the kitchen, Tom. I don't know about you, but I'm going to need a cup of coffee before I can discuss business."

She quickly got a pot of water poured into the coffee maker on the kitchen counter and hit the power switch, doubly thankful she had taken the time the previous night to unpack it and get it ready to go.

Sandy swung around from the coffee maker to discover Tom had turned around one of the chairs from the round wooden kitchen table and was sitting straddled across it, his arms resting lightly along its back, watching her every move. She nervously chewed on her bottom lip and tried to figure out what to do with her hands until the coffee was ready.

"I thought you were living in Columbus or someplace, down in Ohio."

She looked over at Tom and gave him what felt to her like a stilted smile. "Toledo, where I moved right after college. I lived there about four and a half years."

Tom nodded, his eyes never leaving her face. "So, what brought you back to these parts?"

Sandy felt her face grow warm as she tried to decide how much to tell him. Did she want to divulge her personal life to this man she hadn't seen in over eight years? She didn't think so.

"I came back after dad died to settle things and put his house up for sale, and once I came to visit, I decided I wanted to move back."

Tom eyes locked on hers, and Sandy was surprised by the look of compassion she read there.

"I was really sorry to hear about your dad, Sandy. He was a great guy."

"Thanks."

She swallowed hard and didn't know what else to say, so turned back to the counter to find the coffee mugs. Once the coffee was ready, she poured two cups—one of which she handed to him.

"Hope you like it black. I don't have any cream, and I don't have a clue as to where I packed the sugar."

She heard his deep chuckle as she handed him the mug of coffee. Their hands briefly brushed against each other, and she felt herself flinch when she felt the warmth of his hand, and then hoped he hadn't noticed. She had purposely spent very little time around men since her breakup with Mitch—especially good-looking men like Tom Brannigan.

"Great," he said, his voice sounding steady. "Strong and black, just the way I like it. Thanks."

After a few sips, Sandy felt ready to show Tom the jobs she needed to have done. The list in her head was long, but she tried to prioritize the 'musts' versus the 'wants.' Until her parents' house sold or she had full-time employment again, Sandy knew she was going to have to watch every penny. The unemployment check she received each month was only a small portion of what she had made when she was working, so she was going to have to be frugal with her spending.

Sandy led him slowly through the house to the living room. "The living room is fine," she said as he followed her. "But," she said as she gestured toward the attached room, "I plan to repaint this room and use it as an office. I want to have my desk over there under the window, with shelves on the wall in the corner behind it."

She stood in the large archway between the two big rooms. "It'd be good to have some doors here so I could close off the room if I wanted to, but I'm not sure I can afford to have it done. I guess it will depend on how much work would be involved."

Tom ran his large hands over the wide oak trim. "This looks as if it's been re-done recently. Was this always an open archway, do you know?"

Sandy felt her lips turn up in a gentle smile of remembrance. "My grandma had heavy drapes hanging here on a rod with round wooden rings. When she couldn't go up and down the stairs anymore, she used this room as her bedroom. But when I was a small girl, I remember there were huge oak pocket doors in this opening. I guess they must have quit working or something, so they got rid of them—and one of the owners since then must have boxed this area in to make it an open archway between the rooms."

Tom nodded and tapped his knuckles on the wood along the side and across the top of the opening. Sandy couldn't help but notice he was tall enough he could easily reach up to touch the top of the archway. She wouldn't be able to reach it even if she stood on her tiptoes, but then, she was short.

"I'll have to see what's under here before I can tell you how much labor and material we're talking about, Sandy. Then the cost will depend on what style of doors you want to install—French doors or solid wood."

Sandy nodded her understanding. "I guess I haven't thought that far ahead." She walked into the hallway and gestured in the direction of the small room off of it. "The bathroom faucets both leak and the kitchen one does too, so there are two more projects."

She walked to the base of the open staircase and took hold of the wooden banister and started up the steps, Tom close behind. "Up here I want clothes closets built in each of the three larger bedrooms. They never put closets in the bedrooms in these old houses. The only upstairs closet is the one here in the hallway, and after you build the other closets, I want shelves installed in it to use as a linen closet, because eventually…," she pointed toward the room at the end of the upstairs hall. "I want this small room made into an upstairs bathroom."

Tom looked around and nodded. "It might not be too costly since I think this room sits right above the downstairs bath."

Sandy watched Tom scribble notes on a notepad, and he took measurements in the bedrooms for closets with a tape measure after asking her exactly what she wanted. Then they went back downstairs and stood in the dining room area between the kitchen and living room. The dining room was relatively empty of furniture since she didn't' have a dining room set yet. Buying more furniture was on her wish list, but for now, the small table she had in the kitchen would have to suffice.

Sandy pointed to the rear dining room wall. "There was a wall of windows here, but one of the previous owners removed them and put in a sliding glass door. I think a wooden deck off the back of the house there would be great." She sighed. "But it's going to have to wait until my dad's house sells."

Tom nodded and made more notes. "I guess my question right now is, Sandy, what do you want to be done first? What're tops on your priority list?"

She dipped her chin as her mind ran through the list again. He was asking good questions. "The plumbing repairs and the painting and shelves in the downstairs office need to be done first—then the doorway area between the two rooms, I guess. I may not be able to afford anything else right now. Oh, and I need to have a washer and dryer installed in the laundry room off the kitchen. I bought a used set locally right before I moved here. The former owners are waiting for me to call them since they promised they'd deliver them when I was ready. And there's a closet in the laundry room where I want some shelves installed."

Sandy took Tom into the small room off the kitchen she was going to use as a laundry room and showed him the closet. He asked a few more questions, took a few more measurements, and closed his scratch pad and returned it to his shirt pocket.

Tom nodded again. "Okay. Well, let me take this info back with me, and I'll sit down and run the figures and compile a written estimate. I should have it for you in a day or so if that's okay."

Sandy smiled. "That will be fine, Tom. Like I said, I'm on a strict budget until I find a job."

Tom gave her a warm smile, and she blinked a couple of times as she looked into his golden brown eyes. She had forgotten how mesmerizing those eyes were. And there were his darling dimples again.

"What type of work do you do?"

She pulled her mind back to his question. "Well, I was a marketing executive in Toledo, but I have a Bachelor's Degree in Business and English from Ohio State, so I'm hoping I can get a job doing something—even if it's not marketing related."

He nodded and stood looking at her, and there was an awkward silence between them before he finally turned to head toward the front door.

"Well, I'll get back with you, Sandy—and it's nice seeing you again."

"You too, Tom."

Sandy held the door open and watched him climb into a dark blue pickup truck with a cap covering the back bed, and 'Victory Construction' painted on the side in bright white lettering. He drove out the driveway, and she turned back to the room behind her to look at all the boxes around her. Heaving a sigh at all the work still ahead, she headed toward the kitchen to fix some breakfast.

But her thoughts immediately turned back to the man who had left her house moments earlier. Of all the people she'd expected to run into right away, who would have thought the first one would be Tom Brannigan—the only boy she'd had a crush on in high school?

CHAPTER 3

Sandy spent the next two days unpacking boxes and settling into her new home. The telephone company finally turned on her landline, so she'd been able to cross one item off her long list of things to be accomplished. Of course, she still had a cell phone, but she'd quickly discovered there was spotty cell phone coverage now she was living in rural America.

Once most of the unpacking was finished, she spent an afternoon getting familiar with what she had always thought of as her grandma's house. It felt strange after all this time to be back in the old house again, but the memories it brought to mind were precious. If she closed her eyes, she could almost smell the Christmas turkey baking in the oven—along with every other food imaginable. Whenever possible, the whole family had tried to be there for Christmas dinner. For Sandy, it hadn't been Christmas until they'd arrived at Grandma Baker's.

She opened her eyes from where she had been standing in the middle of the living room and looked toward the large bay window at the front of the room. Her Grandma's Christmas tree had always sat there with a nativity scene placed on a small table in front of the tree. She could remember her cousins fighting each year over who would get to put the star at the very top of the tree.

The oak wooden fireplace mantel at the end of the room was the favored spot for hanging stockings. Sandy had wonderful memories of sitting on the floor in front of the flames of the fireplace, sipping her grandma's special hot cocoa—with marshmallows, of course. And there had been an old wooden rocker sitting in the corner where Grandma had spent much of her time sitting and reading through her Bible. Grandma's faith in her Lord and Savior had been steadfast, and Sandy and she had spent hours reading scriptures and discussing their meaning.

She sighed. At one time her own faith had been strong, and her relationship with God had been the most important thing in her life. Then she had gone off to college and discovered an entirely different world out there and had slowly drifted away from the church and those beliefs under which she had been raised.

Sandy shook her head. There was no sense worrying about the past and what she did or didn't do. She'd made her choices, and it was too late now to do anything about it.

She turned toward the open wooden staircase. How many hours had she sat on those steps, dreaming about growing up and moving to the big city where she would be able to do whatever she wanted? Well, she'd gotten her wish, and it hadn't been all she had envisioned at the time.

Oh, the innocent dreams of children.

Under the stairway was a little cupboard where Grandma had stored children's books, coloring books, crayons, and other small toys. As a small child, Sandy had spent hours sitting on the floor in front of the little cupboard and reading stories which took her to places she hadn't been able to even imagine back them. Sandy walked over and crouched in front of the cupboard doors, taking hold of the wooden knobs with both hands to open them. She held her breath, wondering what she would find inside. But of course, when she finally tugged on the small wooden doors, she discovered the storage area was empty. She didn't know what she'd use it for, but it was nice to know it was still there.

After doing a little more unpacking, she wandered over to stand at the bottom of the staircase. The steps had looked so much bigger when she was a little girl. But of course, she'd been smaller back then, so it wasn't surprising that the world around her had looked larger than life to a little girl. Sandy placed her left hand on the wooden banister, worn smooth over the years by many hands. She felt a little catch in her throat at the realization that at some time or another, all of her family members had touched this very banister. So many of them were gone now—Grandma, both of her parents, and several aunts and uncles and cousins. She slowly went up the steps, stopping at the third step from the top, and sat down. As a child, this had been her favorite spot. She had sat there many a night when the grownups were still up and conversing downstairs in the living room. They had thought she was in bed, so she could safely eavesdrop while they discussed all those strangely adult things only grown-ups talk about.

Running her fingers lightly over the smooth stairway banister, she stood again and went the rest of the way up the steps and down the hallway, stopping in the doorway of the first bedroom. She had chosen this bedroom for her own, but her bed looked strangely out of place there, as did her modern dresser and another little table she used for a bedside stand. Her more modern furniture was a far cry from the antique furniture she remembered back when it had been Grandma's house. She and her cousins had even had a name for this room's bed—'The Princess Bed'—because of its high carved oak headboard. The wooden suite had also included a tall mirrored dresser, and a fancy marble-topped dressing table with a mirror and upholstered stool. Unfortunately, all her grandma's furniture was long gone—sold to someone else along the way. She'd have to hit the garage sales this summer and see if she could find anything more fitting, plus she also needed furniture for the other guest bedrooms. They were empty right now except for a futon bed and a few boxes of items she hadn't wanted to unpack yet.

Sandy strolled down the hall, stopping long enough to peek into the other three bedrooms. At various times over the years she'd also slept in each of these rooms during her visits. The smallest bedroom though had always been her favorite. In her mind's eye, she could still see the narrow twin bed, pushed into a corner to make more space in the tiny room. Sandy smiled as she looked at the room's small window, remembering waking one summer morning to the sound of a robin flying over and over again into the glass window panes. Being a little girl, Sandy had been frightened and had immediately run downstairs to the kitchen, looking for her grandma. Grandma had told her with a smile that the robin wasn't trying to get in the window to hurt her. The bird was only confused and flying into the window because it could see its own reflection as the morning sunlight hit the glass. She smiled at the remembrance from her childhood as she turned to leave the room. It was funny what memories came back to you when you allowed them.

Sandy walked back into the hallway and opened the wooden door of the only upstairs closet. Her clothes were currently hanging there. Once Tom finished the clothes closet in her room, she'd move her clothes, and he could put the needed shelves in this one. Of course, some things were going to have to wait until her dad's house sold.

And she still needed to find a job.

Glancing out an upstairs window that looked down on the front yard, Sandy saw the upper branches of the towering pine. At least the old pine tree hadn't changed.

She made her way down the steps and out the front door, then crossed the front porch and went down the steps and into the yard. She stood under the canopy of branches of the huge pine tree which hung about three feet from the top of her head. Standing there, she was transported back in time to when she was a small child. Glancing down, she found the ground under her feet littered with the tree's long thin pine cones and leaned over to pick up one, feeling the familiar stickiness. As she brought the cone to her nose, she inhaled the piney scent and smiled at the memories it stirred.

On a whim, she circled the trunk of the tree, running her hands gently over the rough bark while her eyes sought out another remembrance from her childhood. When she finally found it, although not as clear and sharp as she remembered, she sighed in contentment. One more thing that hadn't changed; the cross carved into the bark of the old tree hadn't disappeared. One time she had asked her grandmother where the cross carving had come from, but Grandma had told her she didn't know; it had been there as long as she could remember too. It made Sandy feel good to know this tree still remained unchanged—even if the rest of her life was different.

Sandy turned to look back toward the front of the house and mentally made plans for what flowers she could plant in various spots. Maybe Tom could even make her some flower boxes to put under the windows. What fun it was going to be making the old house hers. She knew she couldn't and wouldn't make the yard look the way it had when she was a child. First of all, she didn't have the same gift for growing things her Grandma had. And she didn't have the time it would require to keep the gardens beautiful. But, she was hoping to eventually put a small flower bed at the side of the house outside the office window where she could enjoy seeing things grow. She had almost forgotten the pleasure in having a garden. She'd lived way too long in a big city. There was a special joy at being in the country where the only thing between her and the big blue skies were the white fluffy clouds. She wanted to find that joy again.

✞✞✞✞

Later that same afternoon, Tom Brannigan was scheduled to drop off his estimates. He had called her the day before to tell her he had them ready, so she was anxious to see the numbers. Once she knew the cost, she would be able to decide what could be done now and what would have to wait. And, she supposed if she was honest with herself, she was looking forward to seeing Tom again. The thought of him hadn't been far from her mind since the first day he had stopped at her house.

Sandy didn't understand her reaction to seeing Tom again after all these years. They'd only dated once; a date Sandy had desperately wanted and looked forward to for weeks after he'd asked her out. Then on the actual date, she'd acted like a silly stuck-up child. She couldn't blame him for not asking her out again.

But what surprised her more was how different he acted now. True, he was older, but Tom had come from a pretty rough home—quite different from her middle-income American life. She had a lot of questions about what he had been doing since his high school graduation when she'd lost track of him, but she wasn't about to come right out and ask him. After all these years, they were essentially strangers. It didn't matter anyway. He was more than likely married with three kids and living a happy life. She had hoped she would have a life of that sort by now, but so far it hadn't happened.

Right on schedule, the doorbell rang, and Sandy hurried down the stairs to answer it, fairly sure it was Tom. It was, and this time he was dressed in blue jeans and was wearing a royal blue polo shirt under his unzipped jacket. It was the end of March in Michigan, and still too cold to shed the jackets. There wasn't any snow on the ground right now, but she knew from growing up in Michigan, they could have another dusting—even into April and May.

She opened the door and waved him in. "Right on time, I see."

He grinned at her and came through the open doorway, handing her a white business size envelope as he walked by her. "Here's what you've been waiting for."

She eagerly took the envelope from him and turned toward the kitchen, waving for him to follow. "Come into the kitchen while I look this over. I can offer you a cookie or two if you're interested."

Sandy heard his chuckle behind her. "I will never turn down an offer for cookies, Sandy. What kind you got?"

She pointed toward a ceramic cookie jar in the shape of a Victorian house sitting on one of the kitchen counters. The counter wasn't in the same place, and the cookie jar wasn't the same one, but she'd made the decision early on that Grandma's old kitchen was going to have cookies in it—even if they were store bought.

"There are some chocolate chip ones in there. When I get time, I'm going to try my hand at baking a batch, although I'm sure they won't be as good as my grandma's."

Tom took a couple of cookies from the jar and carefully replaced the lid, then once again turned a kitchen chair around and straddled it while nibbling on the first cookie, his golden brown eyes watching her all the time. Sandy momentarily lost her train of thought under his scrutiny, then feeling self-conscious, sat down across from him at the table and carefully unfolded the papers she pulled from the envelope. Scanning the contents slowly, she was pleasantly surprised to see the numbers weren't as high as she'd been afraid they might be. Maybe she could afford to get more of the work done than she'd originally thought.

"Hey, this isn't so bad," she said.

She heard Tom laugh from the other side of the table.

"You sound disappointed. Do you want me to pad the numbers to make you feel better?"

Sandy raised her eyes from the paper and laughed nervously as she realized she'd voiced her thoughts out loud, and shook her head at his teasing. "No, no. I mean—I'm surprised. I guess I'm accustomed to prices being higher for everything because I lived in the city for so long. These numbers are excellent!"

She felt her face grow warm as she glanced across the table and saw his eyes studying her again. What was there about this man? Whenever he was around her, she always felt so flustered.

"So, when can you start?"

Tom finished off the last cookie and brushed his hands together to remove any lingering crumbs. "Well, that's what I wanted to talk to you about. I'm in the middle of a rather large job, and it's going to be another month or two before I'm entirely finished with it."

Sandy groaned. This was not what she wanted to hear. She hated to do it, but maybe she'd have to hire someone else to do the work. She couldn't wait two months to get some of these things done. The leaky faucets were becoming a real annoyance.

Tom waved his now cookie-less hand at her. "Don't panic. It's not as bad as it sounds. The things you want to be fixed are mostly small jobs, so if it's okay, I'd be able to work Friday afternoons and Saturdays for you. That way I'll get your repairs done, plus keep working away at my other job. The only thing is, once we get into April, most Saturdays I'll only be able to work in the mornings through the rest of the summer—as I have a prior commitment. Will that work?"

Sandy thought about it for a moment. There wasn't any reason he couldn't work here a couple of half-days a week. The repairs she had for him to do were small things, and apparently the company he worked for needed the larger ones to keep in business. She could understand that.

Tom stood from his chair, and her thoughts were side-tracked by the sight of Boots strolling into the room and wrapping his tail around Tom's jean-covered leg. Mitch had never been a fan of the cat, and Boots had often let it be known he wasn't fond of her ex-fiancé either. Sandy started to get up to put Boots into the laundry room but was surprised when Tom nonchalantly picked the large cat up and held him against his chest, stroking his fur. She let out a sigh of exasperation as she heard Boot's motor start running in a healthy sounding purr.

Traitor.

"Sure," she finally said. "That will work fine—if it's okay with your boss."

Tom grinned at her, and she quickly wondered what he found to be so funny.

"You're looking at him."

"At who?"

"My boss."

Sandy felt embarrassed as a light suddenly went on in her head. How stupid could she be? Tom owned the business. Why hadn't she already figured it out?

"Sorry. I guess I assumed...."

He shook his head. "I know—you assumed someone like me would never own my own business. Right?"

Sandy felt awful. She hadn't meant to insult him.

"I'm sorry, Tom. I had no right to make such a judgment. I think it's great you have your own business. To be honest, I'm a little jealous. How long have you been doing this?"

"'Bout four years. I worked for a while with a bigger contractor before I decided to go out on my own. I'm a licensed plumber and electrician, and a master carpenter. You want to see my credentials?"

He said it in a mischievous tone, and his eyes were friendly as they looked across the room at her, but Sandy knew she deserved far more than a little teasing from him. He had every right to be insulted by the way she'd talked to him. For whatever reason, she wasn't starting out very well with him.

"Of course not, Tom!" She briskly folded the paperwork back up and put it back in the envelope, placing it on the table in front of her. "Well, does this mean you can start tomorrow morning—since it is Saturday?"

He grinned again, and finally put Boots back down on the floor with a fond pat. "All I needed from you was the go ahead. I'll be here at 8:30 tomorrow morning unless that's too early."

Memories of the last time he'd appeared at her door in the early hours of the morning to find her half-asleep swept through her mind. "8:30 is fine. Is there anything I need to do to get things ready for you?"

Tom nodded. "I need you to go into Bradford Mills to the paint store and pick out what color paint you want on the office walls. I can get the other materials I'll need this afternoon. I know the brand names of your faucets, so I'll get those parts—if I don't already have them in my truck. And if you haven't done it yet, you can make the call to have the washer and dryer delivered so I can get them hooked up for you."

She smiled. "Wonderful! I'm way behind on doing my laundry." She stood and faced him. "I do have one more question though."

Tom's eyebrows rose as he looked down at her. "Sure, what's the question?"

"Well, I'm curious; I know your business is named Victory Construction, and I just wondered how you came up with the name?"

He turned to leave the kitchen, and for a moment she thought he wasn't going to answer her question. She followed him until he stopped at the door and then watched as he reached into his shirt pocket and pulled out a business card and handed it to her. Sandy glanced down at it, then back up at him.

"I called it Victory Construction to remind me of our victory over sin like it tells about in the book of I John, chapter 5, verse 4." He gave her a look she couldn't discern. "I'll tell you the whole story sometime when we both have more time. Deal?"

Sandy looked back down at the card and nodded, then watched as he gave her another one of his devastating smiles and walked out the door. Once again she stood in the doorway and observed him getting into his truck and driving away.

Why was it whenever Tom Brannigan left her house, she had more questions?

CHAPTER 4

After Tom's departure, Sandy made a trip to town to order the paint. As she drove toward the small town of Bradford Mills, she decided she'd stop at the paint store first and then go to the grocery store to buy the few items she needed. Downtown Bradford Mills hadn't changed much in the eight years Sandy had been absent. Main Street still held many small shops in the town's two-story brick buildings, most of them built in the early 1910's.

She pulled up in front of the building housing the paint store and parked, making sure she grabbed her car keys and purse before she locked the car. She smiled as she stepped over the curb and onto the sidewalk. The chances of her car being stolen in Bradford Mills were relatively slim, but she locked the car anyway. Old habits were hard to break.

Sandy pulled open the glass door of the paint store which was still housed in an old narrow storefront. A short, balding gentleman she remembered from her childhood greeted her, wearing black slacks and a long-sleeved white shirt with a dark-colored tie.

"Hi, Mr. Watson."

He stared at her over his horn-rimmed glasses. "Don't tell me. Let me see if I can remember who you are."

She grinned and headed down the narrow aisles toward the back of the store where she remembered the paint charts were kept, Mr. Watson trailing along behind her.

"Tom Brannigan told me to stop in and pick out a color for the paint he's going to need. Do you know if I'm supposed to take it home, or is he planning to pick it up, Mr. Watson?"

"Aha! You're Bill and Peggy Martin's girl. I knew it. Heard you'd bought the old Baker place." Mr. Watson seemed pleased because he'd figured out her identity, then added, "Tom told me he's picking it up. He already has another order waiting."

Sandy nodded and focused her attention on the panorama of colors on the wall display in front of her. How was she ever going to choose? She didn't want anything too dark or too bright. Maybe something in a warm tan color? She finally settled on a color called khaki suede. With the wood trim in the room painted a bright white, it would look great. Pulling the chip out of the rack, she headed back to the counter.

"I found the one I want, Mr. Wilson."

Mr. Wilson studied the chip for a moment. "Nice color," he stated. "Do you know how many gallons you're going to need?"

She nodded. "Tom said he thought it would take a couple of gallons. He also said he'd need a gallon of white gloss enamel for the trim."

The older man scribbled her order down on his pad of paper, then glanced back up at her. "They'll be mixed, shook, and ready for pickup when he gets here."

✞✞✞✞

Leaving the paint store, Sandy made a stop at the bank to cash her last paycheck from her old job and then decided to treat herself to a piece of pie at the local diner. She hadn't been there in years but remembered it from high school as being 'the place' where all the townsfolk hung out, especially the teenagers. The family diner was housed in a small brick one-story storefront right in the center of Bradford Mills, thus its name, *Central Diner*.

As soon as she opened the glass door of the diner, she was transported back in time to her childhood. The small bell hanging over the door rang out her arrival upon entering, and Sandy felt a blush move into her cheeks as all eyes in the diner turned to see who was coming through the door. She quickly made her way through the maze of small red tablecloth-covered wooden tables to a booth near the rear of the diner and slid in to take a seat.

She was listening to what had to be a local radio station play a country music tune and only had time to pick up the menu when the waitress appeared. Sandy didn't even look up as she was trying to decide between the cherry and the apple pie.

"Well, I'll be. It's Sandy Martin."

Sandy raised her eyes from the menu to those of the waitress, an older woman in her mid-fifties. The faded blue eyes staring at her looked somewhat familiar, but as she studied the face and ponytailed, dishwater blond hair streaked with gray, she couldn't find a name to go with the face.

"Hi," she finally responded with a little smile.

The older woman gently smiled back at her. "You don't remember me," she stated. "Well, it's okay. Our families weren't exactly sociable back then."

Sandy furrowed her brow as she tried again to place the face. "I'm sorry. I'm trying to remember who you are...."

"Maggie Brannigan," the other woman said with a friendly smile on her face. "I do believe my boy's going to be doing some work for you out at your grandma's old house."

Sandy felt a light switch on in her head. "Of course, you're Tom's mom. It is good to see you again, Mrs. Brannigan."

The smile she felt moving across her face was sincere. It was nice to meet someone who actually remembered her and her family.

Maggie grinned back at her. "It's been a long time." The laugh lines around her eyes and lips deepened as she continued to smile. "You grew up into a pretty little gal, didn't ya?"

There was the familiar feeling of heat spreading over Sandy's face again. Sometimes she hated being a fair skinned red-head. Every emotion was written all over her face for the world to see. It had been awful for her as a shy teenager back in high school, and it still annoyed her as an adult, but she had learned to live with it—mostly because there wasn't anything she could do to control it.

She let out a nervous laugh and turned her attention back to the menu.

"A piece of pie sounds good. Which kind do you suggest, Mrs. Brannigan?"

Maggie waved her right hand through the air briefly. "Oh, call me Maggie—and all the pies here are good. I'm telling you, whatever Mike cooks or bakes is yumptious." She dipped her head briefly as if sharing a secret. "I'm partial to the cherry though."

Sandy grinned. "Then that's what I'll have. One piece of cherry pie and a cup of coffee, please, Maggie."

The older woman took the menu from her and smiled at her. "Comin' right up."

In only a few minutes, Maggie was back with an ample slice of pie with a generous dollop of whip cream resting on top. After setting down the plate of pie in front of Sandy, Maggie deftly flipped over the coffee mug resting on the table and poured out a steamy cup of coffee.

As the aroma of the coffee drifted in Sandy's nose, she let out a sigh of satisfaction.

"Smells great. Thanks."

Surprisingly, the older woman placed the coffee pot down on the table and scooted in the booth across the table from Sandy.

"So, you're back in town—for good, from what I hear," Maggie said.

Sandy nodded, wondering why the woman was so interested in her life. Maybe she was looking for fodder for the small-town gossip machine. Sandy glanced around the almost empty diner. Didn't Maggie have something else she should be doing?

The older woman spoke again, and Sandy looked across the table at her. Up close Sandy could see Maggie's face was lined with wrinkles around the mouth and eyes. She knew she had to be in her early to mid-fifties, but Maggie's face looked even older. Life must have been hard for her over the years.

"I imagine we'll be seeing you at church sometime soon now you're back in town. I heard you're still unattached so you might be interested in our friendly Singles Sunday school class. I'm sure you'd enjoy it. They usually have an outing of some sort at least once a month. My son, Tom, attends their meetings on a regular basis."

When the other woman finally stopped to take a breath, Sandy smiled and spoke up quickly. "Sounds nice."

What was Maggie Brannigan up to? Was she trying to play matchmaker? Sandy had only recently arrived back in town, and she sure didn't need anyone attempting to match her up with someone. She'd had quite enough of men for a while. Then again, maybe Maggie was only trying to make her feel welcome.

The older woman finally stood and grabbed her coffee pot. "Well, guess I'd better get back to work." She reached out her left hand to lightly touch Sandy on the shoulder as she turned to go. "I'm glad you're back in town, Sandy. I look forward to getting to know you better."

Sandy watched Maggie walk back toward the kitchen, and an unidentifiable feeling rushed over her.

Tom's mother, Maggie Brannigan, inviting her to church. Who would have thought it?

Sandy frowned and turned her attention back to the piece of pie on her fork. She hadn't been in a church for years—ever since she left Bradford Mills. She had gone off to college and the big city and hadn't had time for God or church anymore. And somewhere along the way she had drifted further and further away, and the faith she had considered so much a part of her life when she was a teenager had faded away. Maggie Brannigan inviting her to church showed Sandy just how much she'd changed from the young woman who left town all those years ago.

Maggie appeared to be a very nice lady though, and it was heartwarming to have someone to talk with who actually remembered her from her childhood. And from what his mom had said, Tom attended church regularly too.

Interesting.

She picked up her fork and sliced another small bite of her pie and popped it in her mouth, savoring the tart sweetness and the richness of the whipped cream topping. Ah, now this was pie. Not quite as good as her grandmother's, but close enough.

✞✞✞✞

When Sandy arrived back at her house, she spent some time digging through the unpacked boxes in one of the upstairs bedrooms. She was looking for a particular "something," and she knew it had to be in one of the boxes, but for whatever reason, she couldn't seem to find it. Finally, in the last box she looked, near the bottom she found what she was looking for.

Her old Bible.

After cleaning up the kitchen from her dinner, Sandy went back upstairs and changed into her pajamas and bathrobe. Then she went downstairs to the kitchen and sat down at the small table where the light was better and slowly thumbed through the Bible. She had received this Bible from her parents when she was ten years old—the same year she had made the decision to accept Jesus as her personal savior and be baptized. It had been years since she'd even touched the book. A bit of nostalgia swept over her. There had been a time when the words in this Bible were the most important things in her life. But those had been simpler happier times, and somewhere along the way she had put her Bible aside and forgotten all about it.

But when Tom had mentioned how he'd come up with the name of his company it had sparked her curiosity, and now she wanted to find the exact scripture herself. She opened the Bible and tried to remember the scripture reference he'd used. John—no, the first book of John—I John. Pulling the business card he had given her out of her bathrobe pocket, she thumbed through the pages until she found I John. Now, she needed to find the fifth chapter. She finally found the scripture he'd used—Chapter 5, verse 4:

For whatsoever is born of God overcometh the world: and this is the victory that overcometh the world, even our faith.

She went on and read the fifth verse.

Who is he that overcometh the world, but he that believeth that Jesus is the Son of God?

Sandy read the words again and then slowly closed the Bible and sat back in her chair with a sigh. What had happened to Tom that had changed him to the person he was now? He certainly didn't seem to be the same man who had asked her out on a date back in high school. She had known, even then, he wasn't interested in anything other than a good time. They had been from completely different backgrounds, and his friends and her friends were poles apart.

Sandy had been heavily involved with church back then, and in high school, she had been so vehement about her beliefs and values—she'd even tried to get Tom to go to church. It made her ashamed to remember one of the last conversations she'd had with Tom all those years ago. She'd acted so self-righteous as she'd preached to him about how he was wasting his life and needed to get himself right with God.

She sincerely hoped he didn't remember the exchange as well as she did.

Well, it had happened a long time ago, and she wasn't a starry-eyed little girl anymore. Her Pollyanna attitude was gone. Life in the real world tended to do that to a person. She still believed in God, but she didn't think He cared much about Sandy Martin anymore. And she couldn't remember the last time she had attended a church service or picked up her Bible—until today.

Sandy frowned as her thoughts turned to the three years she'd wasted with Mitchell Wright. She had lived with the man for those years, positive he would marry her and make her life a 'happily-ever-after.' She'd had this story-book wedding and marriage all planned out in her mind, and Mitch was the man who would make those dreams come true. When he had finally popped 'the question,' she had been ecstatic. She had almost given up hope of him ever asking. When he backed out of the wedding though, she had decided enough was enough. Even though she had compromised her values and the Christian beliefs she'd been raised with to move in with him without the benefit of marriage, she had always believed she would still have the fairy tale ending.

And if he wasn't going to marry her, she was done with him.

Now it seemed rather ironic to have Tom quoting scripture to her. It was almost as if their roles in life had been reversed. Sandy wasn't sure she liked the feeling.

✞✞✞✞

Later the same evening, Sandy sat propped up in her bed in the upstairs bedroom she had claimed for her own. The day's newspaper was spread across her lap as she carefully read through the job listings. There weren't many—at least there were only a few for which she'd qualify, but she took notes on the promising ones. She'd have to get her resume updated and either email or mail it to them.

When a jaw-cracking yawn caught her off-guard, she folded the newspaper closed and looked at her bedside clock. The yawn was a reminder of how long a day she'd had. She cleaned the paperwork off the bed, fluffed her pillows, shut off the lamp on her bedside table, and cuddled down under the blankets. As she settled in, she felt herself slowly relaxing into the drowsy stage that comes right before deep sleep.

It was only a few moments later when Sandy jerked awake and opened her eyes in a panic as she heard a noise sounding like glass breaking. Her body froze in fear as she strained to listen over the sound of her beating heart for any other noises. She might have almost been asleep when she had heard the sound, but there was no doubt in her mind what she had heard.

Someone was downstairs.

Slowly and quietly, Sandy reached over to the bedside stand and found the flashlight she always kept close by in case of a power outage. She probably didn't need it to find her way to the stairs tonight though as there was an ample amount of moonlight streaming through her bedroom window, but she'd take it anyway. She shivered as she got out of bed and quickly pulled her bathrobe off the end of the bed and put it on, her hands shaking. The hardwood floor under her bare feet felt cold which sent another chill up her back.

It was the last thing she wanted to do, but she knew she had to go down those stairs and find out what had caused the noise she'd heard. Boots was in the laundry room behind a closed door, so it wasn't him wandering around the house. So what had made the noise? Was it a window glass or door glass she had heard breaking? Was someone even now entering her house? She shivered again, but this time from fear.

Sandy had never felt so alone—or so scared. Her friend, Rachel, had been right. She was crazy to have moved out here in the middle of nowhere to live all by herself. She didn't even have a phone upstairs as she'd left both her cell phone and her cordless phone in their chargers on a table at the bottom of the steps.

Sandy sat down on the edge of the bed for a second or two and took a couple of deep breaths and tried to calm her racing heart while she decided what to do. She glanced around the room looking for something resembling a weapon. The only item that even remotely qualified as a weapon was her tennis racket in the corner. Deciding the racket was better than nothing, she quickly grabbed it and the flashlight and tip-toed slowly and carefully from her bedroom, and down the hallway toward the top of the staircase. She paused on the top step and listened again.

Silence.

There was no light from a flashlight coming from below, and no sounds. Maybe she'd been wrong, and the noise she had heard had really been outside. No, she was positive whatever she'd heard had been inside the house. The sound appeared to have originated from the room right below her bedroom which would mean whoever it was, they were in the living room.

Well, there was only one way to find out. She took a deep breath and crept down the stairs, one step at a time, straining to remember where each one creaked.

There had been no more noises from downstairs, and she couldn't decide if that was a good thing or not. Maybe the person had already stolen whatever they had been after and left the house. She certainly hoped so. The last thing she wanted to do was face a burglar in the process of robbing her. What would she do if he had a gun?

She was crazy to be doing this alone!

Sandy finally reached a spot on the stairs where she could see a portion of the living room below. All she could make out in the darkness were the shadows of her furniture.

She chewed on her lower lip while she planned out her next actions, finally deciding to hurry down the last few steps and hit the light switch for the main room, hoping to catch whatever or whoever it was off guard. She'd also have to try and grab her cordless phone off the stand, which would mean putting down either the racket or the flashlight. She decided to drop the flashlight. Sandy took a deep breath and readied for action.

Here goes.

It seemed long minutes passed, although Sandy was sure when she replayed the incident in her head later, only seconds passed as she rushed down the stairs, dropped the flashlight, grabbed the phone, and hit the light switch. She glanced feverishly around the room for anything out of the ordinary while her heart tried to beat its way out of her chest.

Nothing. There was nobody there—no burglar, no bad guy carrying a gun. Nothing.

Then through the moonlight pouring through the window, she saw a dark shape fly at her from the direction of the dining room, and she let out a yell, ducked, and ran for the nearest doorway—which happened to be the bathroom. She slammed the bathroom door shut with a bang and leaned against it while she gulped in huge breaths of air.

A bat!

Sandy closed her eyes as a shudder ran through her. Her greatest nightmare. She was terrified of bats!

Obviously it must have made the noise she'd heard. The bat must have been flying around and knocked one of her little glass knick-knacks off the top of her corner bookshelf. She took a deep breath and sat down on the edge of the bathtub to collect her thoughts and attempt to steady her nerves.

While she waited for her heart rate to return to normal, she couldn't help it when the temptation to giggle swept over her. This was ludicrous. It was only a bat, after all. She groaned as the terror returned. Of all things it could be, why did it have to be a bat?

But now she knew what it was, what was she going to do about it? She wasn't sure she wanted to go out there and battle the thing all by herself. She shivered again. She was terrified of bats, and mice, and snakes.... No, she couldn't force herself to go out there and face it alone. But, what other option did she have?

Sandy looked down at the phone in her hand. She should be able to call someone who could come help her or tell her what to do. Surely there were exterminators in the area who made their living doing just that—getting bats and other varmints like them out of houses. But, who? She chewed on her lip as she looked at the phone. She should have grabbed her cell phone instead of the cordless landline. At least her cell phone had phone numbers saved, although they wouldn't be of much help as the numbers saved were all for people she knew in Toledo. The only phone number she had memorized was Mitch's, and she certainly wasn't going to call him in the middle of the night asking for help with a bat flying around her living room. But if she'd had her cell phone, she might have been able to access the yellow pages online to find an exterminator—although getting one to come out this late at night was doubtful.

She momentarily considered dialing 911, but quickly discarded that idea. If she told them she needed help because a bat was flying around in her house, they would more than likely think it was a crank call and hang up. Then her hand touched the pocket of her bathrobe, and her fingers felt the cardboard resting there.

Tom Brannigan's business card!

She'd stuck it in her bathrobe pocket earlier in the evening after looking up the scripture he'd quoted. She pulled it out and smiled. There was one person she could call after all. But, what would he think of her? She grinned, feeling silly. At this point did it really matter? Here she was, terrified and trapped in her bathroom by a bat. If she didn't want to go out there and deal with it alone, she was going to have to ask somebody for help. A shudder ran through her again at the thought of facing the bat alone. No way!

Sandy punched the numbers slowly into the phone and waited for the ring. She only hoped and prayed Tom was home.

✞✞✞✞

Tom Brannigan relaxed in his recliner, watching the end of the Tigers baseball game. It was a pre-season game and didn't count for anything, and even though he probably should have already gone to bed, he still enjoyed watching the game. When the game finally ended, he hit the button on the remote to turn off the TV and had started to get up from the chair, when the phone rang.

He glanced at the clock on the wall. Who would be calling him this late? His mom? Hopefully, it wasn't bad news. He always dreaded getting phone calls late at night.

"Hello?"

"Hi, Tom. This is Sandy Martin. Sorry to bother you as I know it's late…"

Tom detected a note of panic in Sandy's voice. "Sandy, what's wrong?"

He heard her nervous giggle on the other end. He frowned. What was going on? Was she drunk or what?

"Well, I didn't know who else to call. If you don't want to, I'll understand. But you see, I don't like bats much."

Tom shook his head as he tried to make sense of her rambling.

"What?"

He heard her sigh on the other end of the phone. "I have a bat in the house. I was almost asleep when I heard something break downstairs and when I got down here, I found this bat flying around wildly." He heard her sigh. "I'm terrified of bats, Tom."

"So, where are you now?"

He heard her giggle again. "I'm hiding in the downstairs bathroom."

Tom couldn't help the chuckle rumbling out of his chest. He could envision her hiding behind the closed door while the bat flew around her house, unaware of the trauma it was causing her.

"I'll be right there, Sandy."

"Tom, are you sure? I know it's really late and I hate to bother you, but I didn't know who else to call…and there's no way I can go out there and handle it myself." He heard her groan and could almost feel her shudder through the phone line.

He smiled. At least she trusted him enough to call on him when she needed to be saved from wayward bats.

"Not a problem. Can you get to the door to let me in?"

He waited while it grew silent on the other end of the call and he assumed she was assessing the situation.

"When you get here come around to the back sliding glass door off the dining room. I'll try and get out there to unlock it. It's not too far from the bathroom, so I should be okay."

He chuckled again. "Okay, I'll have my cell phone with me if you need to call me before I get there."

Her voice sounded a little less frazzled when she responded. "Thanks, Tom. I appreciate this so much! See you in a bit."

Tom hung up the phone and headed toward the door of the small house he rented, grabbing his truck keys off the kitchen counter as he walked by. This wasn't exactly what he'd planned on doing this evening, but it was okay.

Anything to save a lady in distress.

✞✞✞✞

As he drove through the downtown area of Bradford Mills and headed out the main thoroughfare to the rural road

Sandy lived on, Tom's thoughts turned again to Sandy. He seemed to have her on his mind a lot recently, and he couldn't decide if that was a good thing or not. To have her reappear in Bradford Mills after all these years had surprised him. He had never forgotten the fiery little redhead in high school who hadn't been afraid to tell him what she thought of him. Now, for whatever reason, it appeared the Lord had brought her back into his life, and he wasn't sure why. He'd been doing fine on his own, without a special someone in his life—not that Sandy Martin was going to be more than a friend, even though the attraction he had felt for her in the past was definitely still there. After his past mistakes though, he wasn't about to go after another relationship with a woman right now. Not for a long, long time—if ever. He was doing just fine on his own—him and God.

But he did have to admit, seeing Sandy Martin again had stirred up feelings he had thought were long gone—even after all these years. So on the drive out to Sandy's house, Tom did what he spent as much time as possible doing now. He prayed.

Lord, I don't know why you brought Sandy Martin back into my life after all this time, but I trust Your wisdom and will for my life. I also don't know why You had this particular incident happen which made her give me a call for help, but if it gives me another opportunity to prove to Sandy I've changed, then it will be worth it. Hopefully, it will help bring her back to You. I feel like she's left You out of her life since she left home, and I want her to remember how much she needs You.

Tom smiled and shook his head as he thought about the task ahead of him, then went back to his prayer. He even chuckled a little as he thought about God's sense of humor.

Thank you for the opportunity to help her out, but I have to admit I sometimes don't understand Your ways. Of all the things you could use to bring us together again, why did it have to be a bat?

It didn't take him long to get to Sandy's road. As he made the turn onto it, he hoped she'd been able to get to the door and unlock it or he didn't know what he was going to do. He hated the thought of having to break into her house for the sole purpose of catching a bat, but he'd do what he had to do.

CHAPTER 5

After Sandy hung up the phone from talking to Tom, she looked at the tennis racket she'd dropped on the bathroom floor and picked it up again, hefting it in her hand. It wasn't much of a weapon, but it would have to do. She took a deep breath and tried to steady her nerves. It was time for action.

Standing, she left her perch on the edge of the bathtub and tiptoed to the bathroom door, opening it just enough so she could see into the living room. There didn't seem to be a bat flying around at the moment, so she took another deep breath for courage and crept into the hallway, then turned toward the dining room in time to see the bat fly through the doorway into the kitchen. She ran across the room and pushed the kitchen door shut with a bang, then released the breath she hadn't know she was holding.

At least the bat was temporarily trapped in the kitchen where it couldn't fly at her head.

She suppressed a shudder and turned toward the sliding glass door and unlocked it. Sandy also turned on the outside light so Tom would better able to see the back steps. She didn't have to wait long before the headlights of his pickup truck pulled in her driveway, and she saw him drive around back of the house and stop. She stood at the door and watched Tom get out of the truck and reach behind the seat for something, then turn and head for the door. Sandy hurried over to open the door for him.

"Thanks for coming, Tom. You have no idea how much I appreciate this!"

He wiped his feet on the small rug on the floor just inside the door. "So, where is the little critter? Or did you already get him?" He grinned at her, his handsome dimple teasing her.

Sandy shook her head and pointed toward the closed kitchen door. "He's in there—not where I wanted him to go, but at least I was able to get to the door to let you in without him dive-bombing me." She felt a shudder run through her just thinking about it.

She pointed at the object in his hand. "A fishing net?"

Tom chuckled. "Hopefully, I can net a bat this time." He slipped some gloves on his hands, grabbed the net, and headed toward the kitchen. "Well, here goes. Wish me luck."

She watched him open the kitchen door a little, slip through, then firmly close it again behind him. Sandy paced the dining room floor while she waited, hoping the bat hadn't made a mess of her kitchen. It would need a real scrubbing in the morning after having a critter loose in it.

In what seemed like only a moment or two, Tom came through the door, pushing it open with his back. His right hand held the handle of the net, while his left hand tied off the opening of the pouch of the net where the bat could plainly be seen. Sandy grimaced at the sight of the creature and hurried over to open the sliding door for him. The sooner the bat was out of her house, the happier she'd be. Standing at the door, she watched Tom walk down the steps and through the backyard into the darkness, then a short time later she saw him walk over and put the net and gloves back into his truck. She let out a sigh of relief, not realizing how much the whole episode had terrified her. But the bat was gone now, and she could breathe again. It was her first run-in with a bat since she was a child—and hopefully, her last one.

Sandy greeted Tom's return to the door with a smile. "Thanks, Tom. The bat sure gave me a scare!"

He grinned at her, his brown eyes twinkling. "I'll check in the morning to make sure the chimney is capped with screen, and I'll also look for any holes there might be in the siding or soffit. There's got to be an opening somewhere where he squeezed in. The little guys can squeeze through even the tiniest hole."

Sandy sighed. It wasn't comforting to know bats were so good at getting into houses. She sure didn't want to have another experience with one anytime soon.

"So, what did you do with it?" She didn't care where it was, but she also didn't want to come across the carcass of a dead bat in her yard in the morning.

He grinned at her again, and she couldn't help but notice an extra sparkle in his eyes.

"Tom, you let him go, didn't you? Oh, great! I'll be up all night chasing bats!"

He chuckled and shook his head. "Bats aren't all bad, Sandy. They eat bugs, you know. Besides, I think the poor fella has had enough drama for this evening. He won't be back to bother you tonight."

Sandy suddenly felt self-conscious as she stood there in her bathrobe and bare feet. She pulled the sash of her robe tighter and felt her face grow warm at the thought of how she must look to him. Almost as if Tom understood, he turned and headed for the door.

"Thanks again, Tom. Please add something onto your bill for the trouble."

Tom shook his head and held up his right hand. "No charge for this trip. What are friends for?" He gave a little wave of his hand as he headed out the door. "See you in the morning. Try and get some sleep. Good-night."

Sandy waved as he got in his truck and left, then locked the door and went back through the house turning off lights before heading back up the stairs to bed. Tomorrow morning would be soon enough to assess the damage done by the bat and clean up the mess. Right now all she wanted was sleep, although getting to sleep after the evening's excitement was going to be a challenge.

✞✞✞✞

Tom Brannigan wasn't easily flustered, nor often caught off guard. Years of growing up and living in a family of boys on the rough side of town had taught him to always expect the unexpected. But when Sandy Martin had been the person to open the door of the old Baker house the day he'd gone there, he'd definitely been caught unawares. Her stunning, curly red hair, green eyes, and creamy complexion with a light smattering of freckles across the bridge of her nose had instantly made him feel young again.

He had heard the old Victorian house had sold again, but he had never envisioned she was the one who had bought it. Last he had heard, she had moved to the city and never returned. He hadn't even been sure it was really her when he'd first seen her on the other side of the screened door. After all, it had been eight years since they'd last seen each other and he was sure he didn't look the same either.

They'd gone out only once during his junior year of high school. She had been a freshman, and the two of them hadn't exactly run with the same crowd, nor lived the same lifestyle, but he had thought she was a cute gal, so he asked her out. She was an honor roll student, sat on the student council, and never got called to the Principal's office unless it was to be rewarded for doing something good. Sandy had been way out of his league. As far as he knew, she probably still was.

Tom, on the other hand, had lived on the wild side growing up. He skipped school so many times during his junior year some of his teachers weren't even certain who he was. It had been a miracle he'd passed his classes and managed to graduate. Life to him had been one big party. And the perky freshman, Sandy Martin, had been an irresistible challenge. It was evident to him on their first and only date though, he had made a huge mistake by asking her out. She told him in no uncertain terms she was not going to smoke cigarettes and expected him to refrain whenever she was around. She had also informed him she didn't drink, and if he thought he wanted to drink in her presence, then he needed to take her home right then and there. There had also been the declaration from her that he needed to get himself straight and spend some time on his knees talking to God. He'd just laughed at her and called her "Sassy Sandy."

She'd been so full of life and intensely loyal to her beliefs. Tom had made fun of her, but truthfully, he'd been fascinated by her even though he was scared to death of her beliefs and all she stood for. Although she had been two years younger than he, Sandy had seemed so sure of herself and her faith. He'd never known anyone else quite like her before or since. After that one and only date, he'd never asked her out again. He hadn't had many smarts back then, but he'd been intelligent enough to know she was out of his league.

It wasn't until he'd endured a destroyed marriage, won his fight against addiction and struggled to find his way back from rock bottom, that he'd found the peace he'd seen in Sandy's eyes all those years earlier. A wonderful pastor had taken the time to listen to Tom's story and had spent hours showing him God's plan for his salvation. It was a gift Tom had eagerly accepted. And the resulting changes in his life were his best testimony. Since his salvation, his Mom had also become a Christian, and their relationship had become precious to Tom.

Now Sandy had suddenly and unexpectedly reappeared in his life. And she still scared him—maybe not for the same reasons, but there was something about her that touched a place in his heart he had fervently protected over the years. Even when he'd married another woman, the memory of the fiery-tempered redhead had never diminished.

His mom had mentioned she'd run into Sandy in the diner one day and talked with her. She'd also hinted how lonely Sandy seemed, and being his mother, had reminded him to be sure to invite her to church. He smiled. There had been a time when church and fellowship with other Christians hadn't been a priority in either his or his mom's lives, but now—God and the Word were more important to the two of them than anything else. They sure had come a long way in their Christian walk.

So, he couldn't help but wonder what had happened to Sandy and her staunch Christian beliefs? And what had brought her back to Bradford Mills now? Surely God had a reason for her coming back into his life. Since she was back though, he'd felt an urgent need to pray for Sandy during his prayer time—especially for her relationship with God. From his brief observances of the woman she had become, he was afraid the teenager he remembered from high school with strong Christian faith and solid convictions was gone. In her place, a quieter, more somber and reserved Sandy had appeared. And Tom had noticed this Sandy didn't seem to enjoy or embrace life and those around her anymore. There was a hauntingly sad look in her green eyes, and it was easy to tell that, or something had hurt her deeply. Because of it, she had pulled into a shell and wasn't the same Sandy he remembered.

So why had she come back to Bradford Mills—was it because she was running away from someone or something? He was intrigued with her, and even though his own defense system told him to steer clear of her, his heart wouldn't listen.

For instance, the night he'd gone to save her from the bat, it had totally unnerved him to see her standing there in her bathrobe with her tiny bare feet. She'd looked so young and cute. And vulnerable. He'd had to struggle to remind himself they didn't know each other well.

Tom shook his head as the thoughts raced through his mind. He needed to remember that what she needed right now was a friend, and that's all he could be to her. Nothing more. But whatever it was that fascinated him about Sandy, he knew he needed to proceed with caution until he knew her better and found out exactly where she stood with God. His relationship with God came first and foremost. He'd been involved with a non-Christian before, and he wasn't ever going down that road again.

CHAPTER 6

Sandy climbed down off the ladder and looked around the living room at the sparkling windows. Well, at least the inside of the windows were clean. The outside would have to wait until warmer weather. Today there was a damp drizzle falling outside and no sunshine in sight. Typical late April weather in Michigan.

The house was starting to come together—finally. She looked in the direction of the office where Tom was hanging the last of the shelving units above the area where she planned to locate her desk and computer. He'd painted the room last Saturday, along with repairing all the leaky faucets in the house. She was looking forward to having her desk, computer, books, and writing supplies all unpacked and moved out of the living room into the newly decorated office. It would make it so much easier to get her work accomplished. And the living room would look like a living room again.

Glancing down at her wristwatch, she groaned. She'd forgotten to keep track of the time, and now she'd have to hustle if she was going to make her 3:30 appointment for a job interview at the *Bradford Mills Daily Press* office. The opening was in Sales—not exactly what she wanted to do the rest of her life—but she couldn't be choosy at this point. She needed a job. Even though she still had several months of unemployment pay coming to her, she knew if she was going to be able to keep up with her bills, she had to have a steady income as soon as possible.

Hurrying upstairs, she quickly changed into a cute dark blue skirt and light blue blouse, dug around until she found her navy blue heels, and went back downstairs to tell Tom she would be back—hopefully before he left at 6:00.

"If I'm not back before you leave, just make sure you lock the door on your way out, Tom."

Tom nodded. "Sure. Hope your interview goes well, Sandy."

"Thanks," she smiled absentmindedly at him and hurried to find her purse and keys as she headed out the door.

✞✞✞✞

Tom watched Sandy rush out of the room, and shortly afterward heard the sound of the back door closing, and her car start. Without Sandy's presence, the house fell silent around him.

He enjoyed working in old houses. They had so much character and their own history to tell. As far as he was concerned, old walls could talk—as could floors and doors. At least they talked to him. As a carpenter, he saw things most people wouldn't even notice. For instance, the pencil lines on a doorframe telling the story of children who had grown up in the house; or worn stairs from the many feet that had trod up and down them; or the many layers of paint or wallpaper previous owners had placed on the walls each time they redecorated. They all told a story, but you had to look carefully to hear the words. This house had a story to tell too, he was sure. It was more than simply Sandy's grandma's house. Her great-grandparents had also lived here for many years, and based on what he saw of the age of the house, there had been several other earlier owners.

He turned his concentration back to the job at hand. In a matter of minutes, he had finished putting in the last screws to install the shelving in Sandy's office. Glancing around the room, he nodded in satisfaction. The room didn't look too bad. The white paint Sandy had picked out for the trim made the room bright and cheery.

Tom smiled as he felt Sandy's cat, Boots, rub up against his pant leg.

"What do you think, Boots? I think it looks pretty good." He grinned at the realization he was now talking to cats. He reached down to pet the top of the gray striped cat's head, feeling the rumble of the animal's purr on contact. Tom wasn't sure why he was drawn to this particular cat since he didn't usually care for them. Maybe it was because this specific one belonged to Sandy.

On to the next project on the list.

Earlier he'd promised Sandy he'd try and get the phone line run into the office for her computer modem. She had been surprised when he'd reminded her she wouldn't have cable access in the country. So she had signed up for internet access from the local phone company and now needed a phone line run to this room. She told him she planned to have satellite installed eventually and would then have DSL internet access. But for now, she'd told him, dial-up internet access was all she could afford. Even though it was better than not having internet at all, Tom couldn't imagine having to go back to dial-up.

Grabbing the roll of phone wire he'd brought in earlier from the truck, Tom headed for the basement. Twenty minutes later and several more trips to the cellar, he finished the job by snapping the cover on the wall phone jack.

Another task finished.

Tom looked around the empty room. It looked good—even without any furniture in it. The hardwood floor shone, and the freshly painted room looked clean and renewed. He'd thought about moving her desk into the room as a surprise, but decided to wait as he wasn't certain exactly where she wanted it.

He picked up the tools he'd scattered across the floor and went through the opening between the two rooms. Looking at the archway as he had many times before, he paused. This was going to be his next project, and he wasn't entirely sure what he was getting into. He stood there for a moment before he finally tugged his hammer out of his tool belt and cautiously pried off some of the wood framing the arch, surprised at how loose the boards were. He jerked and yanked and before he knew it, he had the whole arched area on both sides and the top uncovered. As he looked at the nails and debris on the wooden floor, he frowned. He hoped Sandy didn't kill him for the mess he'd made.

Tom turned his attention back to the opening and studied the old pocket door track in the header of the archway. Too bad the old doors had been removed. He was half hoping he'd find them still in the wall when he uncovered the area. No such luck.

Then he remembered something he'd seen in the basement while he was running the phone line and headed back down for another look.

✞✞✞✞

Sandy's heart was a little lighter as she pulled into her driveway. She didn't know for certain, but she thought she had a good shot at being offered the sales job at the Bradford Mills newspaper. And there was also a possibility of doing some freelance writing for them. It was only a part-time position, but it was a start. And while she was in town, she'd also gotten a lead on another part-time job at the library. If she could land at least one of those jobs, she would have some income again, and it would take a huge worry off her mind.

She was surprised to see Tom's truck still parked in her driveway. Sandy glanced at her wristwatch. It was almost 6:30. She had thought he'd have gone home by now.

She hurried through the back door, kicking off her shoes as she reached the dining room.

"Tom? Are you still here?"

"In the living room," she heard at the other end of the house. "Come here. I've got something to show you."

Sandy walked through the door leading from the dining room to the living room and stopped in surprise, her breath catching in her throat. Tom stood in the archway, propping a massive wooden door up against the wall. She couldn't believe her eyes.

"Tom! Where in the world did you find them?"

Tom grinned at her across the room. "When I ran the phone line, I saw these in the basement. I never even thought about what they were until I ripped into the boxing around the archway."

He pointed to the floor. "I'm sorry, Sandy. I guess I got carried away and I've made a real mess."

Sandy waved her hands in dismissal of his worries. The mess on the floor wasn't important. All she could see were the old oak doors. She couldn't believe her eyes, and she gently ran her hands over the vintage raised panel wooden door he was holding upright.

"Oh, Tom. I can't believe you found them. I remember when they still worked."

Tom smiled down at her, and she realized how silly she must look standing there in her bare feet, caressing an old door.

"I can't promise you, but it looks like the track is repairable. We can salvage the doors for sure, and if I can get the tracks working again, it sure would be cheaper for you than having to install regular doors. And it would help keep the originality of the house. What do you think?"

She found herself grinning at him as joy swept over her. "Well, I'm all for the cheaper part. And if you can salvage these beautiful old doors—that would be wonderful!"

Tom nodded, and then gazed at her with a look on his face she couldn't read. "I forgot to ask; how did the interview go?"

Sandy shrugged. "I'm hoping I'll get the job at the newspaper, but I'll know for sure Monday. But I did get a lead on another job opening at the library. Both are only part-time, but they would be better than nothing."

"Well, that's great news!"

Sandy nodded and unconsciously, reached up to pull a cobweb from Tom's brown wavy hair. The gentle look he gave her made her face flush, and she quickly stepped away from him and gestured toward the doors.

"But this is the best news I've had all day. I can't tell you how much it would mean to me if you are able to make these old doors work again."

She whirled around on her bare feet in a little dance of excitement. "It feels like Christmas!"

CHAPTER 7

Two weeks later Sandy sat at her computer, working on a piece for the local newspaper. It was another Saturday morning, and Tom was upstairs working on building a closet in the north bedroom—her bedroom. Since he'd finished the items on Sandy's downstairs list, the upstairs was next to remodel.

She looked around her office in appreciation for his work. The room was comfortably set up with bookshelves and her desk, and now that the huge oak pocket doors were useable, she was more than happy with the result. Tom had worked a miracle as far as she was concerned by being able to salvage the old track and doors. And since she'd moved her desk out of the living room, it was no longer a catch-all for her books and office items.

She had even thought about having her friend, Rachel Foster, come visit her one of these weekends, although she would have to find some furniture for one of the spare bedrooms upstairs before she made the offer. She couldn't invite her when all there was to sleep on was an old futon.

Sandy chewed the end of her pen as her thoughts turned back to the man working upstairs. So far, Tom had been the exact opposite of what she had heard about contractors/carpenters. He had shown up like clockwork each Friday at noon and every Saturday morning bright and early, to work on her project lists.

She had become accustomed to having him around, and her brain enjoyed the sound of his hammering and sawing while she worked on her writing projects; although her heart wasn't sure if it was a good idea having him around her this often or not. The sight of the five o'clock shadow across his cheeks and the sleeves of his work shirt rolled up showing off his muscular forearms was enough to send her mind into a tailspin. She had forgotten how attractive he was.

Sandy lifted her head and glanced toward the office doorway as she thought she heard Tom's deep bass voice calling her name. She hurried to the base of the staircase in time to hear him call her again, right when he appeared at the top of the steps.

"Sandy, I hate to bother you, but I have a question."

Right then the front doorbell rang. Sandy smiled up the stairway at Tom and held up her index finger.

"Hold that thought. I'll be right back."

She hurried over to open the front door, this time not even peeking out first to check and see who it was. How quickly she'd reverted to the simpler ways of life here in the country. She still had that thought on her mind and a grin on her face when she yanked open the front door. The smile on her face froze when she saw who stood on her porch.

"Mitch?"

Her former fiancé, Mitchell Wright, stood on the other side of her screen door, dressed in light colored tan pants and a long-sleeved dark blue shirt, looking as out of place as he apparently felt.

"Mitch, what are you doing here?"

He was wearing his classic charismatic smile she knew from experience usually won the attention of every female around.

"Hey gorgeous, I came to see you! Wasn't easy to find you, I might add." He pulled the screen door open and came through uninvited and gave her a quick kiss on the cheek as he walked by her. She saw his eyes turning and taking in everything in the room around him.

Her first thought was how both she and the house were a mess. Then she took a deep breath and got her wits about her. She hadn't invited Mitch here. This was her house and her new life. It didn't matter anymore what he thought as he had absolutely no control over her life. The bigger question was though, why was he here?

Mitch stood with his hands clasped behind his back and looked her over. As his steely blue eyes roamed over her from top to bottom, her face warmed in embarrassment. How had she ever stood to be around him?

She took a deep breath for courage and faced him head-on. "So, how did you find me, Mitch?"

He grinned at her a little too broadly. She recognized it now as his 'aren't you excited to see me?' grin. Well, she wasn't happy—at all.

"Your good friend, Rachel, gave me your address. Unfortunately, she didn't tell me how much you were out in the middle of nowhere. I thought I'd never find the place."

"Rachel hasn't been here yet, so she couldn't give you directions," Sandy stated as she spotted Tom out of the corner of her eye, who had moved to the bottom of the stairway. At the same time, Mitch caught sight of him.

"Well, who do we have here?" He went over and stuck out his hand. "I'm Mitchell Wright, an old friend of Sandy's."

Sandy saw Tom glance over Mitch's shoulder at her, but couldn't read his expression. She watched him tentatively shake Mitch's outstretched hand.

"Tom Brannigan."

Mitch turned back toward Sandy with a sneer on his face. She frowned at him as she realized what he was thinking. This was a nightmare. She knew how Mitch's mind worked and she didn't want him to consider anything unsavory about Tom's purpose for being there.

"Tom's a local contractor. He's remodeling the upstairs for me, and," she couldn't help herself and added, "He's an old friend from my high school days. I've known him for years."

Sandy noticed Tom's lips twitch into a little smile as he raised an eyebrow and glanced over at her. She gave him a look she hoped he could read as the call for help that it was, then frowned and turned her attention back to Mitch who was saying something to her.

"I was really sorry to hear you'd left the Toledo area, Sandy. You've made a big mistake though, running away and hiding."

Sandy felt her back stiffen. She was so tired of hearing people telling her she was running away by moving here. "I left town because I needed a change, Mitch. And there was nothing for me there; absolutely no reason for me to stay."

"Aren't you going to invite me in?" Mitch asked as he motioned toward the living room.

Sandy shook her head firmly. "No need, Mitch. You aren't going to be here that long."

✞✞✞✞

After Tom had shaken hands with this guy who was obviously Sandy's old boyfriend, he felt reluctant about heading back upstairs. He had seen the look of panic in her eyes and could tell she was unnerved by the man's unexpected appearance at her front door.

He turned his back to the two of them though and tried to allow them a little privacy while still being within yelling distance if things got out of hand and Sandy needed him. For some reason, he didn't like this Mitch fellow much—nor did he trust him. Truth be known, he was more than a little curious as to the story between the two of them. It was obvious something had happened to Sandy to hurt her, and he couldn't help but wonder if this guy had something to do with it.

Tom dug a screwdriver out of his tool belt and busied himself with taking the switch plate cover off the stairway light switch. There was absolutely nothing wrong with it, but hopefully, no one would notice he wasn't actually doing anything constructive. It was a task he normally could have done in a few seconds, but because of the circumstances, he took his time turning the screwdriver slowly to back out the screws. Even though Tom didn't want to hear their conversation, it was hard not to listen to the voices of the two people in the nearby room raised several times. He strained not to chuckle as he heard Sandy turn aside Mitch's request to sit down, stating he wasn't staying long enough.

Go, girl!

Here was the red-haired, fiery-tempered, Sassy Sandy he remembered!

Mitch was talking to her again in a smooth, silky voice. The guy sounded like he was a real sweet talker to the ladies when he wanted to be. It was easy for Tom to tell though, he was a jerk. Tom had run into plenty of men like him in his lifetime, and he didn't have much use for any man who didn't respect women. Thank goodness Sandy had broken up with him.

Sandy was talking again, and Tom slowly screwed the switch plate cover back on while he listened.

"Mitch, if you recall, you're the one who decided you didn't want to get married. Maybe at the time, I was disappointed, but since then I've come to realize you did me a huge favor."

Wright's voice took on a whiney sound as he continued. "Sandy, it wasn't a case where I didn't want to marry you. I wasn't ready. I told you why."

"Oh really, and how many more years would it take before you were ready? After you'd run around and spent all the time you wanted with your other women? I'm not the least bit sorry it happened. You getting 'cold feet' was the best thing that ever happened to me!"

Tom couldn't hear what Mitch said back to Sandy as he'd lowered his voice considerably. But Tom didn't have any trouble hearing Sandy's answer.

"Mitch, you're a selfish, egotistical person. You don't care about anything but what you want. Now I didn't ask you to come here, but I am telling you to leave. Now!"

He saw Sandy jerk open the front door and motion with her hand for the man to leave. Tom turned and faced the couple, willing to jump in if necessary to make sure Sandy's wishes were followed. There wasn't any argument from Mitch though, and he headed out the door, smiling his perfect plastic smile all the way.

"All right, Sandy. You'll get your way, but someday you'll see you made a big mistake by turning me away. I won't wait around for you to change your mind though. I have other fish to fry."

Even Tom was surprised by her answer. "Then go fry them!" And she slammed the door closed for extra emphasis.

As the sound of the banged door reverberated through the house, Tom watched her warily. She stood completely still with her back rigid, although she looked pretty shaky to him. He glanced out the window long enough to see Mitch get in his car and back out the driveway and leave.

Tom finally felt he had to move, so cautiously walked over behind Sandy and lightly tapped her on the shoulder.

"You okay, Sandy?"

✞✞✞✞

Sandy jumped a little at a touch on her shoulder, then took a deep breath and turned to see Tom standing behind her, wearing a look of concern. She laughed nervously and nodded, still too emotionally shook up to speak. She couldn't believe the feelings seeing Mitch had stirred up in her. The intense pain he had brought to her by dumping her had resurfaced just at the sight of him. After a second or two, she was able to swallow, then took a deep breath, pushed her wayward hair out of her eyes, and looked up to see Tom still standing there looking at her, his golden brown eyes studying her carefully.

"Sorry you had to be witness to that, Tom."

Tom grinned at her, his eyes sparkling. "The guy's a real jerk, huh?"

Sandy laughed along with him and felt a cathartic release. She was so relieved Tom had been here when Mitch showed up. Even though he hadn't said a word, it had been reassuring to know he was there if she'd needed him. How strange; the presence of one man could bring her fear and pain while the other offered her such comfort and peace.

She sighed again. "What. An. Understatement," she stated slowly.

Tom juggled the screwdriver in his hands. "I'm here if you want to talk about it."

She nodded, sniffed a little, and then reached over to a nearby table to grab a tissue from the box. After she blew her nose and wiped her eyes, she gave him a weak grin, feeling a familiar embarrassment sweep over her.

"You always seem to see me at my worst, Tom. You must think I'm a shrew."

She was surprised by his response as he laughed out loud in response.

"You're hardly a shrew. And honestly, it was kinda nice to see Sassy Sandy reappear after all these years."

Sandy found herself laughing with him. *Sassy Sandy.* Tom had called that back in high school when they had gone on a date, although back then she was sure he hadn't meant it as a compliment. Now it sounded like he did, and she actually enjoyed hearing the name again. There was no doubt she had earned the nickname from him due to their one and only date.

She had been, as her father had put it many times, quite a little spitfire during her teenage years. It made her sad to remember her dad was gone now and she couldn't apologize for all the times she'd lost her temper and stomped out of the room and slammed her bedroom door behind her.

She couldn't remember the last time she'd lost her temper—until today. Telling Mitchell Wright off had felt better than good and now he'd left, she finally felt free of her past.

Tom walked back toward the staircase, but instead of going upstairs, he surprised her by sitting on the third step up and waving in her direction.

"If you want to vent your frustrations, I've been told I'm an excellent listener."

Sandy smiled at him again, thinking what a considerate man he was. How and when had he become such a nice guy?

"Okay," she finally agreed and walked over to sit down on the bottom stair step, turning sideways as she had as a child, with her back against the wall and her knees drawn up and turned so she could look up at him as she talked. She was a little bigger than the last time she had done this but was pleased she still fit—even though it was slightly more cramped than she remembered it.

She heaved a huge sigh. Where did she begin?

"You're right. Mitchell Wright is a jerk. He has always been a jerk, and will always be a jerk, but when I first met him I was so enthralled with the knowledge he was interested in me, I overlooked that small fact. Guess I wasn't very smart.

"As you probably noticed, Mitch is a smooth talker—it must come from the business he's in—but anyway, he knows how to wine and dine prospective clients to win their favor, and he does the same thing with women to win their hearts. I've seen him in action with other women, but for some reason when he came on to me the same way, I thought it was the real thing."

She frowned as the painful memories swept over her. "We dated a few months, and then he asked me to move in with him. We lived together for three years. I was willing to wait at home when he had to go out of the country on his so-called 'business' trips. Even when I found out there was always another executive going with him—and even when I discovered it was usually a woman—I was willing to believe him when he said nothing was going on.

"Then he finally did what I'd dreamed about ever since I first saw him; he bought me a beautiful diamond ring and asked me to marry him. It was perfect. He took me out to a fancy restaurant, and after we ate a beautiful candlelit meal, he had the musicians come over and play my favorite romantic song." She let out a sarcastic laugh. "Then he got down on one knee and pulled out this fancy jeweler's box, told me he couldn't live without me, and asked me to become his wife."

Sandy took a breath. Maybe this was liberating—talking to someone about what had happened. Even though she had told some of it to Rachel, she had never told anyone the whole story before, and it helped her look at things differently. She should have been able to see Mitch wasn't a man to commit himself to any woman for the rest of his life, and it was evident he didn't really love her. Otherwise, why would he have pushed her to move in with him without offering marriage from the beginning? She should have known and should have refused him from the start. She'd been raised to believe living together without marriage wasn't acceptable, and she was sure it had hurt her dad considerably when she'd made the decision to move in with Mitch. But all the 'should haves' didn't change what had happened.

"Anyway, I said yes, and we started making wedding plans. I ordered the dress and the flowers, and reserved the church. I'd even started addressing the invitations when he came home from work one evening and said we needed to talk. The bottom line was—he'd changed his mind. He told me he wasn't sure he was ready for marriage."

She bit down on her lower lip as she kept her eyes trained on the tips of her tennis shoes. "Obviously, he wasn't. I'm not sure he ever will be, but I do know if he is, it won't be with me." She sighed. "I cried buckets and felt like my life was ruined as if there was nothing good anymore. Then I decided he was a jerk pretending to be a man, and I was wasting my time wishing I'd married him. I moved in with Rachel for a couple of weeks until I could get back into my old apartment building. Now, I'm upset the most about wasting three years of my life trying to have a relationship with the man."

Sandy thought of something and grinned and looked sideways up the steps at Tom. "How many more times were you planning on taking that switch plate cover off and putting it on again, anyway, Brannigan?"

He chortled loudly, and she joined him, laughing so hard she almost fell off the step. Oh, but it felt good! It had been way too long since she'd enjoyed a good laugh with a friend.

"I was hoping no one would notice. Do you think he did?" Tom finally asked when he'd quit laughing long enough to talk.

She giggled. "Are you kidding? Mitch Wright doesn't know one end of a screwdriver from another. He didn't have a clue what you were doing."

Sandy smiled and released another cleansing sigh, and glanced up the steps toward him. "Thanks, Tom. Thanks for the talk, and thanks, for…being here. I can't tell you how much it meant to me knowing I wasn't facing him alone."

Tom grinned down at her from the upper step, his cute dimples making their appearance again. "If you want honesty, I have to tell you I really wanted to punch the guy in the face. It took all my self-control to let you handle it on your own, Sandy."

She nodded, and then looked up at him again. "You did good then. Anyway, thanks." She gazed at him for a moment, wondering if she dared asked him the question uppermost in her mind.

"Okay, I've spilled my guts. Now, how about you?"

Sandy saw his smile slowly fade as his eyes dropped to the screwdriver still in his hand. "Are you sure you want me to tell you about it, Sandy?"

She nodded and gave him what she hoped was a smile of encouragement. "It's only fair, you know. That way I don't get left feeling foolish for baring my heart and telling you about the dumb things I've done over the years."

He gazed down at her a moment with those brown eyes of his and finally nodded. "Okay, but don't say I didn't warn you, Sandy. It's not a pretty story."

CHAPTER 8

Where did he start the story of how he'd arrived at this point in his life? Tom had been praying for an opportunity to share with Sandy what he'd gone through since high school, but he had been so sure it wasn't time yet. Well, the Lord had put him here with Sandy right now for a reason, so it must be time.

He took a deep breath. For her to understand completely, he'd have to go back to the beginning—back to the man she probably remembered from their high school days. It was never easy for him to tell his story—even though he had told it many times before.

"I'm sure you remember I came from a rough family life. My dad was a drinker, and life with him was never easy. We boys and Mom never knew how he would react to us when he came home at night. I have to admire Mom for staying with him all those years, even though he treated her like dirt. Me, I just hated him.

"I couldn't wait to get away from home—away from his meanness and constant need to try and control us. I don't know if you knew it or not, but my dad died of liver failure about seven years ago. My mom was loyal to the man until the bitter end." He frowned. "I was never able to tell him I forgave him. By the time I was to the point in my life when I could forgive him, he was already dead."

He released a weary sigh before continuing. "After high school, I did a lot of nothing—worked a few odd jobs, bummed around, and was basically worthless. I regret to say I did way too much drinking and partying that frankly, I don't even remember. You would have thought I would have learned better after watching it destroy my dad and his life, but I guess I was a slow learner. I got into some bar fights and spent a few nights in the local Bradford Mills jail. Then I met this wild gal named Andrea one night at a party, and she introduced me to a new excitement, a new high. She was a drug addict, and it wasn't long before I was one too."

He frowned and stared into space as he felt the familiar pain in his heart at the memories of all the irresponsible things he'd done and the terrible way he'd treated people—especially his own family. The drinking had been bad enough. He'd found out early on he couldn't handle any amount of liquor, and the drugs hadn't been any different. It had given him a little more understanding about the addiction his dad had suffered and how alcohol had destroyed his life.

"We were married by the local justice of the peace. I don't know why we even bothered getting married, other than I guess we felt we needed each other. We didn't know each other well; we were drug buddies." He shook his head as he remembered the miserable time in his life. "After only a month, she decided she didn't want to be married after all and got a quickie divorce. I honestly didn't care what she did. She was as important to me as a chair in the corner or something."

He cleared his throat. This was tough telling Sandy about his past, even though it wasn't the first time he'd told it. He'd recounted it many times over the years—both in drug and alcohol rehab units, and more recently when giving his Christian testimony. It was a story he often shared with young people to let them know how quickly they could destroy their lives if they weren't careful what they did and the group of people they hung out with.

"I became a person I'm glad you never knew, Sandy. Sin had grabbed hold of me, taken over my very soul, and twisted my life into one of addiction and waste. I was at the bottom of the barrel. The only thing lower than where I was might be the snakes, but I'm not even sure about that."

Tom glanced down at her upturned face and felt a tug at his heart. She was looking at him with such caring in her green eyes; it shook his emotions for a moment. As many times as he'd shared this story, you would have thought it wouldn't be this difficult. But this was Sandy Martin, the cute little gal from high school—and for some reason, because it was her he was telling the story to, it made it tougher to tell. He hated to destroy her view of him, assuming she had ever thought he was a decent human being. He sure hadn't been back in high school. He swallowed hard and made himself continue.

"Thank God, one day when I was in jail, I was visited by a pastor from a nearby church. He's not around here anymore. Last I heard he moved on to the mission field. I've always felt God put him there, right then, just for me. It sure seemed that way to me, because I don't have a clue why he was there, if not for me.

"He said he knew I felt unloved and unclean, but there was One who loved me more than I could imagine and could take my sin and wash it away until it wouldn't exist anymore." He smiled. "To me, it sounded almost magical, and I was so hungry for someone or something better in my life, I didn't care. I asked him to tell me more, and he did. Pastor Jefferson pulled out his Bible and showed me scripture telling me Jesus loved me, and God loved me, and God sent Jesus to die on the cross for me—to wash away all my sins with His blood on the cross, no matter how bad they were.

"It didn't seem possible anyone could love me so much, but the Pastor said it was true, and then he showed me more scripture, saying all I had to do was accept Jesus as my savior and ask Him to come into my heart and life and He would change me. The pastor led me in a prayer, and I prayed it with all my heart, pleading God would hear me and turn my life around. Afterward, the man gave me a hug and left me a small Bible and a list of scripture to read if I ever doubted Jesus loved me."

He smiled, and as he reached the end of his story, the peace he had found back then washed over his soul again, just the way it did every time he recounted his story. "That was the beginning of my life, Sandy. I started reading the Bible whenever I had free time. I couldn't get enough of God's Word. I was so enthralled with all the stories and the love God has for us."

Tom took a deep breath as he continued. "I eventually got out of jail, landed a real job, and began taking night classes at the local community college. I started going to church on Sundays along with my mom, then attended Wednesday night prayer meeting and Bible study. I discovered a world I never knew existed. Six years have passed since then, and I've never turned back. My old life is gone, and I can honestly sit here and talk about it like it was another person because it was; this sinner before being saved by the grace of Jesus' blood on the cross."

Tom looked down to see Sandy wiping tears from her eyes. He sighed. He hadn't meant to make her cry or feel sorry for him, but maybe telling his story to her would remind her of her own faith.

"Don't cry for me, Sandy. The Lord was good enough to accept me when I wasn't acceptable to anyone else. You were right for giving me a rough time all those years ago. You could see where I was headed with my life, and you warned me. I didn't listen. I'm sorry I squandered my life for so long, but hopefully, I can help someone else along the way, so they don't waste theirs."

She turned her lips up in a little smile and nodded at him. "Someone like me."

"Well, that wasn't what I meant, but yes—I guess I hate to see you waste your time believing you should have married him. If I remember, you were the one all those years ago who told me to get on my knees and get my life straight with

God. I sure wish I'd listened to you back then. It would have saved me from lots of misery."

She nodded. "I was hoping you didn't remember." She frowned. "I was a pompous little brat back then, wasn't I?"

He chuckled. "I wouldn't describe you that way, Sandy. You were a young woman with your heart and mind in the right place, and I was a screwed up idiot who didn't have a clue what was important in life."

Sandy looked up at him and then pulled herself to her feet. "Funny, how life is. Now you're the one who seems to have your act together with God, and I'm the one wondering what I'm supposed to do next."

Tom stood and came down the steps to stand in front of her. Maybe now was the time to broach the subject of returning to church. As far as he knew, she hadn't been going since her return—at least she hadn't been to the church where she had formerly gone. He knew because her old church was where he now attended.

"God hasn't gone anywhere, Sandy. He's still right here, waiting for you to come back to Him." Tom stopped before he said more, not wanting to sound preachy to her. "Tell you what; tomorrow is Easter Sunday. What better day to return to church and your first love? Just consider it, okay?"

She nodded but didn't say anything more, and it was obvious to Tom she was done talking about it when she changed the subject.

"A long time ago you yelled down the steps about a question you had. Now would be a good time to ask it—if you can remember what it was, that is."

He laughed. "Hey! Be nice! I'm only a few years older than you. I was just going to ask you a question about what type of doors you want on the upstairs closets. Let's go up, and I'll show you why I asked."

Tom started up the steps, hearing Sandy's footsteps behind him. It was time to stop discussing their pasts and get back to work.

CHAPTER 9

Sandy rolled over in bed and looked at the clock on her bedside stand. Why was she awake so early? It was Sunday morning—the one day she could sleep as late as she wanted. Then she remembered Tom's words of the previous day.

Today was Easter Sunday.

After lying in bed a little longer staring at the ceiling, she rolled out of bed and padded down the stairs, wishing as she did most every morning that Tom had already installed the upstairs bathroom. After splashing a little water on her face, she headed to the kitchen and started the coffeemaker. She was awake anyway; she might as well get ready and go to church. Maybe she'd even be early enough to attend the singles Sunday school class Maggie Brannigan had mentioned to her. It had been a long time since she'd sat in a Sunday school class. Her heart did a little flip at the realization Tom might be there too, but she kept telling herself his presence didn't have anything to do with why she was going to the bother of attending church. It was Easter, after all.

A little over an hour later she knew she wasn't going to get there in time for Sunday school, but she would get there in time for the worship service. Grabbing her purse and her Bible, she took one last look at herself in the mirror. There was no new Easter outfit to wear, but it didn't matter. The people attending church this morning hadn't seen her in years. Most of them probably wouldn't even know who she was.

Sandy drove through Bradford Mills to the other side of town to the small church she'd attended as a child with her parents and grandmother. Pulling in the parking lot caused Sandy another one of those déjà vu moments. She'd had several of those since her return to Bradford Mills.

There were quite a few cars parked in the lot, but it was by no means full. She had thought there would be more people here since it was Easter Sunday, but then many people didn't attend church as frequently as they had when she was a child. Case in point, it had been years since she'd been in a church building other than for a funeral or two and a couple of weddings.

A few people were standing outside the open doors of the church, visiting with each other—as people always seem to do before the service. She walked through the double doors into the entryway, then down the short hallway toward the wooden double doors of the sanctuary. Several men in suits were there, handing out bulletins, and smiling and welcoming people. Suddenly Sandy felt out of place. Perhaps it had been a mistake for her to come. It had been foolish for her to think she was going to be able to revisit her childhood faith by coming back to church.

She hesitantly accepted one of the bulletins, took a deep breath, and went through the doorway into the sanctuary. As she entered, her eyes scanned the room. So far she didn't recognize anyone, although there were several elderly women seated in pews near the back of the church who looked vaguely familiar. Maybe they had been friends of her Grandma.

Sandy mentally caught herself before she started looking for her mom and dad. They had been so much a part of this church and would usually have been sitting in one of the pews and talking with their friends. Mom was gone, as were Dad and her grandmother. All the familiar family faces were no longer present to greet her and offer surprised looks at her return. There was no one here anymore who remembered the little girl who had attended Vacation Bible School every summer or taken part in numerous children's Christmas pageants all those years ago.

She was tempted to turn around and leave. Then one of the older women smiled at her, and she was suddenly reminded of her own grandmother. Maybe she'd stay after all.

Sandy remembered precisely where she had sat as a child with her parents, and where her grandmother and uncle and his family had always sat. This morning she chose to sit halfway up near the center aisle on the left-hand side. There was no real reason why she wanted to sit there, other than no one else was sitting there at the time. She just hoped she wasn't taking anyone's regular seat. She watched as people continued to file in, couples with young children and babies, older couples, and teens. There were a few faces she thought she remembered but wasn't sure she could put names with all of them. She saw Maggie Brannigan come in and take a seat halfway up toward the front on the other side of the church. Maggie glanced her way and smiled broadly upon seeing her and Sandy smiled back. At least she knew one person in the congregation.

After scanning the bulletin for a moment or two, she glanced around one more time and noticed her cousin, Kate, seated near the back with a towheaded boy about six years old. She was contemplating moving back to sit with her, when a middle-aged man Sandy assumed to be the pastor, walked up the aisle toward the front. About that same time, another man whom Sandy couldn't see very well came from a side door near the baptistery and sat down behind the podium and the other man joined him.

The organist started playing an old hymn Sandy remembered from her childhood. It wasn't the older woman who had played the organ in her childhood memories. Sandy knew Mrs. Gillespie, a woman small in stature, but larger than life when she sat down behind a piano or organ, had passed away several years earlier. Sandy had taken piano lessons from her for years but had eventually quit as her interests had moved to other things. The truth was, she hadn't been very good at it; she had never come close to reaching the ability of Mrs. Gillespie.

Sandy pulled the hymnal from the holder in the back of the pew in front of her and opened it to the first song they would be singing as listed in the bulletin, "Christ the Lord Is Risen Today"—one of her Easter favorites.

She glanced up as she heard a man's familiar bass voice welcoming them to the service, only to find her eyes lock with those of Tom Brannigan. There he was, standing behind the podium in front, preparing to lead the congregation in the first song. She saw his face break into a huge smile as his brown eyes landed on hers and she felt her face grow warm. She hoped he didn't mention her name or she would crawl under the pews all the way back out the door. Thankfully he didn't, and the organ started the beginning refrain.

"Let's all stand, please, for "Christ the Lord is Risen Today," Tom instructed the congregation.

Sandy stood with the rest and tried to concentrate on the words of the old hymn. By the time they'd arrived at the chorus, there was no doubt in her mind as to why Tom was leading the songs. He had an incredible singing voice. There was no end to the surprises about this man.

After the hymn ended, Tom asked everyone to bow their heads as he gave an opening prayer. Sandy listened to the words coming from this man who had changed so much from the one she remembered and sighed as a feeling of peace washed over her at his words. It had been a long time since she'd taken time in her life to talk to God—or even think about God, for that matter. She took a deep breath and released it, feeling some of the worries of her life slip away. It had been a good decision to come to church this morning.
Maybe Tom was right. Maybe she needed to turn back to God. She'd tried it on her own and wasn't doing so well.

After Tom's "amen," he announced it was time to welcome each other to the service, and people around Sandy started talking, shaking hands, and greeting each other. Sandy felt awkward standing there alone until a teenage girl who had been sitting in the pew behind her timidly stuck out her hand to shake. Sandy grinned and eagerly returned the handshake.

"Good morning. Are you visiting?" the young girl asked with a shy smile. Sandy guessed her to be about fourteen, with long straight auburn hair pulled back into a ponytail and wearing a dress much shorter than Sandy would have dared to wear when she'd been a teenager.

"Good morning," Sandy said back. "I'm not exactly a visitor. I grew up in this church."

Before she had a chance to say much more, others were waiting to shake her hand. Her cousin Kate made her way across the aisle and gave her a quick hug, whispering in her ear she was glad she was back, and they'd have to get together soon. Maggie came over and quickly gave her a smile and hug before moving on to greet others. When Sandy turned back around to make her way back to her seat, she realized Tom was standing behind her, waiting to shake her hand.

She felt his large hand clasp her smaller one. "I'm so glad you came!" he whispered as if it were a secret. "I'd sit with you, but I have to lead songs right now."

Before Sandy had an opportunity to respond, he let go of her hand, gave her a quick wink, and turned to head back up front. She noticed the others making their way back to their seats and realized the time of welcome had come to an end, but thankfully she was feeling a little less out of place now than she when she'd first arrived. It was a friendly and welcoming group of people at this church, and she understood now why her parents had stayed here for so long.

They sang two more hymns, and then a young man walked up to the podium and gave the announcements for the week, followed by the pastor saying a prayer before the ushers passed around the offering plates. After the offering, there was another hymn, then the pastor (which the bulletin said was Pastor Donald Armstrong) stepped behind the podium to speak.

As the pastor started his sermon, Sandy suddenly realized Tom had slid into her pew from the opposite side of the church and was now seated next to her. She gave him a nervous smile and reached for her Bible on the seat between them. It was going to be difficult to concentrate on the pastor's sermon with Tom Brannigan sitting next to her, but she was going to do her best.

Sandy turned her attention to what the Pastor was saying and rustled through the pages of her Bible to find the scripture for the day's sermon. Today's topic was the story of the morning when Mary came to the tomb where Jesus was buried, and Sandy found herself so caught up in the Pastor's words before she realized it the service was drawing to a close. The old story she had heard a hundred times as a child seemed so much more real to her this morning, although she couldn't put her finger on why. Perhaps it was because it had been so long since she had heard the Word.

Tom gave her a smile before he left the pew to return to his spot behind the pulpit to lead the closing song and she hurried to find the page number in the hymnal. After the concentration she had felt in listening to the sermon, it almost felt as if she were coming out of a trance. As she started to sing with the rest of the congregation, she made a resolution.

It was time for her to start reading her Bible again. She had forgotten what comfort there was between those pages—especially in the Gospels. How had she forgotten? Some of her favorite memories of her grandmother had been seeing her sitting in her rocker in the same house where Sandy now lived, her well-worn Bible on her lap and a look of peace on her face.

Sandy sighed. It had been a long time since she had felt a similar peace. She just hoped God hadn't given up on her.

CHAPTER 10

Sandy sat at her desk in the corner of her home office staring at the computer screen, before a yawn forced her to momentarily close her eyes. She reached out and turned off the computer monitor and the lamp on the corner of the desk, leaving the soft glow coming down the hallway from the kitchen as the only light in the room.

She rested her right elbow on the desktop and plopped her chin on her open palm. She was tired. Even though it had been two weeks since the bat incident, she hadn't been sleeping well. Instead of drifting off to sleep as she'd been able to in the past, she would lay there envisioning a black object swooping over her in the darkness. Tom had promised he'd plugged all the possible entry holes and there hadn't been a repeat sighting of the bat, but she just couldn't feel comfortable once she turned out the lights. Sandy wasn't afraid of much in life, but she was terrified of bats—and mice.

The sound and sweet smell of an early summer evening's soft rain wafted through the open window in the corner of the room. She finally stood and walked over to push the window closed, in case it started to start rain harder during the night. Opening her mouth in another yawn, she sighed. It was time for her to head to bed.

Later as she tried to get comfortable in her bed, her thoughts turned again to the feelings of depression she had been suffering the last few days. The first week or so after attending church on Easter morning, she had been on a spiritual high. The last few days though, she had fallen back to an emotional low spot. Nights had become miserable as intense loneliness swept over her. She struggled tonight as she did almost every night to keep her tears at bay.

What was the matter with her?

She had wanted to get away from Mitchell Wright and her old life and start over again, and she had. Returning to her hometown of Bradford Mills and being around people from her childhood shouldn't make her feel so lost—so lonely. If anything, it should make her feel more secure about her life, she reasoned. That was her whole purpose for moving back here. Of course, living here in her grandmother's house hadn't brought her childhood back, but the house was filled with wonderful memories of happier times in her life.

So, why was she so miserable?

The tears she had been struggling to hold back seeped from the corner of her eyes. What was she missing in her life and where had she lost it? Whatever it was, she wanted it back.

✞✞✞✞

The next Friday, Sandy had the afternoon off and spent most of it outside pulling weeds at the west side of the house. She had been pleasantly surprised to find iris growing underneath the window of her office, and was fairly sure they were planted by her grandmother. It was tough to tell if any other flowers were growing there though, as the weeds had taken over the area.

She stepped back and looked at the side of the house. In addition to the weeds in the iris bed, there was a huge mass of grape vines and English ivy growing up the house near the window. It needed to be taken down before it did further damage to the house and siding, but it wasn't going to be an easy job as there was so much of it. Sandy grabbed hold of the nearest piece and tugged and yanked on the vine until a substantial hunk came loose, then added it to the ever-growing heap of weeds in the yards.

Pausing to rest in the hot late afternoon sun, she surveyed the remaining accumulation of weeds and tangled vines and quickly made the decision to call it a day. She'd been working out there for several hours, and her throat was calling for a drink of water. And even though she'd slathered on sunscreen before coming out, she was feeling the effects of the hot sun on her neck and forearms. The month of May was turning out to be much warmer than she remembered.

She lugged the pile of weeds and tossed them into the nearby wheelbarrow and pushed it around the back of the house to her mounting heap of brush and weeds. Maybe she'd start a compost pile. She'd have to do some research on it.

After a refreshing shower and ice tea and salad for dinner, Sandy was feeling a little more refreshed. While putting her dirty dishes in the sink, she glanced down at her arm and noticed a small red, rashy spot, right above her wrist. She immediately headed to the bathroom where she dug around in the medicine cabinet for some anti-itch cream.

By morning, she was dismayed to see the rash had spread from her wrist all the way up her arm and over to the right side of her neck. And it itched and burned something awful and was turning into less of a rash and more of a series of little boils. She spread more of the anti-itch cream over the affected areas and hoped for some relief. It felt like her neck and arm were on fire, and it was beginning to become very uncomfortable.

Sandy was finishing her breakfast when she noticed a familiar dark blue pickup truck drive around back of the house, pulling a small flat trailer with a load of lumber on it. Tom was supposed to start working on building a deck off the sliding glass doors as soon as he finished the laundry room closet and the upstairs bathroom, and it looked as if he was delivering materials for the job. Sandy grabbed her mug of coffee and headed out the back door, then stood and watched him unload and stack the deck boards.

He placed another pile of boards on the growing stack, and finally turned and glanced her way. She watched him push his sunglasses up on his head as he walked toward her.

"Whoa. What happened to you?" He pointed to her right arm.

She shook her head. "I don't know. It was only a tiny rash last night, but this morning…."

"Were you working outside yesterday?" His stepped closer and his eyes ran up her arm and rested on her neck as he studied the rash closely.

Sandy nodded. "I was pulling weeds under the office window."

She watched Tom tug off his gloves and stick them in his back jeans pocket.

"Go get your purse and lock up the house. I'm taking you to get checked out."

Sandy shook her head. "I don't think…."

"Sandy! It looks like poison ivy, and you are obviously very allergic to it. Until you get some medicine, it's going to get worse and keep spreading."

Sandy saw the look of concern in his eyes and slowly nodded her head in defeat. She was so miserable she didn't feel up to fighting him.

Tom quickly unhooked his trailer from the truck and drove her into Bradford Mills to the walk-in clinic operated by a semi-retired doctor. The receptionist took one look at Sandy and showed her to an examining room. Within half an hour, the gray-haired, soft-spoken doctor had given her a prescription for corticosteroid pills, a huge bottle of calamine lotion, and a package of oral antihistamines, with strict instructions to avoid poison ivy in the future.

"As if I did it on purpose," she muttered as she headed back down the hallway to the waiting room where Tom patiently waited for her. After a quick trip to the pharmacy to have the prescription filled, Tom drove her back home.

"Thanks for making me go, Tom," she said grudgingly as they pulled in Sandy's driveway.

"No problem," he said quietly as they sat in the truck. He turned to look at her, a serious look on his face.

"So, where were you pulling weeds, Sandy? Show me."

✞✞✞✞

Tom had been shocked when he had arrived at Sandy's house to find her right arm and neck covered in a bright red oozing rash. And it had looked to be spreading quickly. He hadn't ever had poison ivy before, but he knew it could be awful for someone who was allergic, so his first thought was to get her to a doctor. Fortunately, she hadn't fought him. If he'd had to, he supposed he could have played 'cave man' and thrown her over his shoulder and carried her to the doctor. Just the idea of doing that caused him to chuckle. He couldn't imagine Sandy allowing anyone, including him, to make her do anything she didn't want to do.

While he was sitting in the waiting room at the doctor's office, he had decided the first thing he was going to do when they got back to her house was find the rest of the offending weed and kill it. Sandy didn't dare have another run in with the poison plant. And if there was some in the yard, there was sure to be more elsewhere on the property. He didn't particularly want to come in contact with it either.

Once they returned to her house and he demanded to know where she'd been working, Tom followed Sandy around the back of the house to the west corner. After she had pointed at the area where she'd been pulling ivy from the side of the house, Tom walked back to his truck and pulled out a large bottle of brush killer. He'd been planning to spray down the area where he was going to build Sandy's deck anyway, so he might as well take care of the English ivy—obviously interspersed with poison ivy—then spray a few more plants in the area. After he'd sprayed down both areas well, he hooked the trailer back up to his truck and finished unloading the rest of the lumber.

He was hoping the remaining poison ivy would have died by the time he got ready to put in posts for the deck and start building it. Fortunately, due to his schedule, it was going to be another week or more before he could start it. Sandy had already requested him to build her shelves in the laundry room closet next. And then, of course, she wanted the upstairs bathroom installed.

And since she was the boss, he thought to himself with a grin, he wasn't going to argue. Especially since the remaining projects continued to keep him in the house with her. Nope, he wasn't going to complain at all.

CHAPTER 11

The next Friday afternoon, Tom grunted as he wedged his tall frame through the doorway of the laundry room closet, cordless drill in his hand. As the last rusty screw backed out of the wall, he put the drill down on the floor and then reached into the closet to pull the clothes bar loose from the brackets. It was no easy task as the bar and brackets had apparently been painted over many times. He gave it a hefty tug and when it finally came loose, gave a sigh of satisfaction and let the heavy wooden bar fall to the floor with a clunk. His fingertips gently ran over the holes left on both sides of the wall. Some spackling compound and sandpaper would soon have those spots smoothed out and ready for paint and no one but he would even know the holes had been there.

Tom glanced over in the corner of the laundry room to see the used washer and dryer he had already hooked up for Sandy two weeks earlier. Now he was working on readying the closet in the room for the requested shelves. It would be an easy task once he tore out all the old hardware from when it had been used as a clothes closet. He turned his attention back to the job at hand and reached to the back closet wall and started to unscrew one of the black antique-looking wire clothes hooks secured to the wall.

While he worked, Tom let his mind wander, as if often did these days, to Sandy. Her list of little jobs was quickly being completed—too fast for his liking. Not that he didn't have other jobs lined up, but this was becoming his favorite work project. He had to admit, even if she was usually in one part of the house while he worked in another part, he greatly enjoyed this time he was spending with her. Even though she was involved with her projects and he was busy working, there were still opportunities to talk with her.

He didn't feel he was making much progress in getting her to open up as to why she didn't go to church anymore, however. After seeing her in church Easter Sunday, he had hoped she had made a decision to mend her relationship with God, but as of yet, she hadn't been back to a service. All he could do was keep praying for her.

Tom threw the loose coat hook to the floor and reached back to remove the second one. As soon as he turned it though, the whole rear wall shifted and came away from the left side corner. He let out a groan. This wasn't good. What was supposed to be a simple closet re-do had the possibility of turning into more of a structural issue. He hoped it wasn't going to be an expensive fix—for Sandy's sake.

He gently pushed on the rear wall was and was surprised when it opened completely, with the right side acting as a hinge.

As if it was a door.

Tom stood there eyeing the opening for a few seconds, then left the room to make a quick trip to his truck. He wasn't sure what he had found in the back of the closet, but he needed more light to see whatever it was. When he returned to the laundry room, he quickly plugged the extension cord he'd brought from his truck into a nearby electrical outlet, then plugged in the trouble light and clamped it on the edge of the opening and pushed the switch to turn it on.

✟✟✟✟

Sandy sat at the desk in her office, staring at the computer monitor while she tried to finish an article she'd promised Mr. Drayton, the editor of the Bradford Mills newspaper. She was having trouble concentrating and she couldn't help but feel it was at least partially due to the presence of the good-looking man working in her laundry room. She enjoyed having Tom around—way too much. At least most of the time. Some days she felt comfortable with him working in the house. Other times when he came to ask her a question or get her opinion about something, she would start to have misgivings about her decision to have him work for her. All those old feelings she'd had for him back in high school were resurfacing, and she didn't know what to do about it. The last thing she wanted right now was to start another romantic relationship. She had gone through the miserable experience with Mitch, and she was determined she wasn't going down that road again for a long time.

The good news though, she didn't have to worry about not being able to afford to have Tom do the remodeling work anymore. Her dad's house had finally sold, the closing having happened just two days earlier, so this house was now officially hers. No more monthly mortgage payments to the bank. No more rent payments to a landlord. For the first time in her life, she finally owned something. Well, she owned her car sitting in the driveway too, but at its age, she wasn't sure how long it would be before she would have to replace it. Hopefully not anytime soon.

Things were definitely looking up for her financially though. She had been offered a full-time position at the library so had been able to quit the dreaded sales job at the newspaper. She was still hoping to be able to provide short news articles for the paper every now and then though. What she honestly wanted was to write human interest stories, but until she became more familiar with the local folks again, she wasn't going to be able to provide many of those.

She turned in her desk chair as she heard Tom's voice calling her name down the hallway, then he stepped into the office doorway.

"Sandy, do you know exactly when this house was built?"

Seeing Tom leaning against the door frame upset her concentration for a second or two until she realized he'd asked her a question.

"Um, which part? This part was built in the 1920's. The dining room area was constructed in the late 1880's or so, and if I remember right, the kitchen and that end of the house is the original part of the house—built sometime before the Civil War. Why do you want to know? Did you find a structural problem or something?"

She gulped at the thought of pouring all of her money into a house with foundation problems. A money pit was the last thing she needed right now. Sandy gasped when Tom strode across the room to where she sat, grabbed her hand and pulled her from the chair.

"Where are we going?" she sputtered. While he wasn't exactly man-handling her, the firm way he took hold of her hand threw her senses and emotions into a tailspin. What was going on? Was he angry with her about something? He kept her hand firmly in his as he strode back out of the room, pulling her along behind him. The only comforting part of the excursion was the grin on his face.

"You have to see this for yourself, Sandy. Telling you what I've found just won't do it justice."

Sandy was uncomfortably aware of her hand still clamped tightly in his large one as they crossed the dining room, went into the kitchen and through the door into the laundry room. He didn't relinquish the hold he had on her hand until they reached the laundry room.

"Tom, what is going on?" She asked as she ran her hands down the legs of her jeans, wondering if her hand had been that sweaty when Tom was holding onto it.

He grinned at her again. "Patience, grasshopper. I want to show you what I've found, but I want to do it the right way—so you'll be as surprised as I was."

Sandy glared at Tom and then glanced around the room in confusion. What exactly did that mean? What surprise?

He was still standing next to her and she felt his strong hand rest on the small of her back as he gently pushed her in the direction of the closet. Sandy looked into the closet to try and see what had Tom so worked up, but couldn't see anything unusual.

It was a closet. What was the big deal?

All she could see was one of his work lamps, clamped on the front door jamb of the closet, lighting up the back wall. Tom had removed the clothes bar from the closet, and it seemed he was in the process of taking out the old black wire clothing hooks from the back wall. What did he want to show her? She looked at him again, feeling frustrated at his interruption. She had work to do, and so did he.

"What am I looking at, Tom?"

He pointed at the back wall. "Take hold of the hook right there and turn it to the left."

She shook her head, not understanding what he wanted. "What?"

Sandy gasped when Tom grabbed her right hand and pull her into the closet with him. It was a tight fit, and she wondered if he could feel how hard and fast her heart was beating with him so close. He was near enough she could smell his aftershave, along with the pleasant smell of sawdust that she always considered to be part of him. Even though he'd been working hard all morning, she still thought he smelled good, and it was all she could do to keep from laying her head on his chest and sighing in contentment.

When Tom gently pulled her hand, her mind slowly came back to why they were in the closet in the first place. He'd said he had something he wanted to show her. Tom firmly guided her hand to the hook in question and helped her turn it a little to the left. She gasped in astonishment as the back wall came loose and opened up to the right as if it were a door. Sandy looked up at his face with what she was sure was a stunned look.

"What happened?"

His smiling face looked down at her, his brown eyes near enough she could see the specks of gold in them. She tried to breathe, but was having a hard time with him so close. He was so close she could easily pull his face down to hers and kiss those lips...

"Stay with me here, Sandy. There's more."

He backed away for a moment, turned off the work light, then returned and clamped it onto the back wall frame. Tom turned to look at her again, the grin still on his face, his dimples standing out and giving his face the appearance of a mischievous little boy.

"Are you ready, Sandy? I'm going to turn the light back on."

She gave a little nod and watched as Tom reached up to push the switch and turn on the lamp, flooding the cavity behind the door with light. Sandy looked in and gasped. In front of them were three stone steps leading down into what appeared to be a room. She looked at him again and didn't try to hide the shock she was feeling.

"What is this room? I never knew it was here!"

He gestured with his hand as if to tell her to go down the steps ahead of him. She started to take a step forward and then stopped.

"Please tell me there are no bats down there, Tom."

Tom was close enough behind her she could felt his breath on her neck and not only heard but felt his deep chuckle.

"I haven't gone down there yet, Sandy. After I found it, I came and got you right away."

He turned her toward him and lightly touched her on her cheek with the palm of his right hand. "I seriously doubt there will be bats in the basement, but if there are, I'll protect you." He grinned at her, his eyes teasing. "There might be some in the attic, however. I haven't been up there yet. If you want, we can go up there and check when we finish here," he teased.

Sandy stuck her tongue out at him and his teasing, released a shudder at the thought of ever meeting another bat, and then braced her back for stepping into the unknown. She just hoped there weren't any mice or rats down there either. The only comfort she had was the feel of Tom's hand on her elbow to steady her as they both carefully made their way down the three stone steps.

They stood in a small room approximately five feet wide and about seven feet long with a stone floor. The walls and ceiling were covered with rough-hewn boards running horizontally, grayed with age. The ceiling of the room wasn't tall, and although Sandy at five foot three inches could stand upright without hitting her head, Tom looked downright uncomfortable as he hunched over to stand in the small area.

Tom's trouble lamp flooded the area with enough light they could see the room was basically empty other than a couple of empty wooden crates turned upside down in one corner and an old wooden barrel sitting in the other. A partially burned candle in a tin holder sat on top of one of the overturned crates.

Sandy turned toward Tom in confusion. "What is this place?"

He shook his head as he glanced around the room. "I was hoping you could tell me. I suppose it could be the original house's root cellar, but I don't know why the entrance was hidden."

She glanced around the room, taking in all the walls and ceiling. "I've never seen anything like it."

Tom looked around too and then turned back to her. "And you really didn't know this was here?"

She shook her head. "Grandma never mentioned it, so I have to believe she didn't know about it either. My mother grew up in this house—so did my grandma. You would have thought somebody would have talked about this room sometime in a conversation over the years if they'd known about it."

Sandy took a deep breath of the cold dry air around her. Maybe it had been a root cellar. It made sense since it was off the kitchen—although back when the house was first built there would have likely only been two rooms. She was still mystified as to why she hadn't known about this little cellar room before though.

She watched Tom go up the steps and unclamp the lamp, dragging the extension cord along with him. He brought the lamp back down into the room with him, rotating it to light up all the corners, and then turned it back toward the steps and entrance again.

Sandy called out when he went to the doorway. "Wait! Move the light back there, Tom." She moved over to the area she wanted him to shine the light on. As Tom turned the light back in the direction of the doorway, she pointed to a spot above the doorjamb.

"What is that?"

Tom handed her the lamp to hold and reached up to pull what looked like a rag from a crack in the wall above the door. He held the bundle in his hand under the light, then gave her the bundle, and took the lamp from her. Putting his right hand on her shoulder, he pushed her gently in the direction of the entrance.

"Let's take it up into the kitchen to look at. I'm tired of stooping over." He chuckled. "If I had to stay down here for long, I'd end up walking around like a humped backed little old man."

Sandy gently held the bundle of rags, and the two of them carefully made their way back up the stone steps and through the closet into the laundry room. Once they reached the main floor, she stood a minute, pushing her shoulders back so she could stand up straight, and quickly ran her free hand through her hair checking for cobwebs and spiders. A shudder went through her again. She certainly wouldn't want to have to spend a lot of time in the little room— especially in the dark.

Tom followed her up the steps and through the opening, pulling the door behind him where it closed with a click. She watched him place the work light on the floor, and then he turned to her with a huge grin like a little boy on his face. She couldn't help but grin back at him.

"Let's go see what we found!" He said.

She looked down at the little bundle in her hand. It was hard to believe it was going to be anything other than a bunch of dirty old rags, but Tom seemed excited by their find, so she decided to humor him. Heading to the kitchen, they both pulled out chairs next to each other and took seats at the table. Sandy carefully placed the bundle on the table in front of them and looked at it. Here in the light of day, it appeared to be a flat leather sack of some kind, tied at one end with a dirty leather string. Her fingers were stiff as she struggled with it, but she was finally able to loosen the string enough to open it.

Sandy looked over at Tom sitting next to her, his face expectant, and she had to hold in her laughter. He looked as if he thought it was going to be a treasure of some sort. She was certain they weren't going to find anything of value. Not in that grungy cellar room.

She pushed the satchel across the table toward him. "You want the honors, Brannigan? I'm almost afraid to reach in there. My creative mind is coming up with all kinds of gruesome things I might pull out."

He laughed and took the satchel from her, grinning all the time. He put his hand in the hole of the sack and pulled out another leather bundle, rolled up and tied with another leather string. She watched as his large calloused hands cautiously untied the string and unrolled what looked like sheets of yellowed paper.

"What is it?" she asked breathlessly. Tom had been right. Whatever it was, it was more than a bundle of rags.

He gently touched the old pages, and she could see from where she sat near him the ink was faded.

"It's hard to say. The pages are so brittle, I'm almost afraid to touch them." He pushed it back at her across the table. "Maybe you'd better be the one to look at it, Sandy. It belongs to you after all, since it's your house."

Sandy hesitantly touched the paper, gently smoothing it out so she could see the words written there. Time hadn't been kind to the pages, and the ink was faded.

"I don't know if we're going to be able to read it enough to know what it is, Tom. It looks really old." She turned back to the beginning of the pages and was able to make out a little of the scribbles. "I think it says, 'This belongs to Darcy.'"

Sandy looked over at Tom. "I wonder who this Darcy person was. And why was this hidden in that room?"

Tom shook his head. "I don't know. Maybe she was a little girl who lived here a long time ago, and it was her favorite place to hide? Do you think you'll be able to read it?"

Sandy glanced through a few other pages, trying to treat the fragile paper with extra care. "I don't know. Maybe I can scan the pages into my computer and then enlarge them. That way I can darken or lighten them as needed."

She gave him a smile as her mind realized they had actually found something unique. "I want to try and see if I can figure out who wrote it—and why it was hidden down there. This is kind of exciting!"

The heat rushed to her face when Tom's gentle eyes rested on her face.

"If anybody can do it, Sandy, you can."

She dropped her head to hide her face from him, feeling more than a little overwhelmed by the feelings rushing through her. The way his eyes looked at her left her feeling...she'd almost thought the word 'loved' for a moment, even though she was sure her imagination was running away with her.

Tom got out of his chair and stood. "Right now though, I'm at the point of re-doing the closet, so you're going to have to make a decision. Do you still want me to build shelves in there?"

Sandy chewed on her lower lip as she thought for a moment. She needed and wanted the shelf space in that room, but without knowing what they had found, she didn't want to destroy the closet entrance.

"I think I want to put the project on hold, Tom, if that's not going to make you angry with me."

He looked over at her, nodded, and gave her a small smile. "I completely agree. We may want to do something different in the closet anyway now we know the little room is down there."

She smiled at how quickly he used the term 'we'—like he had a vested interest in what happened to the closet and the little diary. In a way, she supposed he did since he had been the one to discover the hidden entrance in the first place.

I could have lived in this house the rest of my life and never known it was there.

Sandy felt Tom's hand come to rest on her shoulder and turned to look up at him in surprise.

"You will share what you find in the diary with me, won't you, Sandy?"

She couldn't help but grin at the twinkle in his eyes. "It can be arranged, Thomas." She dropped her eyes back down to the bundle resting on the table. "That's assuming I can actually read what it says."

✞✞✞✞

Tom left a little later as he had another job he had to check out, and Sandy knew until she made a decision about what was going to happen with the closet, he couldn't finish this job.

She spent the rest of the afternoon and most of the evening carefully scanning the pages of the diary into her computer. Some of the pages were in such bad shape she couldn't do anything with them, but most had enough legible writing she was able to get them to scan. About midnight when her eyes began to feel as if they had sand in them, she finally stopped working on the project to go to bed.

The next day was a Saturday, and she was drinking her third cup of coffee when Tom arrived for his day's work. She had touched up and printed off ten pages of the diary and was struggling to read it. So far, what she had been able to decipher confused her more.

Sandy answered Tom's knock on the door and waved him toward the kitchen where she told him to have a seat, then poured him a mug of coffee and pushed a plate of donuts in his direction.

"I need to read some of this to you, Tom, because I am very confused by it. I don't understand why this was down there. I don't know why it was even in this house. I can tell you though from what little I've read, it appears this diary was written by an uneducated woman. It is really difficult to read."

She sat back down at the table and picked up one of the copies she had printed off. "Listen to this."

Sandy painstakingly read the words on the page out loud to Tom.

"'I be Darcy, and dis is my book to writ in. We ain't supposed to read and writ, so I can't tell no body I can. If the Marsa find out, he will beat me or kut off my hand. So I hide my book where nobody find it.'"

She stopped reading and looked across the table at Tom to find him watching her, an uneaten donut held in his right hand, and a look of disbelief on his face.

"Who do you think this 'Marsa' is she's talking about that's going to cut off her hand? I don't understand any of this at all. Do you suppose this is some novel someone was writing or something? It just doesn't make sense."

Tom waved the donut in the air a little as if addressing the room. "Sandy, didn't you tell me you thought this part of the house was built before the Civil War?"

She nodded and then watched as Tom put the donut back down on the plate and sat back in his chair, a slow grin spreading across his face.

"The hidden room is starting to make a whole lot more sense to me now. Do you suppose the diary was written by a slave—a runaway slave? Maybe this house was a part of the Underground Railroad."

Sandy felt goosebumps go up and down her arms as Tom's words registered in her brain. What he was saying was difficult to grasp, but what other reasonable explanation was there for a diary such as this being found in a Michigan basement? Was that what this was all about? Had the diary been written by a black slave girl who had hidden it in the cellar of this house on her way to freedom?

"The Underground Railroad? Do you really think so, Tom? I mean, you would have thought someone in my family would have passed that information down from generation to generation until it got to me, wouldn't you?"

"Maybe they didn't know. Your grandparents and great-grandparents might not have been aware of the history of the original house. It was a long time ago, Sandy." He shrugged, and picked his donut up again and took a bite, then leaned forward in his chair.

"So what else does it say?"

Sandy glanced back down at the page in her hands. The papers suddenly became much more precious to her if what Tom said was true.

The Underground Railroad!

"I haven't read much of it yet. Most of the ink is badly faded, and some of the pages are deteriorated to the point it was hard to even get a good scan of them."

"Sure would be nice to know what the rest of it says. I'm intrigued by the whole thing."

She nodded and then looked across the table and gave him a grin. "I'll make you a deal, Brannigan. While you build some shelving that won't damage the integrity of that very important closet in there, I'll read it out loud to you."

He chuckled, took a final sip of his coffee, and stood, apparently ready to go back to work. "I've already figured out what to do with the closet, Sandy. I spent most of last night coming up with a design. Come on, and I'll show you."

Sandy left the copies of the diary on the kitchen table and followed Tom into the laundry room and watched as he opened the closet door. She got goose bumps knowing the secret just beyond the back wall but turned her attention to what Tom was saying to her.

"This is what I decided I could do to preserve the integrity of the back wall's secret door and still allow you to use this as a supply closet." He glanced over at her as if to make sure he had her undivided attention. "I plan to build a box of shelves on casters—enough smaller than the opening so you'll be able to pull the unit out of the closet whenever you need to get to the hidey-hole, but keep it in the closet behind a closed door the rest of the time." He smiled and then stopped talking as if waiting for her response.

Sandy nodded as she listened to his explanation and tried to envision in her mind exactly what he had planned. It might solve her dilemma. Not only would she still have her needed supply closet shelves, but she would also not destroy something that might lead to discovering more about the history of this house of hers.

"That's a great idea, Tom. Thank you."

She reached out her hand to briefly touch his bare arm, almost jumping as she felt the chemistry between them on contact. Oh dear. She had forgotten that feeling—that indescribable electricity between the two of them. Fortunately, he didn't seem to notice how much it had unnerved her, and it apparently hadn't affected him the same way since his expression never changed. But his eyes appeared to burn into hers before he finally turned his attention back to the closet.

"I'm going out and get the boards cut, drill the necessary holes, and get the unit ready for assembly. Then when I come back in here to put it all together, you can read some more to me from this mysterious diary we've found. I can't wait to hear Darcy's story."

CHAPTER 12

The rest of the morning, Sandy sat on a wooden stool in the laundry room while Tom worked on his closet project. She slowly read the faded words out loud to him from the scanned pages of the old diary, stopping now and then to lend Tom a hand as he assembled the box of shelves he had designed for her closet.

There were several pages at the front of the diary in such bad shape she hadn't been able to copy them. She had only had time to scan a few of the pages of the book the previous night, but she was planning later, when she had more time to adjust settings on her scanner, to try and scan the pages where the handwriting was the worst.

As she slowly read through page after page of the ones she had been able to scan, the story of a young woman's life began to emerge—and it wasn't an existence Sandy could even conceive. The more she read, the more she wanted to know about this young woman named Darcy.

The diary finally exposed the information they had been looking for when they reached a portion where Darcy explained she was a slave in a large plantation house near Charleston. Sandy had stopped reading for a few minutes while she held a board for Tom and they discussed which Charleston it could be, but without more information, it was impossible to know if it was Charleston, South Carolina or Charleston, Virginia—or some other Charleston entirely.

The young woman's master—or *marse*—as Darcy called him was referred to in the diary as 'Marse Robert.' Darcy had been born on the plantation and told in the early pages of her diary of growing up alongside her mistress, Miss Carolyn.

Darcy's job was to take care of Miss Carolyn's needs, and it was because she spent so much time with her mistress while they were growing up that she had learned to read and write, which was almost unthinkable at that time. But, as she had stated in those first few sentences of her diary, she couldn't let anyone know she knew for fear of being punished. Sandy could only imagine what the punishment would have been.

Slowly and painstakingly, Sandy read out loud the words on the pages telling of the daily life of a slave in the 'big house,' as Darcy called it. Darcy never mentioned her father, but she did write a great deal about her 'mama.' And even though she and her mother lived in the main house, she wrote of joyous times spent with her fellow slaves who lived in the slave quarters, during their weekly time of worship or at special times of celebration on the plantation such as Christmas.

She had only made it through a little of the diary when Sandy glanced at her watch. She couldn't believe it was already noon. She knew Tom was planning to work all day instead of quitting at noon like he normally did since he'd explained his usual Saturday afternoon commitment had been canceled.

While Tom went to his truck to retrieve his lunch bucket, Sandy threw together a sandwich for own lunch. They sat around the kitchen table eating and discussing what they had learned so far from the diary. Sandy was amazed at how much Tom remembered from their American History Civil War classes. It was evident he must have been paying much more attention in class than she had been. Or perhaps, he just had a better memory.

"All in all, it doesn't sound like this Darcy's life as a slave was nearly as bad as some of the stories we've heard over the years." Tom took a sip of coffee from his thermos and pointed toward the stack of papers next to Sandy's lunch. "Her owner sounds as if he took good care of his slaves, made sure they had clothes and shoes and enough food, and at least from what she writes, there weren't many beatings or punishments on this particular plantation. Wonder what made her run away? From what I've read, most slaves didn't try to escape as long as they were well treated and felt their owners cared about them."

Sandy swallowed the bite of her sandwich she'd been chewing and looked down at the page of the diary on the table beside her plate. "I don't know why she ran away. Hopefully, we'll find out in the next segment of the diary."

She pointed her sandwich in the direction of the laundry room door. "Will you be able to finish the closet this afternoon?" She grinned at him. "I'm anxious to see how it's going to look and how easy it's going to be to use."

He raised his eyebrows, narrowed his eyes at her, and gave her one of those devastating grins of his. "Yes, it will be finished this afternoon, Miss Martin. And yes, it will be a work of art, and incredibly easy for you to use. Have a little faith, okay?"

✞✞✞✞

Ten minutes later they had finished eating, and Sandy quickly cleaned up the remains of their lunch and headed back to the laundry room to continue reading out loud from the diary. She didn't have to read far on the next page before she could tell the tone of the writing was changing, and the happiness Darcy had enjoyed as a child was gone. Right after Darcy told about having her fifteenth birthday, she wrote that her master, Robert Brown, died after a sudden illness overtook him. Darcy shared how, along with the mistress and the rest of the family, the whole household and the field slaves had mourned his death. She also penned about the uncertainty and fear in the wake of the master's death as the slaves were anxious if some of them would be sold and taken away from their loved ones—and if so, they worried over which ones would be forced to leave.

Darcy's tone became even more frantic after the return to the plantation of 'young Marse Rob,' Carolyn's brother, who had evidently been attending university in the big city. Sandy wondered if he'd had to leave his studies after the death of his father to help his sister and mother run the plantation.

But as the entries continued, the fear in Darcy's writing became clearer—and it didn't have anything to do with being afraid of being sold away from her friends and family at the plantation.

"'Mama says I not to let Marse Rob ever touch me, but I can't get away. He so much bigger than me.'"

Sandy stopped reading and lifted her face and frowned as she glanced across the room to see Tom standing, watching and waiting for her to continue. She swallowed hard.

"I'm not sure I want to keep reading, Tom. I have a sinking feeling I know what's coming next."

He nodded slowly, his brown eyes locking on hers, and then looked back down at the screw gun in his hand.

"I'm afraid we're about to find out why Darcy ran away, but there's only one way to know for sure." Tom pointed at the papers in her hand. "As painful as it may be, you'll have to keep reading."

Sandy sighed, took a deep breath, and turned to the next entry on the copy of the diary.

"'I so scared. Marse Rob kissed me today when I took clean clothes to Miss Carolyn's room. Mama not happy. She scared for me too. Says I have to git away. Where can I go? If I run, they come and take me back.'"

The next entry almost took Sandy's breath away. "'Mama told me Marse Robert my daddy. That means Marse Rob my brother. She says I can't let him touch me. God would send me to hell 'cause it not right. What can I do?'"

"Oh, Tom! How awful. The poor girl." Sandy wanted to cry for the young teenager who had lived through such a nightmare all those years ago.

Sandy heard Tom's sigh from across the room and raised her eyes to meet his. "Well, at least now we know why she ran. Her mother must have realized it was only a matter of time before the son followed in the steps of his father."

She was anxious to keep reading to find out what happened next but realized she was at the end of the pages she had printed off from the night before. She was going to have to scan and print off more pages before they could continue reading. She glanced down at her wristwatch and then waited until Tom finished screwing the last caster onto the bottom of the shelf unit before she spoke.

"Do you want to stay for dinner, Tom—so we can finish reading this thing?"

She almost chuckled as she saw a brief look of shock pass over Tom's face before his expression returned to normal and he gave her a smile she had become more accustomed to. She hadn't thought about it when she'd asked, but it had kind of sounded as if she was asking him to dinner. Surely he understood the only reason she had suggested it was so they could finish reading the diary together, but she couldn't keep the corners of her mouth from twitching up in a smile. Not that she was going to complain. She would really enjoy having the opportunity to cook him a good dinner.

His face broke into a grin. "You won't find me turn down the chance for a homemade meal."

Sandy slid off her perch on the stool and headed for the kitchen. "I hope beef and noodles will suffice," she called back at him.

She heard his chuckle from the other room. "I live on sandwiches, woman. Beef and noodles sounds like gourmet food to me."

It didn't take her long to cook the noodles and open a can of the Amish canned beef she'd purchased at the grocery store the last time she'd shopped. She also found a can of peaches to have with the cottage cheese in the refrigerator. That and slices of bread with grape jelly would have to do.

And of course, there were her freshly baked chocolate chip cookies waiting for Tom in the crockery cookie jar on the counter.

Sandy put plates and silverware on the kitchen table for the two of them, not making a fuss, but feeling a tinge of excitement at the prospect of having an excuse to use something other than paper plates. It had been a long time since she'd had a man to cook for.

Tom poked his head through the door to the laundry room about the time she pulled drinking glasses from the cupboard.

"Should I wash up?" He grinned at her.

"Yup," she replied. "I'm almost ready."

A few moments later Tom was back with a freshly washed face and hands, his still damp, dark brown hair brushed back from his forehead. He took a seat at one of the place settings and waited for Sandy to join him. There was a brief moment of unease before Sandy smiled at him.

"Would you say the blessing, Tom? I'm afraid I'm a little out of practice."

After Tom bowed his head and blessed the food, Sandy watched him dig the serving spoon into the bowl of beef and noodles and scoop a healthy portion onto his plate. It had been a long time since she had cooked for anyone other than herself, and it surprised her how much it pleased her to see someone enjoy her cooking. He must have noticed her attention as he glanced up from his plate and grinned at her.

"I told you before; I don't get homemade meals often. Thank you for the invite." She watched as he took a bite of the hot food, chewed, and swallowed.

"It's really good."

Sandy grinned back. "Eat as much as you want. I sure won't be able to eat it all."

She took a bite of the food on her plate, her thoughts returning to all they had read in Darcy's diary. The young woman's plight was still fresh on her mind. Darcy obviously must have run away from her home in the south and during her journey ended up in the small cellar room below the laundry room. But Sandy couldn't help but wonder what had happened to her when she had left here. Had she been caught, or had she made it to safety—and if she had made it safely out of this house, where had she ended up going? Was that why the diary had been left behind in the cellar—because she had been forced to go back to her life of slavery?

While they ate their meal, Tom and she discussed the contents of the diary. Like her, Tom questioned why the diary was left behind if she'd made it to safety. The only way they were going to know more was to keep reading.

After they had eaten their meal and talked a little more, Sandy smiled as she noticed Tom reach to take another cookie from the plate she'd filled from the cookie jar. If she hadn't lost count, she thought the last one he'd taken made five. It appeared Tom really liked her cookies.

They talked a little longer, and then Sandy stood and started clearing the table. She was pleasantly surprised when Tom offered to help. His closeness caused her more than a little discomfort, and the ease he seemed to enjoy around her only made her more aware of him. Each time his arm brushed up against hers as they both carried dirty dishes to the counter next to the sink, she became more and more aware of him as a man. Those feelings she'd had back in high school were coming to surface again. She was almost relieved when they were almost done, and he told her he'd be in the laundry room, finishing up his project.

A short time later, after taking the time to print off the rest of the pages from the diary, she joined him there. She was almost sad to see there weren't many pages left to read. Sandy took her seat on the wooden stool and resumed reading at the point where they had stopped before dinner.

"'Mama say I have to leave. She made plans to get me away. Can't tell how long it take, but I scared. Scared to stay and scared to run. I never see my mama again.'"

Sandy stopped and took a deep breath as she turned to the next page. This handwritten scrawl was faded worse than some of the other pages, and even though she had darkened the copy on the computer, it was still challenging to make out the words. She continued reading a few more entries about the night Darcy ran away. There was something about traveling down a river in the bottom of a boat, hiding in the straw in a barn at a farm, and riding in the back of a wagon under a stack of hay.

Then came the final entry:

"'I find the house where pine tree with cross cut in bark. The lady here nice and put me in cellar. It cold down here but they feed me and give me candle and blanket. I go to next spot tomorrow night. Tired of running but can't go back. Mama told me it says in Bible God can hide me under his wings. I pray she right'"

Sandy stopped reading as the writing ended. It was silent in the room for a few seconds as the realization hit her.

There were no more pages to read.

"That's the end of what she wrote. There isn't any more." She looked over at Tom. "I wonder if she made it?" she whispered.

CHAPTER 13

Tom watched Sandy's face crumble as she looked down at the papers in her hand.

"I wonder if she made it to freedom," Sandy repeated, her voice no more than a whisper.

He shook his head, knowing some of the same sadness he was sure she was feeling. It was obvious she had taken Darcy's story to heart. "We'll never know, Sandy. We have to assume she did, but there's no way we can know for sure."

Turning from the sight of her forlorn face, he pushed the now finished closet shelving unit through the open closet door into the depths of the closet. It was a tight fit but would give Sandy the needed closet space and still allow her access to the hidden rear door.

"What do you think?" he asked. He pointed at the closet, hoping to get her mind off the contents of the diary.

Sandy hopped off her perch on the stool and came over to stand in front of the closet. He quickly showed her the handles he had installed on both sides of the front of the shelving unit, making it easy for her to simply pull the entire box, which rested on casters, from inside the closet whenever she wanted to. Tom was pleased when her face lit up in surprise.

"I love it, Tom." She glanced at him shyly. "You are so smart! I never would have thought of doing this. I get my shelves and can still get to the hidden door if I want."

She touched his bare arm briefly, and it sent tingles all the way up to his shoulder. "Thank you, Tom."

He gazed at her and nodded, feeling unable to respond with all the emotions sweeping over him. Sandy Martin was becoming way too important to him, and he wasn't ready for the feelings she stirred in him. All he had to do was look into those beautiful green eyes, and he forgot all about his decision to never get involved with a woman again—at least one who didn't have a close relationship with God. He had to remember his promise to stay faithful to God though and stay focused on His Will. He never again wanted to go through what he had gone through with Amanda.

After a few moments of feeling like an awkward schoolboy, Tom looked at the watch on his wrist and sighed. It was later than he thought.

"Guess I'd better call it a day." He turned and started picking up his tools scattered around the room. "Busy day tomorrow at church, you know."

Tom was careful not to look at Sandy again. He was terrified to look at her for fear she would see his heart in his eyes.

God, why are you letting me fall in love with her? She doesn't have the relationship with You that she had as a teenager, so I don't dare let her into my heart. We would both end up getting hurt. Until she finds her way back to You, I need to keep my distance; but it is so hard, Lord. Keep me strong.

Tom quickly gathered his tools and headed through the kitchen to the back door. He needed to leave—fast.

"I'll call you when I know my work schedule for next week to let you know when I can get back here to start on the upstairs bathroom."

He knew he was terse but didn't know what else to do. She had followed him into the kitchen and was standing there looking up at him with those big green puppy-dog eyes. If he didn't get out of here soon, those eyes were going to be his undoing.

"Thank you, Tom. For all you've done," she finally said. "Whenever you can get back here will be okay. I know you're a busy man."

Tom inwardly groaned. He wasn't nearly busy enough, and after spending the whole day with her, he was sure even as tired as he was, his sleep would be disturbed tonight by thoughts of Sandy Martin. He needed to get out of here.

Now.

"Thanks again for dinner, Sandy. It was really good."

He quickly made his way down the steps to his truck where he loaded his tools into the back. It was time to head home to do some serious praying.

✟✟✟✟

Sandy stood at the back door and watched Tom drive his truck down the driveway and leave. He had acted so strangely before he left—as if he couldn't get away from her fast enough. Here, she had been, feeling they were finally developing a nice friendship, but then he had become so distracted all of a sudden. She had seen him glance at his watch just before he fled. Maybe he was late for an appointment or something he'd forgotten, but his quick departure left her feeling lonely, and the house suddenly felt emptier to her than it had in a long time.

She turned back to the copies of the diary pages she had tossed on the kitchen table earlier. The diary held no 'final chapter' to Darcy's story, and the writer in Sandy wanted desperately to know what had happened after she left this house. Had she escaped to freedom, or had she been caught and made to go back to her life of slavery? There had to be some way to find out. Something inside her wanted—no, *needed*—to know the end of Darcy's life story.

Sandy spent a few minutes cleaning up the kitchen and then headed to her office where she spent the rest of the evening looking at the pages of the early part of the diary. The ink was so faded she could only read them on the computer with the photo program zoomed in on the individual words—and even then, some of the words weren't legible. After a great deal of adjustments in the photo resolution, she finally discovered the name of the plantation where Darcy had lived was called 'Camilla'...something. She could only make out part of the name, but at least it was a start. The notepad at her side quickly filled up with tidbits of information she hoped would lead her to more about Darcy and the life she had lived—and where she had ended up after her escape.

Then Sandy turned to the Internet for information. She was thankful she'd finally spent the money to have satellite installed, so she now had DSL. The Internet became Sandy's search engine, and she scoured webpage after webpage of information to see if she could find a southern plantation in Charleston with the name Camilla in it. There was no information on anything in Virginia or West Virginia, so she turned her search to Alabama, Georgia, and South Carolina. There were several hits for a Camilla Plantation. The first one was in Georgia, and she clicked on the link that took her to the listed website and did some research, only to discover it had been owned during the Civil War years by a family named Anderson. So that one was ruled out.

Sandy went to the second link and clicked her mouse. A web page came up with a photo of a stately old two-story white mansion with brick-red shutters and a column-fronted porch. It was the stereotype of what she had always imagined a southern plantation house to be. She slowly scanned through the web page.

The website stated Camilla House Plantation was currently a historical site and was no longer being used as a private home. It went on to say the historical foundation which operated the plantation and provided tours, was in the process of restoring the house and surrounding grounds to its 'original elegance.' Sandy moved the mouse, so the curser rested on the tab on the website marked "History" and clicked.

The link took her to a long article telling the history of the house dating back before the Civil War. The more she read, the more Sandy was convinced she had finally found the right place. It listed the original owner as a Robert Brown who was born in England, and stated the plantation had later been taken over by his son. As she scrolled down the page, there was even a photo of an old tintype showing Robert Brown himself. She stared at the picture and wondered what the man had truly thought about the people his way of life had enslaved. She had to keep reminding herself that back then it was just a way of life for them though.

There wasn't much more information on the website, but she took the time to copy down the email address and phone number for the plantation foundation's curator. Staring at the piece of paper she'd written the information on, she tried to decide if she should send an email or not, to ask if they had any records for their slaves—and if there was anything listed for a Darcy. She knew it was a long-shot, and she couldn't even be sure this was the correct plantation, but she finally decided she didn't have anything to lose by trying.

Sandy quickly typed out an email to Matthew Pierce, the curator of the foundation, in which she explained she was seeking information about a slave who might have lived at the plantation. She asked him if he knew of any written records the family might have kept about their slaves. Sandy explained she was especially interested in a young woman named Darcy, who she thought might have been there right before the Civil War. As Sandy clicked the 'send' button, she wondered if she would even get a response from her email, but felt encouraged that at least she was making an attempt to find the truth.

✞✞✞✞

Over the next week or so, the hunt for Darcy almost became an obsession to Sandy. Why had her diary been left in the basement of this house if she had been able to escape? Did that mean she'd been caught, or had she forgotten the diary in her hurry to go to her next hiding place? Sandy could only wonder and was having a difficult time accepting she might never know the truth.

After working all day at the library, she came home and worked outside in the yard, weeding the old flower beds and trying to keep up with the ever growing grass. After the April rains and the May warmth and the following sunshine, the grass was growing faster than Sandy could keep it mowed. Sometimes she thought having her own home might not have been such a good idea after all. She was quickly discovering it was a great deal of work.

After darkness drove her inside though, she spent the remainder of her evenings online, searching websites having to do with slavery and the Underground Railroad. Like every other student in school, Sandy had learned about it but decided she needed to refresh her memory. She discovered it had been an organization started by abolitionists who had helped enslaved blacks obtain their freedom during the thirty years before the Civil War. Sandy learned those who guided the slaves to safety were called conductors; the slaves were passengers, and the homes or businesses where the slaves were hidden were called stations. If what she had found in Darcy's diary could be believed, her house had once been a station for the Underground Railroad. She was still having a tough time believing that, but the diary was proof.

There were many websites online with maps showing the different routes the slaves took in their quest for freedom. Sandy found it interesting most of the maps didn't indicate a line through her area of Michigan, but they did show a direct route leading to Detroit where the slaves crossed the Detroit River to Canada—and a new life of freedom. All the historical accounts she read, however, stated those who were caught were dragged back to cruel bondage. How many of them had been beaten or sold off to a cruel slaveholder? All she knew was if she had been born into slavery, she also would have been one constantly looking for a means to escape.

Sandy didn't see Tom at all during the two weeks following the completion of her laundry room closet. She had hoped he'd stop around, at least to find out if she had found any new information about the diary. When he didn't stop by or call, she consoled herself with the knowledge that he was more than likely busy working on another big job. She also needed to accept the reality that he wasn't interested in pursuing a relationship with her. If he were, he would be trying to spend more time with her.

It appeared she was destined to be alone. Each time she found a man she thought she might want to have a future with, they always turned out to be someone she didn't want to know after all. Well, that was all right with her. Good riddance. She'd had one terrible relationship with a man who hadn't actually loved her. She certainly didn't need another one—even though for a little while she had hoped Tom was different from any other man she had ever known.

It appeared she'd been wrong again.

CHAPTER 14

Several days later, Sandy was surprised to receive a phone call from Matthew Pierce, the curator of the Camilla House Historical Foundation. When she first heard the bass voice with the smooth southern drawl asking her if she was Sandra Martin, she almost hung up the phone, assuming it was a telemarketer. As if sensing her hesitancy to talk, he quickly explained who he was and why he was calling.

"Miss Martin, I am extremely interested in this diary you have found. I think it would be a fantastic item to add to our Camilla House historical museum."

She smiled as she listened to him drag 'Camilla' out in his southern drawl, and when he said Charleston, it sounded more like Chah-l-ston with no 'r.' Then she frowned at his subtle suggestion she give him the diary.

"Mr. Pierce, I'm afraid I can't give you the diary. First of all, I'm not even sure the slave who wrote it was from Camilla House Plantation. I was hoping you might be able to shed some light on that mystery. And, I plan to turn the diary over to Darcy's descendants."

"Of course," she heard him say quietly on the other end of the phone. "Have you found them then?"

Sandy narrowed her eyes. It sounded as if he didn't want her to find them so he could have the diary for his own precious collection of historical memorabilia. Whether he realized it or not, Mr. Pierce was not winning any points with her, and if she had anything to say about it, he would never get his hands on the actual diary. She might be willing to share photos and digital copies of the diary—eventually; but it would depend entirely on his cooperation. And how much he was willing to help her solve the riddle of Darcy's birthplace.

"Not yet. But I was hoping you would be able to help me," she added in her sweetest, upbeat voice.

It was silent on the other end of the phone for a few seconds. "Well," he said slowly, "I'm not sure how much I can help, but tell me what you know, and we shall see. I have always had a soft spot for mysteries."

She quickly filled Mr. Pierce in on the pertinent parts of the diary, especially the portions noting Darcy's age at the time the diary was written, and the part telling about her mother who also worked at the main house of a plantation whose name started with Camilla, near Charleston. There wasn't any need to tell him everything she knew—not yet.

"I'll tell you what. Let me do some research on this end, Miss Martin," he finally said. "I can search tax records for the property and such and see what I can find—no guarantees, you understand. And it may take some time."

Sandy sighed. Time was something she seemed to have plenty of, and how long it took certainly didn't mean anything to Darcy. Sandy just hoped she would eventually be able to find Darcy's family and return the diary to them. At least, she was going to keep trying until there was no hope of finding them.

Matthew Pierce promised he would get back with her as soon as he could and they said their goodbyes.

✞✞✞✞

The next day, Sandy was surprised to come home from work to discover a message on her answering machine from Tom Brannigan. He asked her to call him back, and she couldn't help but wonder why, after more than two weeks, he'd finally called her. She quickly punched in his cell phone number and waited for him to answer.

"Victory Construction. Tom speaking."

Just the sound of his deep voice made her feel better; until she remembered she was supposed to be angry with him—although, at this particular moment, she couldn't remember why.

"Hi, Tom. You left a message, asking me to call you?"

"Yeah. Hey, when did you want me to finish the upstairs bathroom and start working on the back deck?"

She chewed on her lower lip. So much for believing he was calling for anything other than business.

"Whenever you can fit me into your very full schedule is fine."

There was a moment's silence on the other end of the phone line, and she wondered if he had picked up on her subtle slight. Then she felt bad at taking that tone with him. Even though she hadn't heard from him in weeks and was feeling a little miffed about it, she realized she was being juvenile. The two of them had no commitments to each other, and he certainly didn't have to answer to her for his work schedule. She knew when she'd hired him he was going to have to fit her little jobs in around his larger projects.

"Sorry," she finally said, feeling like she was unfair to him. "You tell me when you can be here and that will be all right."

They talked a little longer, and Tom promised he would be at her house the upcoming Friday.

After hanging up the phone from talking with Tom, Sandy turned her attention to the mail she had brought in and dropped on the kitchen table. Sitting down at the table, she started sorting through the envelopes and magazines. The electric bill had come, along with the bill for her cell phone. Frowning, she tossed them aside. The bills never stopped coming.

There was also another official looking, business-size envelope, bearing the return address of her insurance agent.

She quickly ripped it open, unfolded the letter inside, and groaned as she read the contents.

"What?" she shouted out loud. "They can't do this, can they?"

She glanced up at the clock on the wall. Her local insurance agent's office was closed so she'd have to wait until the next day to rant at them, but she needed to vent to someone about the contents of the letter. Picking up her phone, she quickly punched in the familiar number.

"Tom, you're never going to believe what my insurance company is demanding."

"Sandy. Didn't we just talk?"

"Listen to this, 'We regret to inform you that the results of our recent inspection of your property show the following items need to be addressed in order to continue coverage under your current homeowner's policy. Item #1: The large pine tree in the front yard must be removed as it presents a danger to the dwelling. It is in poor condition and could easily come down on the house, doing significant damage. Failure to have the tree removed promptly will result in cancellation of your policy.'

Tom, what am I going to do? I don't want to take down my tree! It's history. Darcy's diary proves it played an important part in the Underground Railroad. How dare they demand I have it cut down?" Sandy knew her voice had increased in pitch and volume, but the more she read the letter, the angrier she became.

"Settle down, Sassy Sandy." The sound of his calm voice made her more furious.

"Don't tell me to settle down, Brannigan! It's not your tree they want to cut down."

She heard his heavy sigh on the other end of the phone. "Give me a few minutes to clean up, and I'll be right over, okay? There has to be something we can do about it."

Sandy sniffed into the phone as the shock and anger wore off, and her emotions took over. "Thank you, Tom. I'm sorry to bother you...."

She heard him chuckle. "That's what friends are for. I'll be there in a half hour or less. Do you suppose you could feed me a sandwich or something if I show up and act nice?"

What a goose she was. Of course; he had only had time to arrive home from work—as she had. And he probably had plans for the evening, and here she was interrupting his life again.

"Listen, Tom. I'm sorry. You don't have to come over tonight if you don't want to. I mean—I know you have a life and probably have plans...."

"No plans. Although I do have an extremely hungry, grumbling stomach. You will feed me if I come over, right?" She could hear the smile in his voice and couldn't help but grin through her own tears in response.

"I'll feed you, I promise."

✞✞✞✞

An hour later Tom and Sandy were seated around the round oak kitchen table, finishing their dinner of spaghetti, tossed salads, and garlic toast. Tom patted his overfull stomach and picked up the letter he'd glanced at briefly when he'd first arrived.

"I hate to tell you this, Sandy, but the insurance company is probably right. If we ever had a bad windstorm from the right direction, the tree is going to fall directly on the house and demolish it."

Sandy groaned at the words she had hoped he wouldn't say and dropped her head in despair. "I must be able to do something to save the tree. Don't they understand the historical value it has?"

She felt Tom's warm hand reach across the table and touch her arm, almost in a caress. "Sandy, they are a big company located in some big city in another state and don't care. They want to protect their assets by making sure they are protecting yours."

His brown eyes were kind as they looked at her across the table. As she raised her head and looked back at him, she noticed his dark eyelashes and the little lines around his eyes she guessed were from the time he spent out in the sun for his job. He was such a nice guy and had been such a good sport to come over at the last minute to help her deal with this latest emergency.

She blinked a couple of times to get her mind back on the subject at hand. She didn't have time to be distracted by how good-looking Tom Brannigan was. Besides, he wasn't telling her anything she didn't already know, but that didn't mean she had to agree with him. She dropped her head again.

"So, I give up, huh?" she finally managed to mumble.

Sandy knew she was pouting, but the tree wasn't only a part of Darcy's history, it was also a slice of her own. She had spent countless summer days under the shade of the tree's green boughs, collected its pinecones to make Christmas decorations, and she had listened to the wind whisper through the branches on windy fall days, dreaming of what she would be when she grew up. It just wasn't fair! She couldn't believe the tree was going to have to be cut down.

Tom didn't answer right away, but she saw him get a look on his face she recognized from when he was trying to figure out a building project and had an idea.

"You've thought of something, haven't you?" She squealed and jumped out of her seat, hurrying around to give him a quick hug.

He quickly stood and held up his hands in surrender, although she noticed he didn't fight her hug. In fact, his arms encircled her waist, and she felt an unbelievable comfort being held there before she finally forced herself to step back from him.

Tom sighed as if he too were sad to lose the contact with her. Then he looked her in the eye. "It might not help any, but you could communicate with the local historical society and get them on board. And perhaps a call to the local radio station might help—maybe they could do a little remote broadcast out here under the tree while you share what we know about Darcy's story. And of course, you could write an article for the Bradford Mills' newspaper and get some publicity that way. It might help to sway the insurance company if you have some other folks writing letters or calling them and harassing them about saving the tree...."

She hugged him again and gave him a quick kiss on his cheek before she could stop herself. "Oh, Tom. That's an excellent idea! Do you think it will work?"

She felt the muscles of his broad shoulders shrug, and a look in his eyes made her pause. Before she knew what was happening, his lips were coming down to meet hers in a sweet, gentle kiss that took her breath away. When they finally parted, she took a step back from him at the same time he took a step back from her.

Sandy gazed at his face in astonishment. A kiss from Tom Brannigan was the last thing she had expected right then, but she sure had enjoyed it.

"I'm sorry, Sandy." Tom ran his hand across his face as he glanced up at the ceiling, then back at her. "I guess I just got caught up in the moment."

She nodded, still feeling distracted, then went over and sat back down at the table. She needed to get her mind back on the task at hand.

"Anyway, I guess your idea sounds like a good one, and I guess it won't hurt to try."

Over the next hour, the two of them worked out a plan of attack. Sandy struggled to keep her mind off 'the kiss,' but kept reminding herself it had probably happened because Tom was trying to take her mind off her worry about the tree. He couldn't possibly have meant it romantically, could he? Just because she had been rocked to the core by the kiss didn't mean he had felt the same way. But it would be nice to know he was.

Later, as she headed up the stairs to her bed, she shook her head in dismay. Right now, she needed to be worrying about the fate of her tree. She felt as if she was beginning a battle, but hoped with the new ideas Tom had come up with, she would be able to win the war.

✞✞✞✞

On the drive home from Sandy's house, Tom called himself every name for fool he could come up with. When Sandy had called him earlier to tell him about the contents of the letter she had received from the insurance company, he had heard the despair in her voice. It had momentarily thrilled him to know she still felt comfortable in calling him for help, but after she had embraced him when he had come up with possible ideas for saving the tree, he had lost the inner control he'd been struggling so hard to keep.

Feeling her arms wrap tightly around him for the brief moment he had been given, made him want more. So he had acted without thinking of the consequences, pulling her face to his and kissing her. And it had been an incredible kiss. But he had no business doing something like that. Their relationship hadn't developed to that point yet, and might never. Until he knew she had turned her life back over to God and was living for Him, he needed to keep his distance and just be a friend to her. It sure wasn't easy though.

He'd been pleased that at least she hadn't fought the kiss, and for a few seconds, he'd taken her mind off the letter from the insurance company. He wasn't sure if any of his ideas would help, but at least it had dried up her tears and had taken away the forlorn little girl look she'd had on her face when he'd arrived at the house earlier.

But he was going to have to be more careful. After years of being content being alone, he'd come to the conclusion there was only one woman who had the power to break his heart, and that was Sandy Martin.

The next day Sandy called Daniel Drayton, the editor of the Bradford Mills' newspaper. He gravitated toward the idea of a local piece telling some of the histories of the area and gave her the go-ahead to write something up and get it to him. She also called Beverly Titus, the director of the Bradford Mills Historical Society, who 'ooohed' and 'aahed' as Sandy told the story of finding the diary, and the pine tree's significance in the entire episode. Beverly was outraged to find out a large corporation in some big city somewhere would have the audacity to believe they could destroy something so historic. She promised to start writing letters immediately and would contact everyone she knew about the dilemma.

On Tom's advice, Sandy not only contacted the local radio station, but also the nearest television station, and politely explained why she was calling. She talked to a program director who said he'd have to speak to the station manager and find out if it were anything they would be interested in covering. When he said he'd get back with her, she didn't feel optimistic about the outcome, so was shocked when the station manager himself called her the next day on her cell phone while she was at work. He wanted to set up a time for a reporter and film crew to come to the house and shoot a piece about the diary, the hidden door, and the significance of the tree in the Underground Railroad.

Sandy hoped all the publicity would somehow carry some weight with the insurance company and the tree could be saved. Several local business people—including Beverly Titus acting as Director of the Historical Society—were writing letters to the company, asking for reconsideration of their stance due to the tree's historical significance. Sandy had also penned a letter pleading for leniency in the hopes the tree could be saved.

Now she had to wait and see if any of it helped.

CHAPTER 15

Rachel Foster, Sandy's friend from Toledo, finally visited two weeks later. Sandy had been looking forward to her visit for months and had been planning for it for weeks. She'd even found some furniture for the upstairs guest bedroom at a local sale and had taken a large amount of pleasure in decorating the room for Rachel's visit.

Rachel arrived on a Friday night, coming with a flurry of hugs, luggage, and small talk which kept them up until the early hours of the next morning. Sandy set her alarm as she knew Tom would be arriving about nine o'clock the following morning to finish the work on the back deck and didn't want to oversleep.

Though she hadn't gone to bed until about one a.m., she found she was wide awake by eight o'clock, even without the alarm going off. By the time she saw Tom's pickup pull into the driveway, she'd dressed, eaten breakfast, and was arranging the ingredients and materials on the kitchen table for making her grandma's chili sauce. This summer she'd had to purchase the veggies at the grocery store, but she was hopeful next summer she would have her own garden full of tomatoes, peppers, onions, and more. She had no idea why it was called chili sauce, as it didn't have any hot chili peppers in it. It was really more of a mild salsa; much sweeter than any she'd ever found on the grocery store shelves.

When she had been packing up the stuff from her dad's house before selling it, she had been thrilled when she found her mom's old recipe box. In it were many hand-written recipes for things she could remember her Grandma had made over the years. She hadn't kept much of her parents' stuff, selling all but a few pieces of furniture and some items with sentimental value she had packed away to look at later. But when she'd found the box of recipes in her parents' kitchen cupboard, she had quickly taken it home in excitement. Sandy could remember her mother telling her many of the recipes had been passed down from her grandma, and her grandma's mother before her.

By the time a sleepy-eyed Rachel, dressed in sweatpants and an overlarge Ohio State University sweatshirt, wandered through the kitchen door, Sandy had chopped all the vegetables but the onions in preparation for making the relish.

"Good morning, sunshine," Sandy grinned, sniffing her runny nose and wishing she had a free hand to wipe the tears from her eyes.

Rachel stopped inside the door, took one look at Sandy's face, and gasped.

"Sandy, what's wrong?"

Sandy laughed through the tears. "Nothing's wrong, silly." She pointed the tip of her knife at the offending vegetable. "I've been chopping onions."

Rachel yawned. "Ah, that's what I smell!" She pulled out a chair and sat across the table from Sandy and made a face. "I hope that's not my breakfast."

Sandy gave her a smile and then turned to scrape the rest of the chopped onions off the cutting board and into the large pot on the stove. "I'm making chili sauce. Let me get this cooking, and I promise I'll make you a real breakfast." She turned the burner on under the aluminum pot, placed the lid on top, and then turned back to the table to clear up the mess she'd created.

"Did you sleep well?" she asked her friend a short time later, scrubbing her hands well at the kitchen sink before pulling a carton of eggs out of the refrigerator and turning back to the stove.

"I did until the hammering started out back. What's going on?"

Sandy grinned, cracked a couple of the eggs into a bowl, and then lightly whipped them with a fork.

"It's Tom Brannigan, my contractor. He's finishing my deck."

She glanced over her shoulder long enough to catch another yawn and saw Rachel glance out the back window toward the deck.

"'Your contractor,' huh?"

Sandy saw her grin.

"Quite a hunk. But does he have to be out there so early?"

Sandy laughed as she tossed a little shredded cheddar cheese and chopped ham and veggies into the egg mixture in the pan.

"It's ten o'clock in the morning, Rachel. It's hardly early." She chose to not respond to Rachel's obvious search for more information about Tom.

In a few moments, the omelet was done, and she slid it deftly onto a plate and placed it on the table in front of her friend, then grabbed the pot of coffee and poured a mugful of the potent brew into a large mug for her.

"Eat," she ordered. "And drink some coffee." She smiled, feeling motherly toward her friend. It was obvious her friend was out of her element here in the country. Rachel was a city girl through and through. "It's a beautiful day, and you've already missed half the morning."

Sandy grinned as she heard the other woman groan, then she reached for her own mug of coffee and took a sip. She watched Rachel blow on a forkful of omelet, then pop it in her mouth and chew.

"Mmm, this is so good. Why can't I cook like you?"

Laughing, Sandy turned back to the stove and took the cover off the chili sauce pot long enough to stir the steaming, boiling concoction with a wooden spoon. "You could if you ever took the time to learn."

She took a sip of coffee from her own mug and then turned toward the back door when she heard a light knock.

"Come on in, Tom," she called out.

He came in the door, his presence instantly filling the room. Wearing his trademark t-shirt and jeans and a day's worth of whiskers across his face, he appeared even more rugged than normal. But he sure did look good to her; really good.

For a few seconds, the two of them stared at each other before the sound of Rachel clearing her throat brought Sandy back to the present. Sandy felt her face flush, and she quickly dropped her eyes.

She busied herself by turning back toward the coffee pot on the counter and nervously grabbing another mug. "Good morning, Tom. You want some coffee?"

His deep voice came across the room. "I'll have to pass this time, Sandy, but thanks."

She turned back in time to see Rachel smiling up at Tom, who was giving her friend a smile back, those beautiful dimples of his showing off. Jealousy reared its ugly head and Sandy had to stop herself from overreacting. She was silly. Tom was just being his usual friendly self, and Rachel was her best friend. So why did she unexpectedly feel jealous of the way Tom was smiling at the beautiful blond?

Tom turned his brown eyes back on her, and she forced a smile to her face. No way did she want him to know how much it bothered her to see her friend flirting with him. She was having a tough enough time knowing how to act around him ever since he had kissed her. Jealously was the last thing she needed right now.

"I wanted to let you know—I have the deck almost finished, but need to run into town to the lumberyard to get some more deck screws. I should have it wrapped up by lunchtime." He headed for the door. "Nice to meet you, Miss Foster." He glanced back at Sandy again. "I'll be back soon."

Rachel waited until the back door closed, then turned to Sandy with a grin on her face.

"Oh, he's a hunk alright. So what's the history there? Is he single? Something tells me he's much more than 'your contractor.'" Rachel raised her hands in the air to make quotation marks with her fingers as she said the last two words.

Sandy dropped her smile, pulled out a chair and sat down, suddenly feeling deflated. There was no way she was going to share her innermost feelings with Rachel, but it sure would be nice to be able to talk with somebody about Tom. Her feelings where he was concerned had her so confused.

"He's a friend from high school. No big deal."

Rachel grinned and chewed the last bite of her omelet. "So, did you date him back then?"

Sandy's fingers traced the words "Michigander" on her mug and slowly nodded. "Once. It was a disaster."

She heard Rachel's soft chuckle from the other side of the table. "Couldn't have been that bad. He's still talking to you."

Sandy lifted her eyes to see her friend's eyes studying her closely.

"Oh wow. You really like him, don't you, Sandy?"

Suddenly everything Sandy had gone through for the past months hit her, and she dropped her shoulders in resignation. Nothing had ever gone right for her. Why should this? Tom Brannigan wasn't the least bit interested in her in that way. It was obvious. Since he'd kissed her, he avoided her like she had some sort of disease or something.

And anyway, she refused to set herself up to be hurt by a man again.

Ever.

"He's a good man, but I'm sure neither of us is interested in a starting a relationship. We're friends, Rachel. That's all."

Her friend grinned back at her over her coffee mug. "Right. Keep telling yourself that, girl. Sooner or later, you might start believing it."

✞✞✞✞

After Sandy finished canning the chili sauce and they had eaten some lunch, the girls drove into Bradford Mills, so Sandy could show Rachel all the sights of a small town. Sandy had never compared her hometown with larger cities along the lines of Toledo until she saw it through the eyes of her friend. Rachel kept commenting on how 'quaint' it all was. Sandy wasn't sure whether to take her friend's remark as a compliment or not but decided it didn't matter. Rachel was only visiting. Sandy was the one who had to live here, and she was perfectly happy with the small town atmosphere of Bradford Mills. In the few months she had been here, it had become home, and now she couldn't envision living anywhere else.

When they left town and got back to the house, it was to discover Tom had finished the deck, cleaned up all his tools, and left. As Sandy slid open the screened door and stepped out onto the fresh wood of the deck, she sighed in appreciation. Tom, as always, had done an excellent job on the project. The deck boards were placed at an angle to the rest of the house which gave the deck more of a design feel. He had built a railing around it with hand-made spindles, and there was a wide set of steps at the one end which led down to the backyard. It smelled like fresh-cut wood and instantly reminded Sandy of Tom. This was probably the last project she would be able to afford for a while so she wasn't sure when she would see him again, which saddened her more than she would have thought.

Rachel helped her bring her dad's old gas grill around from the small outbuilding where Sandy had been storing it. Then Sandy carried a couple of folding lawn chairs up from the basement. She also made a mental note to buy a nice table and chairs for the deck now it was finished.

As the evening shadows moved across the backyard, the two of them grilled hamburgers and hotdogs and ate a relaxing meal on the deck. Sandy finally had time to fill her friend in on what had happened since her return to Bradford Mills. Rachel had been fascinated when Sandy had shown her the hidden room earlier in the day and wanted to hear the whole story of what she had found out about Darcy since then.

"I don't know if I will ever find her descendants, but I'm going to keep trying. The diary should go to them, whoever they might be."

Rachel took a bite of the potato salad on her paper plate and nodded. "That is so neat, Sandy. It's kinda spooky down there, but it's cool when you think about this house being used for the Underground Railroad once upon a time, and I can't believe nobody in your family ever knew it!"

Sandy nodded. "I know. It's hard to believe it was there all along."

She placed her empty plate on the deck floor underneath her chair.

"So, Rachel Foster. How have you been? The first night you got here, all we did was talk about the house and what I've been doing, and I've kept you so busy since then, we haven't had much time to talk about what's been going on in your life."

Sandy watched Rachel swallow a bite of food and drop her eyes to where her fork pushed the rest of her food around on her plate. Something was obviously bothering her friend and had been ever since she'd arrived. She wished she knew what was going on under the blonde mane of hair. Each time Sandy tried to talk seriously with Rachel, she found the topic being changed. Well, not this time. She was determined to get to the bottom of whatever it was.

"Not much, I guess," Rachel finally answered.

The lightning bugs in the yard were starting to flicker their little lights as Sandy looked out across her backyard. She took a deep breath and decided to try again.

"So, are you seeing anyone special now?" Sandy finally asked. Maybe that was what was bothering Rachel. Sandy knew Rachel had been dating a couple of different men when Sandy had still been living in Toledo. None of them had been serious as far as she knew. But then again, maybe that had changed, and things weren't going well with whoever she was seeing now. Sandy knew all about heartbreak after her association with Mitch.

Rachel nodded. "I have been seeing somebody, but didn't know if I should talk about it or not." She glanced over at Sandy, a pleading look Sandy didn't understand in her eyes.

Sandy frowned and leaned forward in her lawn chair. "You don't seem very happy about it. What's going on, Rach?"

She heard Rachel's sigh. "I've gone out a few times with Mitch."

Sandy gasped and stared at her friend in shock. "Mitchell Wright?" she ground out the words. "Are you crazy, Rachel? Why in the world would you have anything to do with that scumball?"

She stood up and stomped across the deck to stand at the edge, her hands resting on the top of the railing with her back to her friend. She glanced behind her long enough to see tears in Rachel's eyes. Sandy shook her head as despair washed over her. Even though she was trying to understand, she couldn't. What was Rachel thinking?

"Why, after what he did to me—why would you want to go out with the man?"

Rachel sniffed. "I like him, Sandy. And he's been so kind to me." She shook her head firmly. "I saw the way he treated you when you guys were together, and he doesn't act that way with me at all. He hasn't even asked me to move in with him, which is good because I'd never do it."

Sandy spit out her words in reply. "Yet. He hasn't asked you to move in with him *yet*! Rachel, he's a jerk. He will take and take from you and give nothing back in return. And he will never be loyal to you and your relationship."

She went over to stand in front of Rachel and leaned over, taking her friend's hands in hers. "I don't want to see you get hurt by this guy. And I can guarantee, you will."

Rachel looked up at her. "The thing is, I really, really like him. I think he might be the one I've been looking for all these years."

Sandy dropped her friend's hands and stood up, feeling as if she'd been slapped. How could she make Rachel understand?

"Has he told you he loves you?"

She saw Rachel shake her head. "No, but we've only been dating a couple of months. It's too early for any expressions of love." Her chin came up. "But he has been kind to me, Sandy. I'm telling you, he's changed. He's even been attending church services with me."

Sandy blinked in disbelief. Mitch had been going to church with Rachel? Hearing he was actually attending a church was surprising. Maybe...no, she couldn't believe he had changed. He knew Rachel was a Christian and was using religion as a way to manipulate Rachel's feelings.

She saw Rachel get a wistful look on her face as a smile appeared. "He didn't even kiss me or try to hold my hand until our third date."

Turning away from Rachel, Sandy stood rigidly. Her friend was obviously smitten; there wasn't any sense in trying to change her mind. Mitchell Wright was going to hurt her too, and there wasn't anything Sandy could do to stop it from happening.

"Please be careful, Rach. Don't be too trusting of the man, okay? All I can tell you is, he will hurt you and then toss you away like yesterday's newspaper—and I care about you way too much to see it happen."

After the evening's discussion, the tone of the weekend changed. The conversation between them for the rest of the night was stilted, and Sandy was thankful when it was late enough to go to bed.

The next morning at the breakfast table, she wasn't surprised when Rachel announced she wasn't going to be able to stay as late as she'd originally thought but was heading back to Toledo before lunchtime. Sandy nodded resolutely at the realization that Mitch had taken something else from her; her friendship with Rachel would never be the same.

CHAPTER 16

Waiting had never been one of her strengths, but Sandy managed to stay busy with other things to help keep her mind off all the negative things in her life, including the fate of an old and extremely tall tree in her front yard.

Her cousin, Kate, invited her to a party at her house one evening where she would be selling purses and jewelry. Sandy knew the last thing she needed was another purse, but in a weak moment she fell in love with one particular bag the salesperson was showing, and she decided she couldn't live without it. The party was a good distraction for her though, and it was fun to meet some other women from the church and the community. Maggie Brannigan had also been in attendance, and between her and the other woman, Sandy was starting to feel a little less of a stranger to Bradford Mills.

After everyone else had left Kate's house, Sandy spent some time helping her cousin clean up the house and catching up with her news. She and Kate had been close while growing up as they were only three years apart with Sandy being the eldest. There had been a point in their lives when they had almost been inseparable—more like sisters than cousins. But time and life in general had interfered, and they had lost touch—until now. Sandy was very thankful she had at least one family member left in Bradford Mills with whom she could spend time.

While they washed up the few dishes, Kate shared a little of her past since high school. She didn't have much to tell Sandy other than to say she had her son now and was happy in her job working as a receptionist/secretary for a local attorney. The young woman standing before her, with her blond hair cut in layers in a shoulder length cut, was as soft-spoken and gentle as Sandy remembered. It was evident though, while Sandy had gone to the city and received a college education and began her life with a good job, back here in Bradford Mills, Kate had struggled.

Sandy wondered who Robbie's father was, but didn't feel comfortable coming right out and asking. In the back of her mind was the picture of when she had seen Tom and Kate together right after church Easter Sunday morning. Tom had squatted down in front of the boy, intent on talking with him, and the little boy had looked up at Tom like he was his hero. She had no proof and hated where her mind went, but she couldn't help but wonder; was Robbie Tom's son? And if he was, why wasn't Tom doing the honorable thing and claiming him? Maybe Tom wasn't at all who he pretended to be.

She mentally shook herself and turned her attention back to what Kate was saying.

"I guess I need to go get Robbie from my mom's house. I so appreciate she was willing to take him a while tonight so I could have this party."

Sandy absentmindedly nodded in agreement.

"Hey Sandy, I keep forgetting to ask—why don't you come to Robbie's baseball game on Saturday afternoon? He'd love to have you there, you know."

Kate was looking at Sandy expectantly, waiting for an answer. Sandy thought for a moment. Was there any reason she couldn't go? Maybe it would do her good to get out of the house and spend some time at a fun event with other people her age.

"Sure, sounds great. What time and where is it?"

Kate gave her the specifics, encouraged her to wear plenty of sunscreen, bring a lawn chair, and come prepared to clap and cheer the youngsters on.

"You'll have to remember though, these kids are still learning, so it's nothing like watching professional ball. But we have a very good time. And the coaches make it fun for the kids, which is what it's all about at this age. I am so thankful for that."

Sandy nodded and grinned. The more she thought about it, the more fun it sounded.

"I'll be there. You can count on it."

✞✞✞✞

It was a mid-June, hot and steamy Saturday afternoon when Sandy drove into the gravel parking lot at the Bradford Mills recreational ball fields. The place was packed with cars and pickup trucks parked around the two baseball diamonds. Games were getting ready to start at both diamonds, and after she pulled her folding lawn chair out of the trunk, she headed in the direction of what she hoped was the right game. She was relieved when she saw Kate waving her over to an area behind the backstop where a multitude of parents and chairs were already sitting. When she got closer, Kate moved her chair over a little to make room for Sandy's.

"I saved a spot for you," Kate said with a grin on her face. "The kids are still warming up, so you got here just in time." She reached over to pat Sandy's hand resting on the arm of her chair. "I'm so glad you came."

Sandy grinned back. She didn't know what to expect at one of these things, but if all these people turned out for this event on a hot summer day, it must be worth it.

Shortly afterward, little brown-haired Robbie came running over to his mother. Sandy grinned as she watched him. He was already sweaty and dirty—and the game hadn't even begun yet.

"Mom, the game's gonna start soon."

Kate pulled a bottle of water from a nearby cooler. "I know! And Cousin Sandy came to watch too. Isn't that great?"

Robbie grinned over at Sandy and her heart did a little flip as she saw a familiar looking little dimple appear in his smiling cheek.

"Cool! Thanks for coming!" He turned to run back to the makeshift dugout. "We're gonna win!"

Sandy laughed along with Kate as they watched the boys all hurry back to their respective positions to get ready for the game to begin. Then Sandy saw the man she assumed was Robbie's coach come out of the dugout with a clipboard in hand, and call the boys over. He was wearing a matching baseball t-shirt and shorts and wearing the same color baseball cap as Robbie. As she watched him interact with all the boys, it looked to her as if he paid particular attention to Kate's son.

It was Tom Brannigan.

She sat through the whole game, clapped when appropriate, and cheered when she thought she should. But her heart wasn't in it. It was hot and dusty, and she was miserable and wished she'd never come.

But maybe it was better she knew the truth and accepted it. Evidently, Tom Brannigan wasn't the man she had thought he was. All this time he talked about having changed and how he was now a Christian and wanted to do what the Lord told him to do. Yet, it looked to Sandy as if he had a son he wasn't claiming or taking responsibility for. What was she supposed to think about that?

Even though he hadn't told her so, it was obvious to her now she was here that coaching this boys' baseball team had been the reason he hadn't been able to work at her house Saturday afternoons. But coaching a little league team didn't make up for leaving Kate and Robbie in the lurch. And how could Kate smile and act so friendly to him when it was obvious the guy had used her and then thrown her away?

Sandy was disgusted with herself—for starting to hope, to wish—for having thoughts about Tom Brannigan in a romantic sense. What was wrong with her? Did she have a death wish when it came to men or something? First Mitch and now Tom. Well, she wasn't going to fall for this one. She was going to keep it friendly and strictly professional with Mr. Thomas Brannigan from this point on.

She wasn't going to set up her heart for getting hurt again. Once was enough.

CHAPTER 17

Before she left for work Monday morning, Sandy received an unexpected phone call. It was Matthew Pierce from South Carolina, and she instantly caught the sound of excitement in his voice.

"Miss Martin, I've found some information I believe will make you very happy."

Sandy held her breath in expectation as she waited for him to continue.

"I've found your Darcy listed on a 1855 tax list—well, I have to assume it was your Darcy. You said you thought she was about 15 years old when she wrote the entries in the diary you found, correct?"

"That's correct. Do you really think it's the same Darcy?"

She listened for the response on the other end of the phone and couldn't help but wonder about the appearance of the man who belonged to the wonderful soothing southern drawl. He sounded about her age, maybe a little older. Was he tall, short, dark, or blond? Sandy gave her head a shake and tried to concentrate on what he was telling her.

"I believe the information I have found is for the same girl. She is listed directly after a woman named Alice, age 32. I admit that's pretty young to have a daughter who is age 15, but then they had their children young back them—especially the slaves."

Sandy scowled as she thought of the circumstances surrounding some of those 'early children.' Alice hadn't been able to choose when she would have her daughter but instead had been forced into a liaison with her owner—a relationship she more than likely hadn't welcomed.

"I'm so glad you were able to find her, Mr. Pierce. At least now I know where she was originally from."

She heard his deep chuckle on the other end of the phone before he continued. "Wait, there's more."

Sandy caught her breath. More?

"I found Darcy, age 15, listed in the estate records of Robert Brown, her original owner here at Camilla House Plantation. He died in 1856 and left quite a large estate. Listed is," Sandy heard the shuffling of papers on the other end of the phone. "'to daughter, Carolyn, one negro woman named Alice, and her daughter, Darcy.'"

She gripped the phone tighter in her excitement. They had actually found her—well, Matthew Pierce had found her! Sandy was thrilled but took a deep breath to steady her heart so she could listen to the rest of his report.

"Unfortunately, back then the estate inventory only listed the first names of all the slaves, but you did say you thought Darcy was the personal servant of the daughter of the household, correct?"

Sandy nodded before she realized he couldn't see her. "Yes, she talked about Miss Carolyn in her diary—and she mentions her mama, although she never lists her name." She took a deep breath. "Thank you, Mr. Pierce. I believe you've found my Darcy."

"Why don't you call me, Matthew, Miss Martin?" His deep voice resonated over the phone line. "This Mr. Pierce stuff is starting to make me feel prehistoric."

He chuckled, and Sandy laughed along with him. He was making a concerted effort to be friendly; she supposed she could do so also. Besides, she did enjoy the way he said 'Chaahs-tun' instead of Charleston.

"I will call you Matthew if you'll call me Sandy."

"I would be honored," he replied in his drawl.

It was quiet for a few seconds while Sandy tried to digest all the information he had thrown at her. Then she heard Matthew's voice again. "I hope this information helps in your search, Sandy."

"Oh, it does, trust me." She sighed. "Thanks to you, I now know where Darcy came from. Now I have to try and find out where she went after she left my basement. I'm not sure how easy that's going to be."

Her momentary joy at finding a part of Darcy's past evaporated as the truth hit her. They might never be able to find out where she went next and if she succeeded in reaching freedom. It was like a gigantic jigsaw puzzle and every time she found one piece, it left another gaping hole where another portion was missing.

"I promise I'll keep searching for more clues on this end, Sandy." There was a short pause before he continued. "And the Camilla House Historical Foundation would definitely be interested in adding the diary to our collection—if you can't find her family, that is," he quickly added.

Sandy had to grin at the expectant sound of his voice. It was easy to tell he wanted the diary. Well, time would tell who ended up with it. She certainly wasn't ready to admit defeat in the quest to find Darcy's family, so she wasn't going to relinquish it yet.

"I can't promise you the diary itself, Matthew. But I can guarantee you will receive photos of it all—regardless of what happens to the original." She thought for a moment. "I might even be willing to bring the copies down there and deliver them in person, so I can see the place for myself."

She could almost hear the smile in the deep voice that responded on the other end of the phone.

"It would be a pleasure, Miss Martin. I do believe I would enjoy meeting you."

On Saturday afternoon, Sandy drove into Bradford Mills to visit the local historical society, housed in a huge Victorian mansion next door to the more modern community library. She was determined to find more information about what happened to Darcy after she left the hidden room in her basement. If she had made it to Canada, maybe Sandy would need to start the hunt for her there. Hopefully, the Historical Society would have some idea of how to go about such a search.

The Director of the Historical Society, Beverly Titus, a petite woman in her early sixties with very short graying hair, was working behind the counter when Sandy entered through the heavy wooden doors at the front of the building. She greeted Sandy with a handshake and many questions about her search for the writer of the diary, along with more inquiries about the fate of Sandy's pine tree.

"I want you to know, I contacted all our society members and they have promised to write letters to our congressmen and other dignitaries, asking for leniency for the tree. We can't let this big corporation destroy something so historic!"

Sandy couldn't help the little smile creeping across her face at the thought of trying to get the governor to grant a stay of execution for a pine tree but genuinely thanked the older woman for helping her in the battle to save the tree.

Then taking a deep breath, Sandy explained her reasons for her presence there today. Beverly quickly led her over to a table where several ugly looking machines sat. They had large screens that looked similar to a computer monitor on top, and large flat bases with glass covered plates in front. Beverly sat down in front of one and pulled a nearby chair closer, gesturing for Sandy to join her.

"This is a microfiche reader. I'm going to get some files for you to look through—Canadian census records from 1861 and further on. I'll show you how it works. Someday we hope to have all these documents stored digitally so we can just look them up on the computer, but for now this is all we've got," she added as she stood back up and walked away.

Sandy sat down in a chair in front of the machine, wondering what she had gotten herself into. She couldn't imagine it was going to be easy to find someone in a census taken a hundred and fifty years or more earlier, but she had to hope Beverly Titus knew what she was doing.

Beverly was gone for a few minutes and when she returned she was carrying several small boxes.

"I decided we needed to start looking for her before 1861. You said you thought she ran away in the mid to late '50's, right?"

Sandy nodded and watched Beverly pull out several sheets of what she assumed were microfiche film from the box and place one of them under the glass plate on the base of the machine.

"Well then, I guess she probably married shortly after her escape. A young Negro woman alone wouldn't have survived long—even in Canada. If she crossed the Detroit River like many of the runaway slaves did, she would have ended up in Windsor. Let's start there, shall we?"

Together they combed through the marriage index for Windsor. Sandy was flabbergasted to see all the Browns and wondered if they even stood a remote chance of locating the right one. Why couldn't the last name they were looking for be a little less common? Fortunately though, after about fifteen minutes, they finally found what they were looking for.

Darcy Brown, bride; Marriage date 25 April 1860; Location: Windsor, Essex, Ontario; Spouse, Eli Wilson; Parents: Alice Brown

For a minute Sandy could do nothing more than stare at the words on the screen before her. She'd found her—well, at least she'd discovered Darcy had safely arrived in Canada—and had married there. It was a beginning. She grinned over at Beverly in amazement.

"You found her!"

The older woman smiled back at her and patted Sandy on the arm. "*We* found her."

Beverly showed her how to print off that particular page of the index, then removed the piece of film and replaced it in the box. Sandy couldn't help but wish there was some way to have a copy of the actual document instead of a copy of the listing in the index but decided at this point, she had better be thankful for what information she was able to find.

"Now we start searching census records," Beverly patiently explained. "Canadian census' were taken every ten years, similar to ours here in the U.S. Theirs were odd years from ours, though. Our census years were 1850, 1860, 1870, etc. Theirs were 1851, 1861, 1871, etc." She smiled as she flipped through the microfiche sheets.

"We'll start looking at 1871 in the index and see if we can find the Wilson family listed. If we can't find them in the 1871 census, we'll go back and look at the 1861 census. But I'm assuming you're looking for her children, and more than likely, there wouldn't have been any born yet in the 1861 census."

Again, Sandy was dumbfounded at the number of Wilsons listed in the index. How in the world would they ever find the right one? Beverly explained they were fortunate because they also had a first name for Darcy's husband, so it narrowed their search. There was an Elijah Wilson, along with two Eli Wilsons. Age-wise, the first Eli Wilson was too old as he was shown in the index as being in his fifties. Beverly pulled up the page that had Elijah Wilson listed, and when they finally found him, they realized he wasn't the correct one either as he was born in England. One Eli Wilson remained to check. Sandy was tempted to cross her fingers for luck as Beverly fiddled with getting the next piece of film loaded, and then turned the round knob on the machine to zoom in.

Sandy took a deep breath. She didn't know what they would do if this Eli wasn't the correct one.

She watched as Beverly twisted the knob a little more to make the document clearer...and there he was.

Eli Wilson, age 32, male, born in the United States. Married, Ethnicity: African.

Sandy almost let out a whoop of joy until she remembered she was in a library of sorts where other researchers were quietly working. Instead, she gave Beverly a giddy grin.

"It sounds like it's him. What do you think?"

Beverly absentmindedly nodded her head and scrolled down a little further where it listed the household members. As she turned the round knob to focus in on the page better, Sandy felt an even larger grin sweep over her face.

Name: Darcy Wilson, age 31, female, born in the United States, married, Ethnicity: African

Also listed were three children: *Caleb, age 6; Prissy, age 4, and Tillie, age 2*, all born in Canada.

"Aha!" Beverly stated. "Now we know we've found the right one!" She hit the button to send the page to the printer and turned to look at Sandy with a huge smile on her face. "Isn't this fun?"

Sandy had to agree. This could quickly become addictive—looking through the records of people who had long ago passed away, but had at one time or another mattered to someone. Again she felt she was trying to find the fragments of an enormous puzzle.

After another search, they found Eli and Darcy listed in the 1881 census, still living in Windsor, although there were now only two children listed: Caleb, age 15 and Prissy, age 14. When Sandy asked why Tillie wasn't listed, Beverly pointed out she more than likely died between the 1871 and 1881 census. Sandy felt a sadness sweep over her—even though it had happened so long ago. Darcy had gone through so much pain as a child, and then to also lose a child of her own; how had she been able to bear it all?

Sandy glanced down at her wristwatch and saw it was almost closing time for the society's office, so they didn't have a chance to do more searching. She frowned in disappointment as she remembered she had to work the following Monday so wouldn't be able to come back right away. But Beverly promised she would continue the search and would let Sandy know what she found in the future census records. She said she would also search out church records and whatever Canadian birth and marriage records she could find.

"We'll find Darcy's family—one way or the other," Beverly assured her.

As Sandy headed for home, she felt a renewed sense of optimism. It was beginning to look as if they might actually be able to trace Darcy's family! What had seemed to be an insurmountable task in the beginning was starting to sound like a real possibility.

That night as she readied for bed, she couldn't help but wonder if she should update Tom on the progress of the search, then let out a sigh as a heavy sadness swept over her. She wasn't looking forward to talking to Tom again after seeing him with Robbie at the ball game. The realization Tom Brannigan could very well be Robbie's father had left her more shaken than she'd thought and she wasn't looking forward to talking with him anytime soon.

She had promised to keep him informed though, but it didn't take much to talk herself into waiting. Surely it made more sense to delay until she had more information about the search for Darcy. Even though she knew she was putting off the inevitable confrontation with him, she couldn't help wanting to protect her heart. The less she saw of Tom Brannigan right now, the better it would be for her.

CHAPTER 18

After work the next evening, Sandy spent an hour or two working at her computer, writing the beginning of an article telling what she knew so far about Darcy's story. She was going to approach Mr. Drayton, the editor at the newspaper, to see if he would be interested in publishing it. Her hope was it might also gain her some additional publicity to save her pine tree.

Since she didn't have to be to work at the library until midmorning the next day, she took the printed pages of her article in hand and drove into Bradford Mills and parked in front of the brick one-story building housing the newspaper. She entered through the glass door entrance and stood in front of a counter where she immediately asked to see Mr. Drayton. After a short wait, she was instructed by the young receptionist to go back to his small office, which looked to Sandy to be so disorganized she wasn't sure how he managed to accomplish anything. Files and paperwork covered every flat surface of the old wooden flat-topped desk, and the small table holding his computer monitor and keyboard were plastered with sticky notes.

"Have a seat, Miss Martin," he said, pointing toward the only wooden straight-backed chair not covered with stacks of newspapers and books. She sat down tentatively, wondering if the old chair would even hold her.

Glancing down nervously at the file folder in her hand, she had visions of being laughed at and thrown out of the editor's office in disgust at her writing. Maybe she should forget the whole idea. He was a busy man and probably wasn't going to be interested in what she had written anyway.

No. For Darcy's sake, she had to at least try.

"I appreciate you taking the time to see me," she began. Licking her lips nervously she took a deep breath and clasped her hands tightly on the folder she held to try and stop them from shaking. "I have something I wondered if you would have the time to read. I thought it might make a great local historical human interest story for the paper...."

Mr. Drayton held out his hand for the file. "Sure, sure, I'll give it a look. Can't make any promises, you understand. Why if I printed everything coming across this desk, I'd have been run out of town a long time ago."

Sandy nodded her understanding as she passed the folder across the desk to him. "Of course, I understand. I would appreciate your input on it though." She stood to leave. "Thank you again, Mr. Drayton. You have a beautiful day."

He opened the folder and waved at her briefly as she headed out the door. "Stop in anytime, Miss Martin. Happy to see you again."

✞✞✞✞

After she left the newspaper office, Sandy headed back to the Bradford Mills Historical Society to check in with Beverly Titus, hoping to find out if she had any more information on Darcy's family. When she arrived, she found Beverly working at one of the large tables in the main room with an elderly woman, a large record book opened in front of them. As soon as she saw Sandy come through the door, Sandy heard Beverly speak softly to the other woman.

"Excuse me, Meredith. I'll be right back."

The older woman hurried over to greet Sandy, a frustrated look on her face. "I'm sorry, Sandy, but I haven't had time to do anymore looking for your Darcy and her family. I can't believe how busy we've been!"

Sandy laughed at the dismayed look on Beverly's face and held up her hands, trying to reassure the older woman.

"Don't worry about it, Beverly. I was in town and thought I'd check in." She nodded toward the elderly woman still waiting patiently at the table for Beverly to return. "You have plenty to do, and there's no rush. Just be sure and let me know if you do find anything though."

"Of course! Thank you for being so patient." Beverly touched her lightly on the arm, then turned and went back to her mission.

Sandy turned to leave the building, feeling somewhat deflated, but understanding she wasn't the only one looking for pieces of historical puzzles. Another day or two wasn't going to make much of a difference.

✞✞✞✞

When she returned home from work that evening, she had no more than come through the door when the phone started ringing. She was breathless from hurrying to answer it and when she finally said, "Hello," she was surprised to discover Mr. Drayton from the newspaper office on the other end.

"Miss Martin. May I call you Sandy?" Before Sandy had an opportunity to consent, Mr. Drayton had already moved on. "I wanted to get back with you on the article you brought in this morning. This is fascinating stuff. You actually found a diary in your basement belonging to a runaway slave? And your insurance company wants to make you cut down the tree that led slaves to freedom? Outrageous, if you ask me. Well, what I want to tell you is," Sandy held her breath, almost afraid to hear where this was going. "I want you to do more with this story. I'm going to send you to that plantation in South Carolina to get photos and more information. Then I want you to come back to Bradford Mills and write additional articles. We'll do a weekly write-up to update the readers on the progress of your search while it's in progress. This is great stuff. News stories like this are what sell newspapers. What do you say?"

Sandy took a deep breath, trying to grasp what Mr. Drayton had said to her. "Are you telling me you're going to pay for me to go down to South Carolina and find more information?"

"That's exactly what I'm saying, girl! I want you to learn all you can about this Darcy gal and her life in the south during the years before the Civil War. You'll need a good camera, so stop here at the office to pick up one of ours, so you can get some shots of the plantation. I'm also counting on you to find out what happened to her once she escaped—after she left Bradford Mills. I'm willing to pay you for your time, Sandy, but I also expect you to make it worth what I pay you."

Sandy grinned. "Of course. Thank you for this opportunity, Mr. Drayton." She stumbled over her words, not knowing what else to say, but he wasn't done talking yet.

"Come into the office tomorrow morning to pick up your airline ticket, and we'll finalize plans for the articles. I don't want to waste any time. We need to get this thing written so it can be in this next week's issue—the week after that at the latest."

Sandy hung up the phone from the unexpected phone call and did a little dance in her kitchen. She had a writing assignment; a real writing assignment—and not just any old one. The newspaper was actually going to pay her to go to South Carolina to find out more about Darcy Brown.

✞✞✞✞

It didn't take her long to pack a bag with enough clothes and personal effects to get her through a few days away from home. She contacted the library to explain why she was going to need to take a few days off from her job there. Fortunately, her boss was willing to give her the time off when she found out what was going on. She, like everyone else who had heard the story of Darcy from Sandy, was enthralled with the idea that a house in their small community had once been used to hide escaping slaves.

Sandy also called Beverly at the Historical Society to let her know she wasn't going to be around for a while due to a newspaper assignment. Sandy didn't tell her where she was going as she didn't want Beverly to start asking questions at this point. The newspaper was the one who was paying for her trip, so they were going to have first dibs on any information she found.

She also put a call into Tom, and when he didn't answer, she left a voicemail message. It had been a couple of weeks since she had actually talked to him, but she thought she should let him know she wouldn't be around for a few days, and she wanted him to know where she was going so he wouldn't worry. She knew that was just wishful thinking on her part though. Tom Brannigan didn't appear to be too concerned about her, or he wouldn't be avoiding her. Then again, she guessed she had been doing her best to evade him too. Now he'd finished the work at her house, she had no reason to see him. She had thought it would be a relief when he wasn't around all the time, but instead, she had found she missed his quiet presence. And she had even caught herself a couple of times, wishing he'd still been working around her house so she could have gotten his opinion about something.

She shook her head and sighed. She had spent way too much time worrying and wondering about Thomas Brannigan.

It sounded as if some time away from Bradford Mills would do her good.

Later that evening she put a call through to Matthew Pierce in South Carolina to make sure he would be available for the promised tour of Camilla House when she arrived. It put a smile on her face to hear his eloquent southern drawl on the other end of the phone, and he acted genuinely pleased to find out she was coming to see the plantation.

"What fantastic news, Sandy! We don't have a tour scheduled the day after tomorrow, so I'll plan on spending most of the day with you—showing you all around the house and grounds. There isn't anyone in all of Charleston more knowledgeable about the place."

Sandy smiled at the almost cocky tone of his voice. Matthew Pierce seemed quite full of himself.

"Sounds great, Matthew. I can hardly wait to see it."

✞✞✞✞

Two days later found Sandy on the road at five thirty in the morning to get to the airport—Toledo Express Airport in Ohio—in time for her flight. She could have flown from Detroit Metro but had always appreciated the less hectic atmosphere of the Toledo Airport.

She was more excited than she had been about anything for a long time, but she was also extremely nervous. This was a tremendous opportunity to write something—not only for a local newspaper—but, if it were good enough, there was also the possibility she would be able to have something published in a larger historical publication. She was going to do whatever she could to make sure she did it right.

Unfortunately, there were no direct flights from Toledo to Charleston, so she had to fly from Toledo to Chicago, Illinois in order to catch a connecting flight to Charleston International Airport. Both flights were uneventful, and Sandy spent most of the hour and a half of the second flight sleeping due to her early morning commute.

When she arrived at Charleston she hurried to the baggage claim area to find her bag and headed to the car rental facility in the main terminal where they had a car waiting for her. She took a map out of her purse and punched the address of the bed and breakfast where she was staying into the rental car's GPS. Mr. Drayton had thought of anything she might need, and the trip looked to be enjoyable, although she had to keep reminding herself it was a work assignment and not a vacation.

It only took her about fifteen minutes to reach the large historic district of Charleston. The brochure had stated the large three-story Federal style 'house-turned-bed-&-breakfast' was centrally located to the finest restaurants and antique shops. Sandy was pleased to discover there was also off-street parking for her rental car.

After dragging her bag from the back seat of the car, she made her way up the front porch steps—mentally correcting the word in her mind. In this part of the country, it was referred to as a 'piazza.' She walked through the front door where a wooden plaque announced she was to enter—no need to knock—and stepped into a foyer, which was apparently considered the lobby. A long, polished cherry desk sat at the side of the entry, with a massive elegant Italian black marble fireplace in the wall behind it. Sandy raised her eyes up where elegant chandeliers hung from large ceiling medallions. The house was stunning, and she couldn't imagine ever having an opportunity to live in someplace so huge and elaborate.

A woman who looked to be in her early sixties, with very short silver hair and wearing black slacks and a bright blue blouse, bustled into the room with a smile on her face. She moved around the desk and walked briskly toward Sandy, her hand outstretched for a shake.

"Welcome to The Cardinal House. I'm Josephine St. Claire, the proprietor. Do you have a reservation?"

Sandy smiled and shook the offered hand with her free one. "Hi. I'm Sandy Martin. I believe Mr. Drayton from the *Bradford Mills Daily Press* made reservations for me."

Ms. St. Claire led the way over to the large book spread open on top of the desk. She quickly took a seat and pulled the book toward her.

"Let's see. Yes, right here you are. 'Sandra Martin.' It appears the room is already paid for by a business credit card. You're here on business then?"

It was hard to not notice the inquisitiveness in the woman's eyes. Sandy got the impression however, her hostess wasn't nosey, but genuinely cared about her guests.

"I am—plus I'm here on what you might call a personal quest, Ms. St. Claire."

"Oooo, how mysterious!" Josephine laughed. "But please, call me Jo. Everyone does."

Sandy smiled back at this woman with the infectious smile and the bright green eyes behind her glasses. "And I'm Sandy."

She glanced at the grandfather clock in the entryway. "I know check-in isn't until 3:00 and I'm early, but I was wondering if I could drop off my luggage until I return later to 'officially' check in."

The older woman waved her hands gracefully through the air. "Oh, that's just for the brochure. We offer concessions to those rules when people arrive earlier than planned. When you're coming from out of town, you never know exactly what time you'll arrive. You are more than welcome to check-in now and leave your luggage in your room."

She walked over and tugged open a drawer in the desk and pulled out a key ring. "Here is the key to your room. If you follow me, I'll get you settled."

Sandy dutifully trailed after the older woman as they walked down the hallway and up a beautiful carpeted open stairway. She tried to pay attention to what Jo was telling her about the history of the house while also taking in the loveliness of the place with its wainscoting, wide plank hardwood floors, and crown molding. Jo told her the house had been built in the 1800's and had been in the same family until the early 1960's when it had fallen into disrepair. Her parents had purchased the house and lovingly restored it to its former beauty, and after their deaths, she had decided to make it into a bed and breakfast.

Jo opened the door to Sandy's room and motioned for her to enter first. It was a huge room with sunshine streaming through the floor to ceiling windows. Sage green damask draperies hung at the windows, and the wooden floors glowed in the sunlight. Sandy's eyes were immediately drawn to the huge canopy bed—the bedding in the same sage green flowered pattern as the draperies—a tall wooden armoire, and an Oriental rug. Even though there was a flat-screen TV in the corner, the room had been lovingly decorated with what she assumed were period reproductions.

"You have a private bath through this door," Jo continued as she led Sandy into another room. "There are plenty of fresh towels and such, but if you need anything, please let me know." Jo led her back to the main room and pointed at what looked to be an exterior door. "There is a private entrance, so you don't have to come through the main part of the house. It leads out to your own piazza with steps leading down to the parking area. It is well lit and very safe, so you shouldn't have any trouble, even if you return after dark."

She patted Sandy's arm lightly. "I'll let you get settled, but remember if you need anything at all or have any questions about the Charleston area, please let me know." Jo turned to leave and then turned back. "Oh, and afternoon tea is from 3-5 p.m. Breakfast is served in the dining room beginning at 8:00 a.m. We have several delicious items on the menu for you to choose from, along with juice, fresh fruit, and good southern coffee! We don't have many staying here right now, but I promise I will take good care of you. So please, let me know if you need anything." She smiled again. "You have a very good time here in Charleston."

Sandy had read somewhere Charleston had been voted 'America's Friendliest City' several times. If all the residents were as friendly as Josephine St. Claire, the city was well deserving of the designation.

After her hostess left, Sandy flopped on her back on the huge bed and let out a sigh of contentment at being in such a stunning room. It would be all too easy to get side-tracked by all that Charleston had to offer in sight-seeing, but she needed to stay focused and remember why she was here. This wasn't a vacation, and she had a limited amount of time here, so she was going to have to use it wisely.

She went into the bathroom and quickly ran a brush through her unruly locks, washed her hands, and touched up her makeup and lipstick. Checking her purse to make sure she had the camera and her notepad with her, she headed out the door to her rental car. It was time to find someplace to grab a quick lunch, and then see if she could find the Camilla House Plantation.

Her quest to find out more about Darcy Brown was about to begin.

CHAPTER 19

After leaving The Cardinal, it didn't take Sandy long to find a coffee shop nearby where she was able to purchase a chicken salad sandwich and latte. She sat for a few minutes at a table on the sidewalk in front of the shop, watching people stroll down the moss-draped, tree-lined streets. She took a deep breath of the humid air and beamed a little smile. It felt as if she had been transported to a different world.

Finishing her lunch, she threw her sandwich wrapping and empty latte container into a nearby trash bin and headed back to her rental car. It was time to go to the plantation and get this show on the road. She was thankful for the GPS as it led her through street after street, across a river, and through the countryside down rural roads. Sandy supposed she would have managed, but it was doubtful she could have found the plantation as quickly with only directions and a map.

As she drove through the stone gates and down the paved drive between the lines of moss-covered live oaks on both sides, she got her first glimpse of the stately old two-story white mansion. It stood proud and white with brick-red shutters. Its white columns and two-storied porches gleamed brightly in the South Carolina sunshine.

She pulled into the paved parking area to the right of the house and quickly left her air-conditioned car to have the heat of a Charleston afternoon hit her in the face. It put a hot Michigan summer to shame. This was real heat.

Sandy strolled across the almost empty parking lot, looking around her at the beauty of the residence. White, pink, and red Azaleas blossomed around the house. The green lawn was neatly trimmed, and several concrete benches were strategically placed around the area. The sound of several songbirds could be heard in the trees above her. It was a peaceful, quiet place, and even more so because the regular crowds of tourists were absent on this day. It appeared that other than for the workers around, she had the whole plantation to herself today.

Sandy turned her attention to a tall man headed in her direction she guessed to be Matthew Pierce. He was dressed casually in tan colored pants, and a white shirt, open at the throat with the sleeves rolled up. As he neared, she couldn't help but notice his tanned face and arms. It was easy to tell by the look of him; Matthew Pierce didn't spend all of his time indoors behind a desk.

"Sandy?" he called when he was near enough for her to hear.

"Yes," she called back, walking a little faster. "You must be Matthew," she finally stated as they drew near to each other.

She quickly shook the offered hand, noticing the warmth and firmness of the handshake, and the blue eyes of the man staring back at her. A slight breeze caught a few strands of his light brown hair and blew it across his forehead. He quickly reached up and pushed it out of his eyes.

"Welcome to Camilla House Plantation. I trust you didn't have any trouble finding us?"

Sandy laughed at the twinkle in his eyes. "I would have if not for my trusty GPS." She quickly fell into step with Matthew as he directed her down the wide brick walk leading through the front gardens of the house.

"I thought we'd start in the main house, if it's okay with you, Sandy." His blue eyes glanced over at her, and she tried and failed to stop the blush she knew was sweeping over her face.

Oh my! Matthew Pierce was a flirt, in addition to being an incredibly handsome southern gentleman. She was definitely in trouble.

They chatted back and forth about the house as Matthew led her up the wide wooden steps, across the columned porch, and into the house. Sandy was in awe as they slowly walked through the rooms. Each one was filled with early American antiques and fine porcelain. As Sandy gazed at the Chinese tea set gracefully sitting on the tiny antique side table in the parlor, her thoughts immediately turned to Darcy Brown.

"Are all the furnishings original to the house?"

Matthew lightly touched the side table with his fingers. "Not everything. This table and china set are, however. Those items not original to Camilla House have been procured from other homes of the same period. None of them are reproductions."

Had Darcy walked through these same rooms a hundred and sixty years earlier? Had her bare brown feet trod these same wooden floors, crossed these ornate carpets, and had her hands washed the exact tea set she saw here? Even in the heat of a late June day in Charleston, a shiver went down Sandy's back. She was close to finding the truth about Darcy Brown and what happened to her—very close.

She could feel it.

Matthew's deep voice brought her back to the present. "As I told you on the phone, I checked Robert Brown's estate records, and I did find a slave named Darcy, age 15, listed in the estate records of Robert Brown, who would have been her original owner." He walked across the room and picked up a manila file folder sitting on the mantle. "I made a copy of the page from the estate records for you with the information."

Sandy stared at the paperwork in his hand before finally accepting it from him. She was almost afraid to see what it would tell her. She opened the manila folder slowly, and then picked up the paper inside. Halfway down the page were the elegantly hand-written words Matthew had read to her over the phone: '*to my daughter, Carolyn, one negro woman named Alice, and her daughter, Darcy.*' She quickly blinked away the tears she could feel forming in her eyes, then looked up to see Matthew's kind eyes studying her.

"Are you okay?"

She nodded. "I'm fine, really—just feeling a little overwhelmed at actually being here." She sniffed a little, took a deep breath, and lifted her chin. This was not a time for tears. She had a job to do.

Placing the paper back in the folder, she closed it and looked up at Matthew. "Did you find anything else about Darcy?"

He shook his head. "I'm afraid not, but I can show you where her mother is buried if you're interested." She felt him take hold of her elbow and turn her toward the wide open staircase. "But first, I'm going to give you the full tour of this beautiful house."

They went up the broad stairway, the thick burgundy-colored carpets underneath their feet muffling their footsteps, then down a wide hall with rooms on each side. Sandy stopped periodically to look in each one, noticing all the doorways were roped off so you could only look into the room, but not enter. When they reached the last one on the left, Matthew opened the door and motioned for her to enter before him.

"We typically rope off the doorways so our guests can't actually enter the rooms, but considering your mission, I'm making an exception in this case."

Sandy smiled over at him. "Thank you. I can't tell you how much this means to me."

She slowly crossed the threshold and entered the large room. A marble-mantled fireplace stood at one end with a huge canopied bed at the other. Several upholstered chairs and small antique tables and a chest sat around the room, and a multi-colored quilt covered the bed. A headless manikin stood in the corner, wearing a hooped tan and gold silk ball gown, decorated lavishly with satin ribbons, pearls, and lace. It was a beautiful dress and spoke of the lifestyle of the privileged southern plantation owner's family.

"This was Carolyn's room," Matthew said quietly, his eyes steady on her face.

Sandy swallowed hard. As her mistress' personal slave, there was no doubt. Darcy would have been in this room.

"I know it isn't generally allowed in a house where you charge admittance, but may I take some photos? I'm working on a newspaper article, and they would be helpful...."

He smiled and waved his hand as if dismissing her worries. "Of course. You're right though. We don't allow our regular visitors to take photos. We prefer they purchase our brochures and booklets to financially support the Foundation. But in your case, I'm more than willing to make an exception. Please take as many as you wish."

She let out a breath she hadn't realized she was holding. "Thank you so much, Matthew."

Sandy pulled the camera out of her purse and started snapping photos, starting with the dress, then moved on to take pictures encompassing the entire room. She probably wouldn't use them for the article, but they would come in handy to help her remember all she had seen this day while she was in the process of writing it.

As she neared the fireplace mantel, her eye was caught by a small silver, oval-shaped frame holding a picture of a young woman with dark curly hair worn up on top ofher head. She wore a pale blue dress and was a beautiful young lady.

"Is that Carolyn?" she asked as she walked toward the fireplace.

Matthew nodded. "It's actually a hand-painted portrait on ivory. From her father's paperwork, we discovered it was commissioned by a local artist right before the war."

Sandy looked at the small painting of the young woman and snapped a couple of photos of it, hoping the expensive camera Mr. Drayton had given her to use would capture a good likeness of the tiny portrait.

"Carolyn lived here with her brother after her father's death. She finally married after the war. After Charleston fell to Union forces in February 1865, the house was damaged when Union soldiers set fire to the rear section where the kitchen is located. Fortunately, the family and servants were able to get the fire out before the whole place burned."

Sandy felt his eyes on her as she prowled around the room, photographing things she thought might prove interesting to her readers.

"Who did Carolyn marry?"

"She married a son from a neighboring plantation family—Caleb Dorsey. They moved to Charleston as he owned a large mercantile there. They had three children—two boys and a girl. Carolyn died of consumption at the age of 38."

Sandy turned to look out the floor-to-ceiling window, gently pushing aside the dark green, heavy damask draperies to better see what lay beyond. The window looked out over the rear gardens, and she could also see outbuildings, which she assumed were the barns and stables. In the distance were several smaller buildings.

"What are those little buildings way over there?"

Matthew came over to stand next to her, his arm brushing against her elbow and causing her to take a step back.

"Those are the slave quarters. Do you want to see them?"

She nodded her head slowly. "Yes, but would Darcy have lived there if she was a house servant?"

He thought for a moment. "She was probably born there and lived there as a child, especially if her mother hadn't been taken into the house yet. But Darcy would have lived in the attic in the servant quarters here once she started serving as Carolyn's personal servant."

"Then I'd like to see the attic first if it's okay with you."

He nodded and led her from the room. They went down the hall and up a small dark and narrow stairway which took several sharp turns before ending in a large gabled room. It was a dark area and quite Spartan in comparison to the rest of the house below. There were cots and small benches, and several hooks on the wall where Sandy assumed the slaves would hang what few pieces of clothing they had.

Sandy lifted her camera to take photos of the space around her. Here was where Darcy lived and slept until she made the fateful decision to run away.

"I can't imagine the life she must have suffered here," she said quietly, feeling somewhat depressed at seeing how forlorn the area looked.

Matthew nodded somberly. "Slavery was a terrible thing. But on the whole, I believe most owners took good care of their slaves. It was in their interest to have them healthy and strong and able to do their work."

She pursed her lips and stopped herself from responding with what she thought about slavery and the things owners thought they were allowed to do to those slaves. There wasn't any sense getting into an argument with Matthew Pierce about something that happened more than a hundred fifty years earlier.

Sandy looked around a little more and then turned to go back down the steps. There was nothing here to give her more information about Darcy, and the attic was a hot, depressing place.

"Let's go look at the slave quarters then."

As they went back down the stairway, Matthew continued to relate to Sandy the history of the low country where the plantation was located. He explained the house and grounds were often rented out for weddings. Sandy looked around at the extravagance of the house and its furnishings and nodded in understanding. She could easily see where a bride would appreciate the authenticity of the place, and the romantic notion of being married at an old southern plantation house would be a great drawing card.

They walked through the rest of the house and out the rear door to cross the gardens, then strolled down a grassy path through the cooler shade of more moss covered oak trees toward the little white houses she had seen from

Carolyn's room. Sandy looked around her in awe. She could have stepped into a movie set during the Civil War, and she half expected to see several of the black servants step through the open doors of the slave quarters to greet them.

To call them houses was being generous—small shacks seemed to be a better description. A row of four small, simple frame houses sat before her. They had planked wooden doors, but no windows—only open hinged shutters over the window openings.

"We are also in the process of repairing and restoring these buildings as an example of what they were like during the years of slavery. There were many more than these four, of course, but most of them were beyond saving."

He sighed. "We're trying to preserve them for future generations to see. It was a terrible time in our country's history, but we can't ignore there was slavery here at one time. The African-Americans helped to build our nation and aided South Carolina in becoming what we are today. They are as much a part of our history as anyone else, and we intend to honor their part in making this nation great. And it is important for our children and grandchildren to know how they were treated in order to understand why the war was fought in the first place."

Sandy took a few photos of the outside of one of the structures, then stepped up the stone steps and into the first small pine framed house. It was hardly more than a shack, sparsely furnished; there was even less here than what had been in the attic. There was a simple wooden bed frame in the corner, a wooden chair, and a small wooden table. The rough wooden plank floor was swept clean, and the brick fireplace was empty. Whitewashed walls were the only bright spot in the room.

"You probably don't know which one Darcy's family would have lived in." It was more of a statement than a question.

He shook his head. "Sorry, no. There's no way to know, I'm afraid."

Sandy took several photos of the inside of the slave quarters and turned to leave the room. There was nothing of Darcy here and the sadness she felt at being in the small shack left her feeling more depressed than the attic room had. How had the slaves felt to have lived in such sparse conditions when they saw how their owners lived on a daily basis?

After leaving the slave quarters, Matthew led her through a small grove of trees to an area with a split rail fence around it. Sandy quickly recognized it as a graveyard.

"This is the slave cemetery," he stated, his voice hushed as they went through the low gate.

There were no large marble monuments here—no fancy urns for flowers. A few small square stones were marking some of the graves, but most were bare of any markers other than some simple wooden crosses. Matthew led Sandy around the perimeter of the cemetery to a spot near the back where he stopped in front of the small gray marker, a little larger than the rest.

Alice, 1827-1866

Sandy sighed. Darcy's mother hadn't lived long after the emancipation of her people. How sad. She couldn't help but wonder about the care this grave appeared to have been given in comparison to the rest of the cemetery. Even the tombstone was a little larger, a little less plain. It was easy to tell that someone—either in the family or someone else on the plantation—had cared for her a great deal. Although there was no way to know for sure, Sandy liked to think it was Carolyn Brown who had seen to it that Darcy's mother had been recognized as an important part of the plantation.

Matthew spoke quietly as he gently took her elbow and led her back out of the cemetery. "The graveyard was extremely overgrown when the Foundation received ownership of the plantation. I'm sure you noticed we've painstakingly restored as much of the remaining tombstones in the cemetery as we could."

Sandy automatically nodded her head, her mind still back at Alice's grave. The body of Darcy's mother lay there. Darcy had never had the privilege of visiting her mother's place of burial to put flowers on it in the same way Sandy was able to do with her own mother whenever she wanted. She couldn't help but wonder if Darcy had even known when her mother had died. Chances were she hadn't, as she hadn't been living in America at the time. How difficult it must have been for both of them to be apart.

She and Matthew headed back across the yard and spent some more time wandering around the grounds of the house. In addition to the azaleas blossoming, there were hibiscus, mimosa, Southern Magnolias, daylilies, and row after row of stunning roses in every color imaginable. There were also multitudes of the beautiful Camilla plants for which the plantation was named—with their dark green shiny leaves and blossoms in every color of the rainbow. Sandy's emotions leveled out as they strolled through the beautiful gardens, and she took many photos of the lovely blooms. There was also a reflecting pool and a small fish pond with water lilies and pampas grass growing around it, and the smell of jasmine and gardenia floated through the air around her as she and Matthew walked down the brick paths through the gardens.

By the time they returned to the house, Sandy was feeling less depressed and paused several times to take a few photos of the front of the old home. The Foundation had done an excellent job so far in their restoration project, but a house this large and old was going to continue to need a large amount of upkeep. She was glad they weren't letting it fall into ruin as so many of the old plantation homes had been allowed to.

Sandy turned back to Matthew. "Thank you so much for taking the time to show me around and letting me take photos. I appreciate it, and I'm sure my readers will also."

He took hold of her hand and smiled, and her stomach did a little flip at the apparent interest showing in his blue eyes.

"Well, you can repay me by allowing me the pleasure of taking you to dinner tonight at one of our finer establishments here in Charleston."

Sandy shook her head slowly. "You don't have to do that...."

"I know I don't have to—I want to." His blue eyes were pleading.

She smiled. "Okay. I would be pleased to have dinner with you."

They set a time and decided the easiest thing was for him to come to The Cardinal and pick her up and go to the restaurant from there. As Sandy drove down the drive with the view of the old mansion in her rearview mirror, she felt light of heart and excited to see what the evening would hold.

CHAPTER 20

After a quick shower and changing into a long flowery skirt and colorful blouse, Sandy felt ready for the evening. While she waited for the time of his arrival, she entered all her notes and photos into the small laptop she had brought with her, taking the time to begin her article. The story was starting to fall into place.

The only thing missing was an ending.

From what she and Beverly had found, they knew Darcy had made it to Canada and freedom, and had married Eli Wilson and had borne children. They didn't know when she had died, or where her children and grandchildren had ended up.

Sandy did some quick calculations in her head. If Darcy had lived to her early 70s, she would have died about 1916. That meant there was no one still alive who would remember her. It saddened her to think about it. But the story of her life could have been shared down through the generations by her own family. Hopefully, the young slave girl who had escaped to freedom hadn't been entirely forgotten.

✞✞✞✞

Matthew Pierce arrived right on time to take her to dinner. She was relaxing in one of the white wooden rocking chairs on the front piazza, discussing The Cardinal's many flower gardens with her hostess, when he arrived. He was sharply dressed in a pair of dark blue dress pants, crisp white shirt, and tan sports coat, and looked particularly handsome.

She said goodbye to Jo and took Matthew's offered hand as he led her down the steps and walked her to his car.

Conversation was stilted in the car, and Sandy found herself feeling uncomfortable. Perhaps she'd been foolish to accept Matthew Pierce's dinner invitation. She didn't know him or much about him—just that he was the curator of Camilla House. But by the time they reached their destination, a huge two-story brick Victorian house turned restaurant whose sign promised an upscale southern cuisine, she was starting to feel a little more relaxed. The restaurant was a magnificent place, with a smaller dining room on the first floor and two larger elegant dining rooms on the second floor. The walls were decorated with framed photos telling the history of Charleston, and Sandy had to restrain herself from walking around the room to get a better look at them.

After they were shown to their table in a quiet corner near one of the ceiling-to-floor windows, they discussed the weather, her schedule for leaving the next day, and his future goals for the plantation. By the time their food order had been placed on the table in front of them on pale blue plates bearing the name of the restaurant along the outside edge, Sandy was feeling much more relaxed.

"So, have you found any helpful information here about your Darcy?" Matthew asked between bites of his steak.

Sandy finished chewing a delicious bite of her own nut crusted salmon before answering. "Being here has given me more of a feel for the place—more of a sense of how she must have lived before she ran away." She smiled at him. "And of course, I have you to thank. I appreciate you taking the time to show me around Camilla House."

Matthew took a sip of his water and smiled at her across the top of the glass. "It's my job." He grinned. "Although in your case, it wasn't work at all. I do wish you were able to stay longer though."

The unspoken words were loud in the room. It was obvious he was attracted to her. But did she feel the same way? Suddenly another man's face intruded on her evening, and she found herself comparing Matthew Pierce to Tom Brannigan—even though she kept telling herself she had no right to do so. Tom was a friend, nothing more. But Matthew's smooth talk and gentlemanly airs didn't hold the same appeal to her that Tom's honest smile and handsome ruggedness did. But then, Tom wasn't available to her—was he? If he did have a son with Kate, he needed to work on building a relationship with them, and she needed to forget daydreaming about having more than a friendship with him and move on with her life. She let a small sigh escape before she turned her attention back to her date for the evening, and struggled to catch up on what Matthew had been talking about.

As chocolate chunk bread pudding arrived for their dessert, Sandy tried to concentrate on the man across the table from her. He wasn't Tom Brannigan, but he was her escort for the evening and had been helpful in finding more information about Darcy Brown for her. The least she could do was be polite and listen to what he was saying.

After dinner, they strolled a short ways down the tree-lined streets before walking back to their car. It was a hot and humid evening with the aroma of food wafting on the breeze from the numerous restaurants, and the smell of flowers planted along the way. Somewhere in their walk, Sandy found her hand being held in Matthew's.

Once they walked back to the car, he drove slowly through the busy streets on the way back to The Cardinal. The conversation had died to a minimal as the evening came to a close. It had been an enjoyable evening, but Sandy was ready for it to be over. It had become tiresome to keep smiling at him because frankly, she wanted to go back to her room and go to sleep so she could go home the next day.

After he parked the car in The Cardinal's small parking area and turned off the ignition, Sandy turned toward him.

"Thank you for a beautiful evening, Matthew. And also, thank you again for taking the time out of your busy day for the tour of the plantation. I really appreciate it."

"So, tomorrow you go back to Michigan?"

She nodded in the gathering darkness. "Yes, I do. But thanks to you, I now have enough information to do an article justice. At least, I hope my editor feels the same way," she added with a little laugh.

It was silent for a few seconds before Matthew reached out to pull her into a quick kiss, which left her breathless only because it was such a surprise. She certainly hadn't expected it. She barely knew the man. As she pulled away, she put a smile back on her face.

"Thank you again," she stammered as she opened the door and quickly exited the car.

She hurried to the bottom of the steps leading up to her room and only turned around once to lift her hand in a little wave as she heard Matthew start the car to leave. It was far better to not have any unfinished ties to South Carolina. He had been a nice man, but the sparks weren't there.

Frustratingly, the only thing she had on her mind when Matthew had kissed her was Tom Brannigan. And how she wished he'd been the one on the other side of that kiss.

✞✞✞✞

The next morning, after a leisurely breakfast consisting of raspberry stuffed French toast, fresh fruit, coffee and juice on the front piazza with her hostess, Jo, Sandy was feeling refreshed and ready for the flight back to Michigan. Even though it had been a short trip, it had been great to visit a part of the country she had never seen before, but now she was ready to go home.

Home.

Sandy could hardly wait to get back to her house and started some serious work on the article. She was also curious to find out if Beverly at the Historical Society had been able to find any more information.

If she was going to honest with herself though, she was really looking forward to seeing Tom again to tell him about her trip to Darcy's birthplace. That had to be the reason she found her thoughts turning to him so often. She couldn't and wouldn't let her emotions fall for someone like Tom—someone who had hurt her own cousin and didn't want to take responsibility for his actions. What type of man did that sort of thing? Obviously, one she didn't want to become emotionally involved with.

No matter what her heart kept saying.

✞✞✞✞

The flight was uneventful, and the drive home from Toledo thankfully felt short to her, but it was late afternoon when she finally drove her car into her driveway. She let out a sigh of relief. It had been exciting to go on the trip, but now it felt good to be home.

She quickly pulled her luggage from the back seat where she had tossed it and unlocked the back door of her house to let herself in. Traveling was all right, and she'd enjoyed having the opportunity to see where Darcy had been born and raised with her own eyes, but the old adage about there being no place like home was true as far as she was concerned.

Sandy dropped her luggage on the dining room floor and was greeted by Boots meowing as he rubbed against her leg. She quickly reached down and scooped up her little friend, snuggling his softness against her chin.

"Hi-ya, Boots. Did you miss me?"

After spending a few minutes checking to make sure the cat still had food and putting fresh water in his bowl, she went back out the door to the mailbox near the road to collect the last two days' worth of mail. Strolling back to the house, she quickly thumbed through the envelopes. Most of them were bills or junk mail, but there was another letter from the insurance agency. She let out a groan at the sight of it.

What now?

She slit open the back of the envelope with her fingernail and unfolded the letter. Scanning through it quickly, she let out a sigh of relief. It sounded as if the insurance company was giving her some time—and for a while at least, the old tree had a reprieve. Due to the 'historical value' of the tree, they were paying to have a forester come and look at the tree to discern if it should or could be saved, or if their initial decision had been accurate. It wasn't much, but right now it sounded good to her. If nothing else, it bought them some more time.

Sandy quickly unpacked her suitcase and set up her laptop in her office, pulling her notes out of the laptop bag. It was time to get to work on the article as she knew Mr. Drayton was going to expect something from her soon now she was home. Looking through the photos she had downloaded to her laptop, she was instantly transported back to the attic where Darcy had more than likely lived before she ran away. The photos of the slave shanty made her remember how depressing it had been and how it was such a stark contrast to the lavishness of the 'big house.'

She'd been working about an hour and was getting ready to stop working to fix some dinner when she noticed the light blinking on the answering machine sitting on the table in the corner. Walking over to push the 'play' button, she smiled at the sound of Beverly's voice from the Historical Society.

"Sandy, I'm so excited. I've found Darcy's family—well, really her son's family—living in Ottawa, Ontario. They evidently moved. I also found death records for both Darcy and Eli, and now know where they are buried. If you want to stop in the office when you get back, I've made copies of all the documents for you. Hope you had a great trip! Call me when you get home!"

She couldn't help the smile spreading across her face as she listened to Beverly's infectious excitement. Sandy could hardly wait until she got her hands on the paperwork which would hopefully show what had become of Darcy's family.

Too bad she hadn't seen the light blinking earlier while the historical society office was still open. Oh well, it would have to wait until tomorrow.

CHAPTER 21

Sandy decided she was going to have to wait an extra day to go see what Beverly had found on Darcy since she was on a deadline and had to finish the article for the newspaper first. So, she worked the next day fervently to write and re-write the piece, wanting to make sure it was perfect. She also knew Mr. Drayton would want to include a few photos, but was having a difficult time deciding which ones to give him, so finally burned a cd for him with all of them on it and left the choice to him.

Finally, Friday morning Sandy drove into the *Bradford Mills Daily Press* office to drop off the cd, along with the finished article. She had written and re-written it until she felt she was giving Darcy's story the proper voice. It was a news article, but it was also a story about a real person who had lived and loved and died, and she wanted the readers to be able to relate to what the young black woman had been through as much as was possible through the written word. The article as a whole was long enough it would need to be run as a series of items over a period of several weeks. She knew Mr. Drayton was expecting to increase their readership and subscriptions by having a continuation of a human interest story to hook them in as readers. Sandy just hoped both he and the readers would be happy with the finished product. Unfortunately, Mr. Drayton was out of the office when she arrived, so she left her article and the cd with his secretary for his return.

After finishing her other errands, Sandy made her way to the nearby grocery store to make the needed purchases to fill up her cupboards again. Walking down the cereal aisle, she ran into her cousin, Kate. After exchanging hugs, she glanced around for her cousin's young son.

"Where's Robbie?"

Kate grinned. "He's at a friend's house. It was his first big all-night stay over. I wasn't sure how he would handle it, but I never heard a word from him last evening, so I guess they were kept so busy by the parents, he never had time to miss me." She frowned. "Unlike me. I've discovered a quiet, empty house isn't all it's cracked up to be."

Sandy smiled. "Won't be long and he'll be all grown up. You'll need to get used to the 'empty nest' feeling someday."

"Yeah, well I'm not in any hurry."

Her cousin's laughter warmed Sandy's heart. It was good to hear and lifted her spirits as well. Even though Sandy was sure it hadn't been easy, Kate seemed content with her small town life.

Kate pushed her cart out of the way of another shopper and then turned back to Sandy. "So, what's going on with you, cuz?"

Sandy took a couple of cans of green beans off the store shelf and added them to her growing pile of purchases in the grocery cart.

"I just got back from South Carolina where I was sent on assignment for the newspaper." She laughed. "It was a whole lot hotter down there, let me tell you. Michigan summers are much more comfortable!"

Kate and Sandy continued to chat as they slowly pushed their grocery carts side by side down the aisles. Sandy missed the camaraderie she and her cousin had when they were younger.

"Is Robbie all finished with playing baseball?"

She glanced over at Kate briefly, hoping she wouldn't guess as to why Sandy was asking. There had been no phone calls or contact with Tom for several weeks, and she was definitely starting to feel he was purposely avoiding her. Maybe she would have to put forth the effort to go to another one of Robbie's games in the hopes of catching Tom after the game to talk. A part of her heart dreaded seeing him again, while another part yearned to have the opportunity see and talk with him.

"He only has one more game this year. Coach Tompson says he's doing great and has improved a great deal this summer. I'm so proud of him."

Sandy frowned. "Coach Tompson? I thought Tom was Robbie's coach...."

She saw the other woman look over at her in confusion.

"Tom's gone, Sandy. He went to Louisiana with a work crew, rebuilding hurricane-damaged homes. So Bill Tompson is finishing out the ball season as coach. He's doing a great job with the kids."

Sandy looked at her in shock. "When's Tom coming back?"

The other woman shrugged. "Don't know."

A huge sigh of disgust escaped Sandy's lungs. She couldn't believe Tom Brannigan. He'd deserted Kate and their son—again. What was wrong with the man?

"I'm so sorry, Kate. You must be furious with him. He's been spending so much time recently with Robbie."

Kate turned her eyes on Sandy. "It's okay. He made arrangements before he left."

"'Arrangements'?" Sandy ground out between her clenched teeth. What did that mean?

"Yeah, you know—another Big Brother."

Sandy looked at Kate, hearing the words but not understanding what her cousin was saying.

"Big Brother?" she repeated.

Kate gently smiled. "Yes, the organization is great. When the person assigned to your child isn't able to fulfill their obligation and spend time with them, they appoint another Big Brother to take care of it."

She sobered. "I'm sure Robbie will miss Tom, but he will still have someone to take him to movies, go rollerblading with him, and take him out for ice cream. When you're a little boy starved for male companionship, it doesn't matter who the man is, as long as he's there for you."

"But...I thought..." Sandy stuttered over her words, trying to figure out how to ask what she wanted to know without making more of a fool of herself than she already had.

She saw her cousin's eyes studying her for a moment and knew the exact instant Kate realized the thoughts racing through Sandy's mind.

"Oh my! You thought Tom and I....you thought Tom was Robbie's father?"

Sandy nodded her head as she felt her face grow hot from embarrassment, and glanced around the store quickly in the hopes no one else was within earshot of their conversation.

Of course, she had thought Tom was Robbie's father! What else was she supposed to think? It had been obvious to her from the start that Tom cared about the boy, and he seemed to spend quite a bit of time with him. It had seemed odd to Sandy because he didn't spend much time with Kate, but she hadn't thought about that part of it too much until this point. Now, it all made so much more sense. He was Robbie's Big Brother! What an idiot she had been.

Kate laughed, and Sandy flinched upon hearing her laughter. "Oh, Sandy. I'm sorry for laughing, but Tom Brannigan is the last person I would be interested in." She put up her right hand with her palm out at what Sandy was sure was her look of anger at Kate's remark. "Don't get me wrong, Tom's a great guy. But he's not my type."

Sandy had to smile a little at Kate's remark. She had to admit she had never been able to visualize Kate and Tom together. But the relief she felt when she realized Tom wasn't Robbie's father and he and Kate had never been romantically involved was so much more than just the knowledge her cousin hadn't been hurt by him.

She hadn't been wrong about Tom Brannigan after all. He really was one of the good guys.

Sandy shook her head trying to erase the heat of embarrassment flaming across her face again. She could only imagine how bright red her face was right then.

"I'm so sorry, Kate. It's really none of my business."

The other woman patted her arm lightly. "I forgot. You weren't here because you were already away in college, so you don't know the story. And obviously, you're too polite to ask. Guess that's the way we were raised, huh?" She grinned, and then the smile disappeared as Sandy saw her eyes glaze over in remembrance.

"I got pregnant my senior year of high school—right before graduation. It was a teacher—a married teacher," she added almost in a whisper, her eyes dropping from Sandy's. Sandy could see the pain etched there though before Kate looked away.

"He never even knew I was pregnant because he left the school and the state right after the end of the school year. There was quite a scandal about it at the time as the school administration found out he'd been having affairs with several of the senior girls. I was one of many girls he'd been involved with—but unfortunately, I was the one who ended up pregnant."

Sandy quickly reached out to pull her cousin into a hug. "Oh, Kate. I'm sorry for dredging up this painful history for you. I never knew...."

Kate hugged her back and then stepped back, took a deep breath, and raised her chin a little. "I know you never knew, Sandy, so don't worry about it. I'm okay—really. Robbie's a great little boy, and I'm very blessed to have him. My parents were very supportive, and I was able to finish high school and go on to get my associate's degree from the community college and get a good job working for an attorney, so we're doing fine. God has been good to us. I don't know how I would have made it through it all without my faith in God and knowing He was there for me, no matter what."

"You never told Robbie's father about him?"

"No!" Kate quickly shook her head and glanced around the store, then lowered her voice as she turned back to Sandy. "I don't want him to know about Robbie, nor do I want Robbie to know about him. The guy was a creep and used young teenage girls as if we were his personal haram. I guess the school board did contact the state and he lost his teaching credentials. Hopefully, he's not out there somewhere at a high school continuing to treat young girls that way."

Sandy felt her cousin's eyes focus back on her. "And as for Tom..." Kate grinned, and Sandy felt the heat rush into her face again. "I think he likes you, Sandy—more than just a little bit. And if I'm not mistaken, I'm pretty sure the feeling is mutual. So...what are you going to do about it?"

Sandy shook her head in denial at first, then bit her lower lip to keep from smiling, and nodded instead. "Okay, okay. I am more than a little attracted to the man. But if he likes me so much, why did he leave town without letting me know? He just disappeared."

Kate frowned and shook her head. "I don't know. You'll have to ask him yourself. Have you tried calling him?"

"No."

"Do you still have his cell phone number?"

Sandy nodded, the wheels spinning in her head. Her feelings were suddenly in turmoil now she realized she had misjudged Tom and his relationship with Robbie and Kate. Instead of Tom being a womanizer and out to use her cousin and not taking responsibility for his former actions, she had discovered he was the loving, caring, and wonderful man she had thought he was when she had first come back to Bradford Mills. What an idiot she was! And after the type of life she had lived for three years, who was she to judge anybody?

Forgive me, Lord, for my feeling worthy to stand in judgment of others. Only You have that right!

But was it too late to mend the rift between her and Tom? Had she alienated him by her rudeness to the point he'd written her off and wouldn't want anything further to do with her?

"Well then," Kate continued. "I suggest you give the man a call!"

CHAPTER 22

Tom Brannigan swung his hammer to pound another nail into the two-by-six in the framework of the wall he and his buddy were building. He took a moment to take off his baseball cap—the cap he'd received as a coach for Robbie Baker's baseball team back home—and wiped the sweat from his brow with his bare arm.

It was hot here in Louisiana. Correction. Hot didn't even begin to describe the sticky humid air hanging over him like a heavy wet wool blanket, making it difficult to breathe. It was hot in the shade, but when you were out in the sun working, it was like standing in a blasting furnace. He leaned over to take a drink of water from his nearby thermos, but even though it gave him a moment of relief to have the cooler wetness sliding down his throat, it didn't lower the temperature any. He would never complain about a Michigan summer's heat again.

Tom returned to pounding in nails on his end of the wall, knowing Jeffrey Wilkes, a Christian man he'd met working on the job, was working on the other end. Jeffrey was a recovered drug addict who had come to know the Lord about five years earlier and was using his vacation from his job as a Technology Director, to help rebuild houses through the same organization that had brought Tom here. Tom and Jeffrey had hit it off from the first day and even shared the same motel room. Their days were spent working together, and their evenings were spent studying God's word and talking about their lives and how far God had brought them from where they had been, to where they were now.

Tom finished pounding in another nail and paused to look out over the neighborhood which had been so severely damaged by a recent hurricane. Houses were being rebuilt and repaired all over the area and the sounds of saws and hammers echoed all around them. The houses hadn't been much to begin with as it was a poorer area of the community, but when the work crews were finished rebuilding, in most cases they were going to be better than the original houses had been.

As so often happened when he wasn't keeping his hands and mind busy, his thoughts turned to one red-headed Sandy Martin. He sent up a silent prayer for the beautiful redhead who was never far from his mind—praying she was doing well and settling into her new job, keeping busy, and hopefully finding her way back to the Lord.

It had been difficult to leave Bradford Mills, but it had become too painful for him to stay—at least right now. His feelings for her were too strong, and besides—she had made it clear she wasn't interested in pursuing a relationship of any type with him; although he didn't know what he had done to have turned her against him.

He sighed as he thought more about it. He had started avoiding her right after he realized how strong his feelings for her were becoming. Then she had begun avoiding him too, acting as if they weren't even friends anymore. Maybe he should have confronted her before he had left town, demanded to know why she was so upset with him. But he was too much of a coward to put himself through such a painful an experience. Maybe sometime he would find out. In the meantime, all he could do was pray for her and miss her—more than he thought possible.

"Hey, Brannigan. You gonna daydream all day?" Jeffrey's voice boomed across the framework of the house at him, and Tom's head came up quickly.

He felt the tips of his ears turn pink, and he knew this time it wasn't from being out in the sun too long. He'd been caught daydreaming before by Jeffrey, and now it had happened again. The tall heavy-set man walked over next to Tom, his hand coming out to rest on Tom's shoulder.

"You're thinking about that girl again, aren't you Tom?"

Tom pasted a grin on his face and turned away, shaking his head. "Wilkes, you are crazy! Not everybody has women on the brain all the time like you do!" He tried to laugh and shrug aside his friend's hand from his shoulder.

Jeffrey stood firm and didn't leave his side. "Naw, I know that look, Brannigan." He shook his head. "Why don't you call her? At least touch base and ask if she's still mad at you—or find out if you have a chance of going back and working things out?"

Tom reached down to pull another nail from his tool pouch. "Not sure there's anything to work out, Jeffrey. If God wanted us together, He wouldn't have brought me to Louisiana now, would He?"

His friend patted him on the back as he turned to walk away. "Did He bring you here, Brannigan, or were you running away from something or someone when you came?"

Tom turned back to the next nail and tried to dismiss his friend's words, but couldn't shake the words out of his head. Was Jeffrey right? Had he been running away from his feelings for Sandy when he came here? True, what he was doing here was a good thing, and God would approve of it, but was he doing it for the right reasons—or was it just a way to get out of Bradford Mills and away from one Sandy Martin for a while?

He let out a sigh and went back to work. It sounded as if he needed to spend some time with God and his Bible and try to figure out what he was doing in Louisiana—and what he was going to do about a beautiful red-headed woman back in Michigan he couldn't seem to get out of his thoughts.

Sandy's heart started racing on the way to meet Beverly at the historical society's office. It was a Saturday morning, and she could hardly wait to see what information Beverly had found about Darcy's family.

Beverly greeted her as soon as she arrived and pulled her into a private office at the rear of the structure.

"I've made arrangements for one of our volunteers to man the main room this morning so we won't be disturbed. I have all the information spread out here for us to review." She pointed to a large table in the room covered with folders and documents. Sandy grinned at her. It looked like Beverly had hit the jackpot.

They both sat down at the table, and Beverly picked up the first folder in front and to the left of her. "I found Darcy's and Eli's son, Caleb in Ottawa—still in Ontario Province, but quite a distance away from where he was born."

She handed Sandy the census record for 1891 showing Caleb, aged 25, married, with one child, Jacob, age five.

"I also found Jacob in Ottawa in the 1921 and 1926 census. Jacob had a son named Wilbur, along with four other children."

She handed Sandy two more census records to look at.

Sandy saw Beverly glance over at her and frown. "Here's where it gets tricky as we don't have census records available to us beyond 1926."

"Why not?"

Beverly sighed. "Most countries do this to protect the identities of those who may still be living. In 2005, the Canadian Parliament passed a statute which allows for the release of census records once 92 years have elapsed after the data was collected. The legislation restricts the scope of access to genealogical purposes and historical research, but it's still going to be a long time before all the years we want will be available to us."

Looking down at the documents in her hands, Sandy frowned. "So where do we go from here? How am I going to be able to find the family from this point on?"

She heard the older woman's sigh. "Well, we know Wilbur was born about 1910, so we can assume if he lived to be in his seventies, he wouldn't have died until the mid-1980's. If he married and had children, they would have probably been born in the late 1930's or 1940's, and might still be alive."

Sandy shook her head feeling defeat wash over her. "Sounds like lots of conjuncture to me. How am I ever going to find the current generation?"

The only sound in the room for a few moments was the ticking of the antique clock on the fireplace mantel as the two women looked through the papers spread across the table. Sorrow swept over Sandy. To be this close to finding Darcy's family and then to fail, it didn't seem fair.

"If Wilbur's children were born in the 1930's or 40's, that would mean they'd be what—in their 60's or 70's, right?" Sandy asked.

Beverly nodded. "There's no question but what they could still be alive, but I've run into a wall when it comes to being able to trace them any further." She patted Sandy on the arm. "I know you're disappointed, but when you realize how much information we've been able to find, we've done quite well."

Sandy smiled distractedly over at Beverly. She didn't want to sound ungrateful to this woman who had obviously spent a great deal of time working on the project.

"Of course, Beverly. I don't know how to thank you for all the work you've put into this. When I started looking, it seemed like an impossible feat to find her family. You've done wonders in getting us this far."

The older woman grinned at her. "Just remember the Historical Society would love to be able to add the information from the diary to our local historical museum." She quickly shook her head as Sandy started to speak. "I know, I know. The original goes to Darcy's family—as it should. But I would sure love a copy when this is all said and done."

"You'll get it—I promise!" Sandy said, feeling a little better. Beverly was right. They had found much more information than she had thought they would. And Darcy's story wasn't going to be forgotten.

Sandy would make sure of it.

CHAPTER 23

A few days later Sandy had a phone call from her insurance agent, setting up an appointment for the forester person the company had hired to examine her tree. She wasn't excited about the confrontation but knew her cooperation was the only chance she had of saving it.

About 10:00 a.m. the following Saturday morning, a tall, lanky man in his early forties got out of a bright red jeep parked in her driveway and greeted her under the old pine tree. He introduced himself as George Matthews and supplied her with his business card. Dressed in jeans and a dark blue long-sleeved shirt, and wearing a yellow hard hat strapped to his head, he looked the part of a tree man.

They both stood under the shady boughs of the tree, and Sandy watched as the man placed his large hand on the trunk as if feeling for a heartbeat. She caught herself grinning at the thought, but sobered as she saw him tip his head back to look up into the branches.

"What a beauty!" he exclaimed. "This thing's gotta be over a hundred feet high!" He took out a tape and measured around the base of the tree, then again about eye level, marking down his measurements in a notebook he pulled out of his shirt pocket.

Sandy smiled when she saw his eyes fall on the faint outline of the old cross which still showed in the bark, and blinked back the tears in her eyes as she watched him run his large hand over the area.

"So, tell me about your tree," he said as he turned back to look at her.

Sandy quickly wiped the remaining tears from the corners of her eyes and tried to smile at him. It wasn't his fault the insurance company wanted to destroy the tree. He was only doing his job. She quickly related her memories of the tree growing up, and then regaled him with the recent findings of the diary and all the pine tree had represented.

"Wow." He stared at her for a moment, and then gazed back up into the heart of the tree. "What a great story. No wonder you hate to see this old girl go down."

He patted the trunk of the tree again and then turned back to her. "I'm going to climb her and take some samples if it's okay with you. You understand, of course, those samples and my findings are what will decide whether or not the company will allow the tree to stand. I don't make the final decision—I only provide them with the facts."

She frowned and nodded her head, then watched him go to his vehicle and come back with ropes, pulley, and a harness which he put on. He threw the ropes over the lowest branches and prepared to pull himself up into the tree.

As he made his way up to the limb closest to the ground, Sandy stepped back to watch from further away but heard his voice call out to her as he made his way from limb to limb, up the tree.

"Has anyone ever climbed it before?"

As the remembrance of a hot July 4th from her childhood swept over her, she smiled sadly. Back then a young man had actually climbed the tree to place an American flag in the very top. The newspaper had even come out and taken a picture of the tree and her cousin and published an article about it on the front page. She had forgotten all about that incident until now. The young man had been her cousin, Kate's older brother—and it seemed as if it had been a lifetime ago. Charlie had been killed in Iraq three years earlier serving in the Marines.

"My cousin climbed it when we were younger," she finally found the voice to holler back.

Sandy stood in the yard and watched George climb higher and higher, only occasionally catching sight of his yellow hard hat amongst the dark green boughs. He spent about fifteen minutes up in the tree and even though she didn't know what he was doing, she had to assume it had something to do with the various samples and tests he was supposed to be collecting. It wasn't long before she saw him start to lower himself back down the trunk, and she couldn't help but release a sigh of relief when his feet firmly hit the ground. She'd had a moment or two of panic wondering what would happen if he fell while in the midst of his climb or descent. With her fear of heights, she knew she'd never be able to climb trees for a living. Thankfully, he reached terra firma without any incident and picked up his climbing gear. He shook her hand again before he left, telling her the company would be in touch.

She hinted, trying to get a little information on what he had discovered, but all he would tell her was the tree was old—really old.

Sandy sighed. That, she already knew.

✞✞✞✞

The next Sunday found Sandy sitting in her chosen pew at church, waiting for the service to begin. She could hear the soft sound of voices around her as her fellow worshippers visited with each other, but she sat quietly in her seat, praying and readying her heart for worship. When she'd walked in the church door this morning, she had decided today was going to be the day; the day she made her heart right with God.

After a restless night spent tossing and turning, wrestling with her past and what she hoped for her future, she'd finally given up and fallen to her knees at the side of the bed. She'd been battling the feelings for weeks now, and it was time to face them.

When she'd come back to Bradford Mills, she had returned to her beginnings in the hope it would heal her heart. She had expected that by coming home, she would find that elusive peace she had known as a child. But she wasn't the same person she'd been then. She had lived an entirely different kind of life for the past eight years—a life she wasn't exactly proud of.

When she lived with Mitchell Wright without the benefit of marriage, she closed her heart and mind to the truth—the beliefs with which she had been raised. Now she felt shame pierce her heart whenever she recalled those three years of her life. How could she have thought it was acceptable—that she loved him and he loved her, so it was no big deal that they hadn't made the commitment to marry each other when in her heart she had known better? Maybe that was why she had been looking forward to getting married, thinking it would make everything okay and legitimize all she had done in the past.

How could she ever approach marriage with a man—a Christian godly man—knowing she had selfishly turned away from God and her beliefs all those years ago? Sandy knew God would forgive her if she asked, but when it came down to it, she didn't feel worthy of His forgiveness. She couldn't help feeling she had failed God. God hadn't turned His back on her—it had been the other way around.

The previous evening when she had spent time on her knees at the side of her bed, she had poured her heart out to her Lord and Savior, asking for forgiveness and an opportunity for a fresh start. The peace that had swept through her had touched her heart and made her feel more loved than she had in years. She had finally returned to her first love.

After the sermon was over and the pastor gave his final 'amen,' Sandy made her way to the back of the church to shake Pastor Armstrong's hand.

"Pastor, if you have a moment, I would like to have you pray with me."

She saw the surprise, then joy sweep across the older man's face at her request. "I would be happy to. Just give me a moment to finish up here."

Sandy nodded and walked over to the side to wait for Pastor Armstrong to finish greeting the rest of the congregation. When he finally shook the last hand, he turned to her with a smile on his face.

"Miss Martin, I think you've made a decision?"

Sandy smiled at his wording. She had made a decision, that was true; but the decision he was talking about was one she had made many, many years before—when she was just a child.

"Actually, Pastor, I just need to have you pray with me. I accepted the Lord as my Savior when I was a child and was baptized right here in this church. I'm not proud to say it, but I haven't lived for Him since I went away to college. I drifted away and made a lot of mistakes. Last night I asked Him for His forgiveness—again." She wiped a couple of tears from the corners of her eyes. "But I would feel so much better if you would also pray with me...."

Pastor Armstrong took hold of her hand and led her to sit down in a nearby pew. "Sin is a barrier that separates us from a relationship with God, Sandy. But He's just waiting for you to come back to Him." He smiled at her kindly. "I would be honored to pray with you, Miss Martin."

The two of them sat down, and Pastor took hold of both her hands and then bowed his head. "Father God, You know why we've come to You today in prayer. You already know Sandy's heart as she's poured it all out in her prayers to You. I ask for Your forgiveness, Your peace, and Your presence in her life as she goes forth into the world to live for You. We know You are more pleased than we can ever understand when one of Your children returns to the fold—and we rejoice with You and the angels.

Now go with her as she steps forth to do Your will. We ask all these things in Jesus' name. Amen."

"Amen," Sandy said. She took a deep breath and smiled at the Pastor through her tears. "Thank you."

He smiled back at her and patted her on the shoulder. "Welcome back to the family, Sandy. We've missed you."

As Sandy made her way through the parking lot to her car, she felt a lightness in her heart she hadn't felt for many years.

She'd finally come home.

CHAPTER 24

Kate kept hounding her, so after weeks of putting it off, Sandy finally dug out Tom's cell phone number. Chewing on her lower lip, she punched in the numbers and placed the call, wondering what in the world she was going to say to the man when he answered. As it turned out, before she could chicken out and hang up, she was forwarded to his voice mail. She nervously listened to his message and started talking at the beep before she lost her courage.

"Hi, it's me—Sandy. Haven't heard from you in a long time and wondered how you were doing? I've been searching for more information about Darcy and thought you might want to hear what I've found—if you're still interested."

Good question. Was he interested in her at all, or was she wasting her time? But it wasn't a question she was going to ask via voice mail. She paused for a moment, wondering how much more to say in the message.

"Give me a call if you get a chance, Tom. Take care."

She pushed the button to disconnect and let out a sigh. She would never admit it to a soul, but she missed Tom—missed seeing him at her house working on projects, missed the sound of his voice in person or on the phone. Just plain missed him.

Well, she'd done her part in contacting him. Now it was up to him as to what happened next.

The Fourth of July was a Friday so Sandy had an extra day off work and looked forward to a three-day weekend. She had originally planned to stay home and catch up on some of her housework until Kate invited her to go with her and Robbie to the local fireworks display at the county fairgrounds. It was an easy choice for Sandy; spend the day by herself or spend it with friends and family.

"I haven't seen a fireworks display in years," Sandy said when Kate called her at work the Thursday before. "But it sounds fun—I'm in!"

Sitting around feeling sorry for herself wasn't going to accomplish a thing, she decided. Kate was an excellent example of a woman who managed to keep going even after being mistreated by a man. If Kate didn't need a man in her life, she didn't either. Although in retrospect, Kate did have a man in her life. He just happened to be a short little man with a high squeaky voice who had a difficult time sitting still.

Sandy slept late that Friday morning and did a few things around the house. Then about seven o'clock that evening, she hopped in her car and drove into town to the fairgrounds to meet Kate and Robbie. The midway was open with many of the same vendors who would come back later in the summer for the annual County Fair. They each ate a hotdog (mustard only on Sandy's), some fries (with vinegar, of course), and an elephant ear. By the time they'd walked around the fairgrounds and visited with what seemed to Sandy to be the entire town of Bradford Mills, it was starting to get dark, and they slowly made their way to a grassy hillside, a favorite spot of theirs for years to watch the fireworks.

They had no more than plopped down on the old quilt Kate had brought along for that purpose when a man Sandy recognized from church named Ken Murray, greeted Kate. Sandy was surprised when Kate asked him to join them after introducing him to Sandy. Sandy sat quietly with Robbie between her and Kate, with Ken Murray on the other side of

Kate. It was easy to see Mr. Murray was taken with her cousin, who didn't seem to mind his attention one bit.

So much for Kate not being interested in a man.

The fireworks were beautiful, and Robbie and Sandy had a good time 'oohing' and 'aahing' as they watched the big colorful light display. But the evening hadn't turned out to be the bonding time with her cousin Sandy had envisioned. After the show was over, she said good-night to the other three and strolled through the dark to her car, feeling the loneliness sweep over her again. It didn't help her feel any less alone when she passed Kate's car in the parking lot and saw her sitting in the driver's seat with Ken standing beside her car, still talking to her. She was happy for Kate; really she was. She was feeling sorry for herself; that was all.

Truthfully, she was tired of being alone. Surely God didn't want her to spend the rest of her life without a special someone, did He?

Tom's face instantly appeared in her mind. She was so attracted to Tom—even before he'd kissed her. She shivered a little at the thought of the good-looking man. Attraction didn't begin to describe the emotions Tom stirred up in her.

As she drove home, she thought about calling him again. The worst thing that could happen would be he would hang up on her. But by the time she pulled into her driveway, she'd talked herself out of it—again.

✞✞✞✞

Sandy had previously done an online search for any Wilbur Wilsons in Ottawa, Canada and hadn't found anything. Sunday afternoon after attending the morning church service, she decided to search again, widening the search this time to Ontario. In the possible matches, she found an obituary for a Wilbur Wilson who had died in Sudbury, Ontario in 1985. She paid the small fee by credit card which gave her access to the full obituary on the newspaper's website. After pulling the PDF file up on her screen she quickly read through the obituary, starting to get excited the more she read. This Wilbur Thomas Wilson was born June 7, 1910, in Ottawa, Ontario, Canada. It listed his parents as Jacob and Jess Wilson. It also listed his children—two daughters, Rachelle and Trina, and a son, Thom. She quickly hit the print button and let out a squeal, grabbed Boots up in a hug, and spun the office chair in which she was sitting in circles.

After Boots demanded he be put back down on the floor, she turned her attention back to the obituary and Wilbur's children. The chances of finding one of the daughters were slim as most women married and took their husband's names, so would be difficult to trace. There might be a possibility of finding Thom if he were alive since he would still have the last name of Wilson.

She did another search through Canada's White Pages on-line to see if there was a Thom Wilson listed anywhere. There wasn't, but there were three 'T' Wilsons shown in Sudbury, Ontario. Listed were complete street addresses, so she printed off the results of her search. One of those had to be Thom Wilson—she hoped.

So, how was she going to find out which one was the one she wanted?

There was a phone number listed for one of the T. Wilsons, and she even thought for a moment or two about giving that particular one a call but decided against it. How would she feel if she received a phone call from some unknown person asking a bunch of questions about her ancestors? She grimaced. There was no doubt about it; she would simply hang up and not talk to whoever was on the other end.

No, it would be wiser to write them all a letter, explaining why she was writing, and asking if they were related to Wilbur Thomas Wilson, son of Jacob Wilson. She spent the next ten minutes writing and re-writing a brief letter to mail to each of the T. Wilsons listed. The next day she would take them into Bradford Mills on her way to work and mail them, and hopefully at least one of the recipients would take the time to actually read the letter and respond.

✞✞✞✞

The next day on her lunch hour, Sandy picked up her cell phone and punched in the familiar numbers on her keypad for Tom's cell phone. While she waited for him to either answer or for it to go to voicemail, she wondered what she was going to say to him this time. She'd already left a message for him, and he'd never called her back. When the phone went to the sound of his voice in the message, she almost hung up, and then decided at the last minute to reach out to him one more time.

"Hi, Tom," she said, trying to sound cheery. "Not sure if you got my earlier message, so I decided to call back and leave another one." She chewed on her lower lip a second as she tried to come up with more to say. "I think I've found Darcy's family—living in Sudbury, Ontario, Canada. Can you believe it? Of course, I don't know for sure. I've written some letters, and hopefully, I'll hear back with some positive information, so I'll know if I have the right one."

She sighed. Best finish the message and go on with her life. "Hope you're doing well and wearing your sunscreen. Take care, and God bless! Bye!"

Sandy pushed the end button on her phone. Just hearing the sound of his voice recorded in his phone message had left her feeling lonelier than ever. She couldn't keep doing this to herself. Hadn't she learned anything from her botched relationship with Mitchell?

She lifted her chin in resignation. If she didn't hear back from him this time, she wasn't going to call him again. It was too painful. It would be better to forget about Tom Brannigan and move on.

Easier said than done.

CHAPTER 25

Tom Brannigan was sitting in a booth in a small diner with his friend, waiting for their lunch order to arrive when he felt the cell phone in his jeans pocket vibrate. He absentmindedly pulled it out while listening to Jeffrey talk about the new singles Sunday school class at the church they'd both been attending—in particular, his interest in one cute little blond gal named Tracy. When Tom saw the number of the last call, he knew his eyes must have grown larger as his friend quit talking.

"What's wrong, buddy?"

Tom quickly recovered, gave his head a little shake, and stuffed the phone back into his pocket.

"Just missed a call, nothing important."

He glanced up and across the table to see his friend's eyes studying him, his brow furrowed over his bushy eyebrows.

"It's that girl again, isn't it, Tom? When are you going to break down and quit being so stubborn and call her back?"

Tom looked down at his glass of water and then slowly picked it up to take a sip. He didn't know how to answer Jeffrey's question. What was keeping him from calling Sandy? Why was he so stubborn? She had made a concerted effort to contact him twice now, and he had purposely avoided her calls, which was childish—if not downright rude. But what would happen to his heart if he called her back only to find out she was seeing someone else—or what if she wanted to remain 'friends' with him when he wanted to be so much more than just her friend? He was sure his heart wouldn't literally break if she rejected him, but the pain caused by her turning him away might make it feel that way.

Jeffrey wasn't giving up. "So. Call her already!"

Tom gave a little laugh and shook his head. "Maybe later. A busy diner isn't the best place to have a private phone conversation."

He felt his friend's eyes studying him for a while. "True. But don't keep ignoring her, Tom—or you'll lose her for sure."

Tom hesitantly nodded, then turned his attention to his lunch the waitress had placed on the table in front of him.

Maybe he would call Sandy back—just to check in with her to make sure she was okay and find out what was going on with the search for Darcy. From her messages, it sounded like she might be making some headway in locating Darcy's family and he genuinely wanted to hear about it. Also, his Mom had told him several times she was attending church regularly now and was also going to the singles Sunday school class, so maybe she'd finally straightened out her relationship with God. It would make him feel better to know that for certain—even if their relationship never went beyond friendship.

He sighed. It would be terrific to talk with her though. He had thought by coming here to Louisiana it would dull the pain and by now he would have quit missing her so much. No such luck.

As for not losing her; he wasn't so sure but what he'd already lost her. Of course, it was hard to lose someone's love you'd never had. But he couldn't very well tell that to Jeffrey.

✞✞✞✞

Sandy slid into a booth at Central Diner in downtown Bradford Mills and picked up a menu. It was unusual for her to eat breakfast anywhere other than at home, but she'd decided to give herself a treat this morning since she had to come into town anyway. It was a Saturday morning, still fairly early in the a.m., so the place wasn't busy yet. A couple of elderly gentlemen sat at the counter, eating waffles and drinking their cups of coffee—along with sharing all the latest local news, she was sure. Other than that, she had the place to herself—at least until the town started waking up.

Her eyes were scanning the multitude of breakfast foods listed, trying to decide exactly how hungry she was, when Maggie Brannigan appeared at her side, coffee pot in hand.

"Good morning, Sandy!"

Sandy smiled up at Maggie standing there with a grin on her face. Where did she get the energy to be so chipper this early in the morning when she knew she had a full shift on her feet in front of her?

"'Morning, Maggie."

She watched the older woman pour the steaming coffee into the ceramic mug on the table and wondered if she dared to broach the subject of Tom with his Mom.

"Do you know what you want to order yet, sweetie—or should I come back?"

Sandy pulled her eyes off the coffee mug and back to the menu.

"Uh, I guess I'll take the special—eggs over easy and hash browns, please."

Maggie scribbled her order on the little pad of paper in her hand, and then stuck the pencil back in her apron pocket. She reached out and gently patted Sandy on the shoulder.

"I'll put this order in and be right back—so we can chat, okay?"

Sandy handed the older woman the menu and watched her walk away, wondering why Tom's mother wanted to talk with her. Maybe Maggie knew why Tom had left Bradford Mills so suddenly, and better still—when he was going to come home.

It wasn't long and Maggie was back, taking a seat in the booth across the table from Sandy. She gave Sandy a motherly smile.

"So, everyone in town is talking about that tree out to your house. Is it true? Is the insurance company going to make you cut it down?"

Putting the now half-empty coffee cup back down on the table, Sandy nodded. "I'm afraid it is, Maggie. Unless I can get them to change their mind, I'm probably going to have to cut it down." She frowned. "I hate to even think about how much it will cost."

Maggie nodded. "That tree is huge if I remember right."

It was quiet for a moment before Sandy decided to take the plunge. "So, what do you hear from Tom?"

She couldn't decipher the look Maggie gave her but saw a distinct twinkle in the older woman's eyes. Sandy dropped her head, afraid Tom's mother might see more in her own eyes than she wanted to divulge.

"Well, since you asked," Maggie said with a slow smile spreading across her face. "I haven't heard a great deal from him. He did call last week to say it was hot—way hotter than he thought it would be down there." She laughed. "I don't know why he thought it wouldn't be miserably hot. He is in Louisiana after all. I took great joy in reminding him of that."

Sandy laughed along with Maggie. It was now late July and had warmed up considerably here in Bradford Mills too. She couldn't imagine how hot it must be in the south.

She finally asked the question uppermost on her mind. "Did he give you any indication of how much longer he's going to be down there?"

"Nope." Maggie's eyes were back to studying her. "But if you want to know, why don't you give him a call?"

Giving a quick shake of her head, Sandy frowned. "I already left him two messages, and he hasn't called me back."

Realizing she'd said more than she'd intended, she dropped her eyes and felt the heat of embarrassment sweep over her face. What must Tom's mom think of her? It made it sound as if Sandy was chasing after her son. Was she? Because she'd left two messages already, would it seem that way to Tom too?

She heard Maggie chuckle. "I have never known two more stubborn young people."

Sandy brought her head up with a snap and looked across the booth at Maggie. "What are you talking about?"

Maggie smiled at her and reached across the table to gently pat her hand. "I've seen the way you look at my son. And I heard the way his voice sounded when he talked about you back when he was working at your house. You two are dancing around each other like boxers, waiting for the other one to make the first move, terrified to make it yourselves. You're both so afraid of getting hurt again, you're going to miss out on something special God has planned for you two if you don't get your acts together." She chuckled.

Dropping her head, Sandy wondered how much she should tell Tom's mother. She didn't have a mom of her own to talk with, and she'd already talked with Katie and been told pretty much the same thing Maggie was telling her now. How could she explain she was afraid—terrified of being hurt, and scared of hurting Tom?

"I don't know if he's interested in me or not, Maggie. I thought he was involved with someone else, so I pushed him away. That's when he left town. I found out I'd misjudged him, but now I'm afraid I've lost a chance of having any type of relationship with him." She shook her head. "I was in an unhealthy relationship before I came back to Bradford Mills. It ended on a bad note, and I don't want to be hurt again. Besides, I care too much about Tom to lose him as a friend."

Maggie nodded. "So, have you prayed about it?"

Sandy looked up at her in surprise. *Prayed about it.* She thought about what the older woman had said for a moment. Maggie was right. She should be praying about it. Why did she think she could handle the relationship between Tom and her on her own? If God wasn't included in the equation, there would be no real friendship or relationship to gain or lose. Hadn't she already learned her lesson with Mitch?

"No, but I guess I'd better start."

Maggie smiled at her gently, then stood up and began to walk away before turning back briefly to kiss Sandy lightly on the forehead.

"I've been praying for years for Tom's future. Now we have to wait for God to answer my prayers."

Sandy watched her walk back across the diner toward the kitchen, then picked up her fork to finish her breakfast.

Maggie was right. It was time to get God involved through prayer and see what His will was in the situation. She couldn't and shouldn't try to do it on her own.

✞✞✞✞

As soon as Sandy arrived home, she went directly to her phone. She had picked it up from the kitchen counter and was holding it in her hand, ready to punch in Tom's cell phone number when the phone startled her by ringing.

"Hello?"

There was a second or two of silence on the other end before she heard the deep bass voice she'd been missing.

"Morning, Sandy. Am I calling too early?"

Sandy felt the smile she was sure spread from one side of her face to the other, remembering the first morning he'd arrived at her house and woke her by ringing her doorbell.

"Hardly too early, Brannigan. I've already been in town, had breakfast at the diner, and visited with your mom awhile."

She heard Tom's chuckle on the other end of the line. "Now, that's scary—you and my mom 'visiting.'"

"Be nice, Thomas Lee Brannigan. Your mom is a sweet lady, and I won't allow you to bad mouth her."

He laughed, and she heard his voice gentle as he continued. "I couldn't agree with you more. As far as I'm concerned, she's one of the best gifts God ever gave me."

There was an uncomfortable pause in the conversation while Sandy struggled with coming up with something to say. All of a sudden, all the news she had wanted to tell Tom flew out the open windows of her house.

"I'm sorry, Sandy," he finally said, his voice so quiet she almost couldn't hear him.

She shook her head, struggling to understand. "Sorry for what?"

Sandy heard his sigh through the phone. "I'm sorry for leaving town without talking with you—for being a jerk—for not being there to help you. I haven't been much of a friend."

"Tom, don't, please," she hurried to say. "You don't have to apologize. I haven't been much of a friend either."

She heard another sigh before he continued. "Anyway, why I called—in addition to my apology—was to tell you I'll be back in Bradford Mills next week."

Sandy felt her heart do a little flip and the smile was back on her face before she knew it. Tom was coming home!

"That's great! It will be good to see you—I have so much to tell you. I've found out quite a bit about Darcy! Oh, and I'm still battling the insurance company about taking down the tree. And I've been going back to church and gotten involved with the singles group there," Sandy stopped talking as she realized she was rambling.

"Anyway, it will be nice to have you home again," she added quietly.

She heard Tom clear his throat on the other end of the phone, and then made out the sounds of voices in the background. "Well, I need to get back to work, but before I do, promise me when I get home we can sit down and talk—about everything. I'm afraid I haven't been totally honest with you about some things. I need to do some explaining."

Sandy frowned. He sounded so serious. "I promise, Tom. Whenever you want to get together and talk—we can."

Her stomach suddenly felt as if she'd been punched. What if Tom was coming back to tell her he had found the perfect girl in Louisiana? What would she do then? She wasn't sure her heart could survive another blow.

She took a deep breath and lifted her chin. Whatever happened, it was all in God's hands.

"In the meantime, you take care of yourself and stay safe on your way home. I'll be praying for you."

"Thanks, Sandy," she heard on the other end of the line. "I've never stopped praying for you. You take care too, okay?" His sound of his voice was almost as comforting as having him there with her—almost.

"Okay. Bye."

Tom said goodbye and Sandy hesitantly pushed the button, not wanting to end the connection. As the silence of the house swept over her, she sighed and prayed a quick prayer of thanks.

Tom was coming home—and he wanted to talk with her as soon as he arrived. She wasn't sure if it was good news or bad, but either way, she could hardly wait to see him.

CHAPTER 26

"Next week" hadn't been specific enough for Sandy. Did that mean next week Monday, or next week Friday? Or wasn't he sure when he was coming back? Either way, Sandy found herself looking at her watch and glancing at the calendar more often during the next few days.

Not that she didn't have anything else to worry about.

On Wednesday she received a phone call from her insurance agent. As soon as she realized who it was, her heart rate increased. What was the final decision regarding the fate of the pine tree?

It wasn't good news.

The forester had made his report, and because of the age of the tree and due to some disease concerns which would ultimately weaken the tree to the point it was even more dangerous, she had thirty days to have it removed, or the company would cancel her homeowner's insurance policy. After Sandy got off the phone with the agent, her first thought was to call another insurance company and move all her policies. Then exhaling a large sigh, she decided it probably wouldn't matter anyway. They would just send out a different inspector, and he would make another report which would cause the company to form a similar opinion and demand the same outcome.

She'd not only lost the battle, but she'd also lost the war.

Sandy put a call through to Beverly at the Historical Society, wanting her to be aware of the fate of the tree. She suggested if she wanted photos of the tree for the society's records, she ought to come take them before it was taken down.

Her next few phone calls were to tree removal companies, asking for estimates. There was no sense stalling since she was going to have to find an estimate that would fit into her budget. She couldn't even guess how much it was going to cost to cut down a tree this large.

✞✞✞✞

Saturday evening Sandy sat on the front porch in the white wooden swing Tom had installed for her, watching the lightning bugs twinkle across the yard. She'd mowed the yard earlier in the afternoon, walking behind the self-propelled lawn mower for almost an hour before collapsing in a heap on the living room sofa for an afternoon nap. Obviously, she wasn't in as good a shape as she thought she was, but she kept telling herself the more outdoor physical activity she did, the stronger she would become.

It was early evening, the time right after dusk when the world was quiet, but before total darkness swept over the land. It had always been her favorite time of the day. Tonight though, she couldn't help but feel sad because she had no one to share it with.

Immediately her thoughts turned to Tom, and she sent up a quick prayer for him—for his safety while he was still working on the crew down south, and safety when he finally started the trip home. Her mind replayed their last conversation, wondering what he wanted to talk about with her that was so…she couldn't think of a word to describe how he had sounded.

Of course, she had much to tell him about the results of her search for Darcy, and now about the decision regarding the tree. But he had sounded so...different...on the phone. He hadn't seemed angry with her, but he had sounded somber. Whatever it was, she prayed it wasn't too serious.

✞✞✞✞

Sunday brought sunshine and hot, humid weather. Sandy spent some time looking through her closet for something lightweight to wear and wished for the first time the church sanctuary was air-conditioned. She finally chose a pastel flowered cotton sundress and her white sandals, hoping it would be cool enough.

When she arrived at the church, the singles Sunday school classroom was already buzzing with conversation. Sandy said quick hellos to several people she knew from her previous times in class and headed toward Kate, standing near the refreshment table where a few cookies, donuts, and a coffee urn sat waiting. Sandy said a quick 'good morning' to her before pouring herself a cup. Even though it was hot, she knew she needed some caffeine to wake her up. She quickly took a chair next to Kate and sipped her coffee while waiting for the class to begin.

"So," Kate said quietly, sitting next to her. "Did you finally call Tom?"

Sandy glanced at her cousin and shook her head.

She heard Kate's exasperated sigh. "Sandy...."

Sandy smiled and held up her hand to stop her from continuing. "I was going to, but he called me first."

Kate's eyes grew large. "Really!" she also whispered. "So...what happened? Did you guys talk? Is it good between you two now?"

Sandy quickly shook her head. "I don't know, Kate. We talked a little, but he acted so...serious. He said he's coming home."

"Well, that's good news."

"I guess. He said he wants to talk with me when he gets here." Sandy took another sip of the cooling coffee. "I couldn't get a read on how he was feeling, but at least he's coming back."

Kate patted her knee. "I'll keep praying for you two."

Sandy nodded and gave her cousin a little smile as Ken Murray sat down in the chair the other side of Kate and the teacher came to the front of the room. She took a deep breath and turned her attention to the teacher's opening prayer. Thoughts of Tom would have to wait for another time.

✞✞✞✞

The morning worship service was a good one, but Sandy was so distracted by the heat and the number of bulletins fanning the faces of the congregation, she was thankful when it was over. She picked up her Bible and purse from where they sat on the pew next to her and turned to step out into the aisle to leave the sanctuary. She lifted her eyes toward the rear doors and came to a screeching halt, positive her eyes were deceiving her.

It couldn't be them.

Rachel Foster and Mitchell Wright stood at the end of the aisle near the back door of the sanctuary, waiting for her. Sandy gulped, straightened her back, and tried to put a smile on her face as she started following the other attendees slowly walking down the aisle toward the rear of the church.

"Rachel," she blurted out as she reached the couple. "What are you doing here?"

Her friend took hold of her hand and pulled her to the side where they could stand out of the way of the crowd. Sandy noted Mitch stood off to one side, shuffling from one foot to the other and looking exceptionally uncomfortable in his expensive suit.

Good.

"Sandy, I'm sorry to give you such a shock. Mitch and I decided to come to church and surprise you."

Sandy forced a grin to her face, gritting her teeth together in the process. "Well, you surprised me, that's for sure."

Mitch finally stepped forward and moved to stand next to Rachel.

"Is there someplace the three of us can go talk, Sandy?" he lifted his eyebrow in question.

Talk?

What in the world did she have to talk about with these two people—these traitors who had claimed to be her friends, or in the case of Mitch—much more than her friend?

Rachel still had hold of her hand and was clenching it tightly between both of hers. "Please, Sandy. *Please*."

Sandy felt panic sweep over her at the thought of going anywhere with the two of them, then took a deep breath. Rachel looked as if she was about to start crying, and even Mitch had a serious look on his face. She took a deep breath and sent a brief prayer heavenward for wisdom.

Listen to what they have to say.

"I guess we can go to my house," she finally said.

Rachel and Mitch nodded and headed out the door to their car with Sandy making her way on shaky legs across the parking lot to her own. This was a nightmare. What in the world were they doing here—and what had possessed her to invite them to her home, of all places? She looked in her rear-view mirror to see their car following her out of town, and took another deep breath and said a quick prayer. She could do this; she wasn't alone. For whatever reason, God had brought them here today, and with His help, she was going to deal with it.

By the time Rachel and Mitch came through her front door, Sandy had pulled herself together and had her emotions in check. She plastered a small smile on her face and invited them to sit down in the living room. She took a seat in a chair across from them.

"So what brings you two to Bradford Mills?"

Then she noticed they were holding hands, and Rachel had a wedding band on the ring finger of her left hand. Sandy gulped.

They were *married*?

She pulled her eyes up to look Rachel in the face, finding blue eyes looking at her, pleading for understanding.

"Sandy, we felt we needed to come see you. We came to tell you something..."

Mitch interrupted Rachel. "And I came to ask for your forgiveness."

Sandy stared at the two of them. What type of crazy nightmare was she having? Maybe she'd wake up soon to sunshine pouring through her bedroom window, and maybe someday she'd be able to laugh about this. But right now, all she felt was shock.

"What?"

Rachel started to talk again, but Sandy saw Mitch pat her on her knee and shake his head at her.

"Sandy, I treated you terribly, and I want to ask you to forgive me." He held up his hand as if he realized Sandy was about to say something. "I know I don't have any right to ask it of you. But ever since Rachel and I started attending church, and I came to understand I was a sinner, I realized what I did to you, and it's haunted me. My search for forgiveness for my own past sins includes asking you to forgive me. You don't have to, but it would mean so much to me if you could."

Rachel sat next to Mitch with tears running down her face, and Sandy took a shaky breath as she tried to decide how to respond. For some reason, she felt Mitch was sincere. Could he have changed that much? She swallowed the bitter words she wanted to say and instead said a quick, silent prayer.

Lord, what do you want me to do? How can You ask me to do this? I'm not sure I CAN forgive him. God, I need your help here.

Then a verse Sandy had learned as a child recited itself through her muddled brain.

For all have sinned and come short of the glory of God.

'All have sinned'—even Sandy Martin. What made her any better than Mitchell Wright? In what way was her sin any less sinful than what he had done to her?

Another verse came to her mind from the book of Matthew, Chapter 6 and verse 14: *For if ye forgive men their trespasses, your heavenly Father will also forgive you: But if ye forgive not men their trespasses, neither will your Father forgive your trespasses.*

Peace swept over her as she was reminded of God's forgiveness in her own life. How could she not forgive another's transgressions when hers had been equally as bad, if not worse? She had been raised in a Christian home and knew better. Mitch hadn't been raised in the same type of environment. Didn't that make her more of a sinner than him? She took a deep breath.

"You're forgiven, Mitch. But if you hurt my friend, you will answer to me."

She smiled a little as a shocked look appeared on his face. Something told her he hadn't expected her to do it when he asked.

"Really?" Rachel squeaked out. "Even though we got married, you're going to forgive us?"

Sandy nodded and then stood to go over and pull her friend into a hug. "Yes, Rachel. I'm happy if you're happy."

She was shocked to see a trace of tears in the eyes of the man who stood to shake her hand. Maybe he was serious about his search for salvation and forgiveness. If so, their marriage might survive.

"Sandy, I can't tell you how much this means to us—to both of us. Rachel has just about made herself sick, worrying we'd be hurting you by getting married." He shook his head. "Regardless of how you might have felt about me in the past, I honestly am trying to make a fresh start with my life. And I honestly do love Rach. I'd do anything for her."

Sandy grinned, feeling a little evil. "Even face me, huh?"

She laughed as a sheepish look crossed Mitchell's face, and then he nervously laughed along with her.

"Yeah, facing you was pretty scary," he finally admitted with a grin.

The three of them drove back into town to the diner for lunch, and then Rachel and Mitchell left for their trip back to

Toledo. Talking with the two of them, Sandy felt a release of the bitterness she had held for Mitch for so long. He and Rachel appeared to genuinely love each other and Sandy was happy for them. By forgiving Mitch, she had freed herself from her own mistakes in the past.

It was time for her to move on.

CHAPTER 27

Tuesday's mail brought estimates from three different tree removal companies. They were all much higher than Sandy had thought they would be, and she frowned as she realized she would have to take money from savings in order to pay the bill, but the decision had been made, and the tree had to come down.

Wednesday was a hot, humid day. Everyone who came to the air-conditioned library let out a literal sigh of relief as they came through the double doors and the cooler air hit them. Sandy was kept busy all day with the extra foot traffic caused by the reading public and those looking for a cool spot to hook their laptops up to Wi-Fi.

She was so hot that evening she opted for a huge bowl of chocolate chip ice cream for her dinner. Sandy smiled as she licked the last morsel off her spoon. It probably wasn't the healthiest of meals, but it sure had hit the spot. She reached down from her perch on the porch swing to place the now empty bowl on the floor, the spoon making a clunking sound as the bowl connected with the porch.

The call had been made to the least expensive tree company, and they were scheduled to come Saturday morning to take down the pine tree. She still couldn't believe it was going to be cut down. It felt like she was losing a loved one and in a way, she was—a part of her childhood. Sitting on the porch, she tried to imagine her front yard without the tree...and she couldn't do it.

Sandy picked up the now empty bowl and went back into the house to the kitchen. As she sat the dirty dishes in the sink to run water in them, an idea formed in the back of her mind. She didn't know why she hadn't thought of it sooner.

Going to her office, she opened desk drawers until she found what she was looking for—her new digital camera. After borrowing the newspaper's top-of-the-line camera, she had splurged on a better camera for herself. It wasn't as fancy or as expensive as the newspaper's commercial grade one Mr. Drayton had allowed her to take to South Carolina, but it was much nicer than any camera she had ever owned. It not only took photos but also could film video.

Taking the camera with her, she went out the front door, across the porch and down the steps to the front yard. She walked across the grass, turning back occasionally to see if she had put enough distance between her and the tree. She finally ended up down and across the road before she was far enough away. Once there, Sandy started snapping photos of the tree, taking steps closer, and taking more pictures until she was back where she had started—under the tree. Once there, she took photos of the trunk, trying to zoom in on the spot where the faint outline of the cross was located.

She sighed in relief as the day clouded up and a warm breeze blew in. The earlier weather report called for rain to come through the area later and she sincerely hoped the weatherman was right. She was also optimistic it would wash some of the humidity out of the air.

As Sandy stood under the boughs of the tree, memories from her childhood swept over her.

Grandma, why does the tree make a funny noise when the wind blows through it?

The wind is whispering through the tree, sweetie, telling us the story of its life.

Sandy felt tears building behind her eyes and quickly blinked them back to stop their flow, then took a deep breath to steady her emotions. There would be plenty of time for tears later. Right now she had too much to do.

Standing under the towering pine, Sandy flicked the switch on her camera over to video format and filmed the looks and sounds of the wind blowing through the tree branches above her. It was a sound she would never hear again once the tree was taken down, and she never wanted to forget it.

✞✞✞✞

Later the same night, Sandy was already asleep when she was awakened by the sound of wind-driven rain on the roof and the windows of the house. She tried to get back to sleep for a time, then turned over and looked at the clock to see it was already four-thirty in the morning. Chances of getting back to sleep were slim if the storm kept up at its present pace.

Thunder boomed loud enough to rattle the windows, and the lightning flashed so brilliantly in the darkened room, she instinctively closed her eyes to shut out the brightness. She finally turned on the bedside lamp, got out of bed and slipped on her bathrobe and slippers, and started down the stairs.

Then she heard it.

The wind hit the house with a vengeance, and an unearthly sound echoed through the night followed by a tremendous crash. Then the electricity went out. Sandy hurried the rest of the way down the stairs, feeling thankful the morning sky was lightening enough she could see to get downstairs. She hurried over to the front window and looked out, not sure what to expect.

Sandy gasped at the sight awaiting her.

The huge old pine tree had come down—away from the house. About ten feet up, the wind had snapped off the tree and laid it straight across her front yard, the road, and partially into the ditch on the other side of the road, totally blocking the road. She stared at the unbelievable destruction and then had to smile at the irony. God had intervened. The old pine tree had come down, in His time, and in His way.

She went back upstairs to throw on some clothes and shoes and wondered how long it would take before someone from the county road commission would be out to remove the tree from the roadway. And of course, there was no electricity in the area now thanks to her tree falling; not only was her electricity out but also the surrounding neighborhood.

But the insurance company had been wrong. Her house had not been threatened. What the experts hadn't taken into account were the prevailing winds during a summer storm. They almost always came from the southwest, which had pushed it in the opposite direction. Her house had been saved—the tree hadn't.

She grabbed a light hooded jacket from the coat hook near her back door and went out the front door to survey the damage. There was still a cool misty rain falling, but the sky had lightened, and she could see the rosy pink of the coming sunrise in the east.

As Sandy walked the length of the fallen giant, she was in awe. The forester had been right. The old tree had been enormous and obviously had been rotting as was proven by it being brought down so quickly by the storm. Well, it was down now. She didn't have to worry about it anymore.

Sandy went back in the house and had already eaten a cold breakfast of cereal and orange juice by the time the rain had entirely quit and the sun was fully ascended. When she heard several county trucks and the power company trucks pull into her driveway, she hurried back outside.

A number of men carrying chainsaws and wearing hardhats exited the road crew trucks and started working on the portion of the tree blocking the road. One of the men who appeared to be older than the rest and looked to be a supervisor headed toward her.

"Morning, ma'am. Looks like you had some major excitement out here last night."

She smiled weakly and nodded her head.

"Thanks for getting here so fast. I'm sure you have lots of storm-damaged trees to clean up."

He nodded. "A few." He looked at the tree spread across her yard. "But nothing as big as this baby!"

The man gestured toward the tree. "You'll have to clean up what's in your yard, but we'll get it off the road and power lines so the power company can get the electricity back on for you and your neighbors."

She nodded. "Thank you again," she added as he turned to go join the rest of his work crew.

Sandy was getting ready to head back into the house when a familiar dark blue pickup truck pulled into her driveway.

Tom.

He quickly exited the truck and jogged over to where she stood at the bottom of the front porch steps.

"Sandy, are you okay? I heard about the tree on the scanner."

As he came to a stop in front of her, he placed his hands on her shoulders, forcing her to look up at his face. She saw genuine concern in his eyes as they studied her.

"I'm all right, Tom. My tree, on the other hand, isn't doing so great."

Before she realized his intentions, she felt herself being pulled against his chest where she rested her cheek against his cotton shirt. She sighed and allowed herself to relax for a few moments, inhaling and enjoying the smells of his aftershave and sawdust—smells that were all Tom. All too quickly, Tom pulled away and turned to join her in looking at the devastation covering her front yard.

"I'm sorry, Sandy. I know how much you loved the tree."

She sighed and nodded as she left the comfort of his broad chest. "Thanks, Tom. But, it's okay—really. It was only a tree after all, and it was going to have to come down anyway."

Sandy felt his eyes land on her again, and his hand was on her elbow as he turned her toward the back door.

"Can we talk, Sandy, or is this a bad time?"

She glanced over at his face, reading the concern there. "Now's as good a time as any, as long as you understand I don't have any coffee for you. No electricity." She grinned at him. "But I do have cookies."

He smiled enough that his beautiful dimple appeared and she let out a sigh of relief. It was the first smile she had seen from him since he'd arrived. Maybe things would be okay between them after all.

As they made their way into the house to the kitchen, Sandy spoke up. "When did you get back? I was surprised to see you pull in the driveway."

✞✞✞✞

Tom watched Sandy take half a dozen cookies from the cookie jar on the counter and place them on a plate, and then put the plate on the table in front of him. He loved her cookies, but a plate of cookies wasn't why he was here this morning.

"I got home about ten thirty last night," he said as she pulled out a chair and sat across the table from him—too far away for his liking.

He saw her eyes sweep over him as if looking for any changes in his physical appearance. He knew his hair was a little longer than when he had left as he hadn't had time yet to get a haircut but other than that, he thought he looked about the same; well, he had an impressive suntan now covering his arms and neck. There was no getting away from the Louisiana sun.

"So," she said quietly. "How was your trip down south?"

Tom smiled. It had hardly been a trip. He considered a trip something more along the lines of a vacation. This had been genuine work.

"Good. I met a Christian man on the work crew. We shared a motel room and became pretty good friends." He sighed. "It was a lot of hard work, but I'm glad I went and helped out. It's nice to do something where you're able to help someone who has lost everything."

Sandy stared at him with those big eyes of hers, and he swallowed hard. He didn't want her to consider him a hero. He was far from hero status.

He'd done a ton of praying on the drive back from Louisiana and had come to a decision. Tom just hoped he wasn't too late.

✞✞✞✞

Sandy smiled across the table at Tom. "Well, I'm glad you're back. There's been so much that's happened while you were gone."

While Tom nibbled a chocolate chip cookie from the plate in front of him, Sandy filled him in on her trip to South Carolina and all she had found.

"So, I've written letters to the three different T. Wilsons, hoping one of them might be the right one. I haven't heard anything back yet though, so I'm starting to worry I still don't have the correct one."

"Wow," Tom exclaimed as she watched him push the empty cookie plate away from him. "You have been busy."

She saw him look down at the table.

"I'm sorry I wasn't here to help you out, Sandy. I owe you an apology for running out on you."

She shook her head firmly. "You don't owe me anything, Tom."

Sandy was about to confess her misinformation about him and Kate and Robbie when she was interrupted by the phone ringing. She glanced over at Tom in surprise. She had assumed her telephone was out along with the power. Fortunately, she had an old wall kitchen phone that didn't run on electricity and hurried over to answer it.

"Hello."

The deep cultured voice of a man was on the other end. "Is this Sandra Martin?"

She glanced over at Tom, hoping this call wasn't bringing any more bad news. She didn't think she could handle much more right now.

"Yes, it is. Who am I speaking to?"

It was silent for a second or two before the man answered. "This is Thom Wilson, and I received a letter from you stating you had information about one of my ancestors."

Sandy gasped. "Mr. Wilson! Oh, I'm so glad you called." She quickly motioned for Tom to come closer to her. "Mr. Wilson, what was the name of your grandfather, if I may ask?"

She held her breath as he answered. "He went by Jake, but his real name was Jacob Thomas Wilson."

"And what was his father's name?"

There was silence on the other end of the phone again. "Miss Martin, may I ask why you are asking me all these questions? I'm a little reluctant to give out family information over the phone to a complete stranger..."

"Of course, Mr. Wilson. I totally understand." She paused. How did she begin to tell him why she wanted—no needed—to know? "I'm hoping his name was Caleb, son of Eli and Darcy Wilson."

There was silence on the other end of the phone, and for a moment she was afraid she'd lost the phone connection.

"Well, I'll be," the man's deep voice finally said on the other end. "How did you know?"

Sandy chuckled. "Mr. Wilson, I've been looking for Darcy's family for months. You see, I have something that belongs to the family, and I want to personally deliver it to you—along with a story I believe you will find interesting."

She heard his laugh on the other end of the phone line. "If you remember, Miss Martin, I don't live nearby."

"That's okay," she quickly assured him. "I have the means to come and bring what I have to you if you're interested."

"Can you tell me what it is?" he asked quietly.

Sandy smiled. If it were her on the other end of the phone, she would be dying of curiosity too, but she didn't want to spoil the surprise for him.

"I'd rather show it to you when I bring it, Mr. Wilson. When is a good time?"

They talked for another ten minutes or so and made arrangements for Sandy to meet with him the next week. She'd already warned her boss at the library that if she found Darcy's family, she was going to have to take more time off to make the journey to Canada. When she had first approached Ms. Tayler, she had been afraid she would be upset by her wanting to take more time off. But for some reason, she was enthralled with the story of what she had found out about Darcy and the proof that a local residence had been used as a station on the Underground Railroad. Since she had heard her story, she had almost acted as if Sandy was a celebrity of some sort, and had assured her the library was more than willing to give her the time needed to complete her mission.

Of course, it was going to be time off without pay, but Mr. Drayton at the newspaper was covering all her travel expenses. Originally she had thought he would want her to fly, but he'd surprised her by telling her to drive and take lots of pictures on the way because he wanted her to write further pieces on other Michigan historical locations.

When she finally hung the phone back in the cradle, she turned to Tom and let out a whoop.

"We've found them!"

He let out a matching whoop and picked her up and twirled her around until she was dizzy. She finally pushed a little against his shoulders until he released her.

"Okay, enough celebrating. We have a lot to get done if we're leaving on Monday, Tom."

She saw the surprise on his face.

"We? You want me to go too?"

Sandy chuckled. "Seems only fair as you were the one to find the hidey-hole in the first place, wouldn't you say?"

CHAPTER 28

Monday morning Sandy met Tom at the diner for breakfast at five o'clock. Her car trunk was packed with room left for Tom to throw in his luggage. After a quick cup of coffee and breakfast, they were on their way headed north on 127.

Tom took the first shift of driving while Sandy looked at the map and navigated their quickest route. Even though she had a GPS, she still preferred to have a map to refer to.

It was early on a Monday morning, so traffic was light which didn't surprise Sandy. They stopped in Mt. Pleasant for lunch and then were back on the road with Sandy taking a turn driving. By this time it was late enough the traffic had increased, and it took all her concentration to deal with semis and crazy drivers wanting to pass all the time.

Sandy and Tom made good time and reached the southern side of the Mackinac Bridge before dinner time. They checked into their reserved rooms and ate dinner at the hotel dining room as they both expressed they were too tired to go out and find anyplace else to eat. Conversation was mostly about Tom's work in Louisiana and their trip so far, but Sandy knew she was only postponing the inevitable. Eventually, she would have to finish the conversation they had started at her kitchen table before Thom Wilson's call.

They had stopped several times along the way, and Sandy had taken oodles of photos. She also took notes of interesting historical places along the way. Mr. Drayton had expressed interest in articles on historic places to visit in Michigan, so she was going to do her best to provide those for him.

Tom and Sandy were both so tired after dinner, they said their good nights and went to their respective rooms which were right across the hall from each other.

✞✞✞✞

The next morning Tom knocked on Sandy's door early, but she had already been up and was showered, dressed, and ready to go. She was so excited the previous night, it had been difficult for her to get any sleep.

Today was the day they would deliver the diary to Darcy's family.

After a quiet, quick breakfast, they once again headed north. Sandy had estimated it would take a couple of hours for them to get from Mackinaw City to Sault Ste. Marie and from there, another three hours to Sudbury, Ontario in Canada where Thom Wilson lived. Tom and she kept up a friendly dialogue on Darcy and Sandy's trip to South Carolina while the landscape around them changed.

When Sandy could finally see the sun shining brightly off the uprights of the famous Mackinac Bridge on the horizon, she couldn't get the grin off her face. Tom noticed her excitement and when she explained to him the reason for her delight, he told her he couldn't believe even though she'd been born and lived in Michigan most of her life, she had never crossed the 'Mighty Mac.' It was going to be an entirely new experience for her, and she could hardly wait. As the bridge in the distance came closer, it became more evident to her exactly how huge it was. If she remembered correctly, the entire length of the bridge was around five miles long. She was amazed when Tom told her the main towers of the bridge rose over five hundred and fifty feet from the water. Even more astounding was the realization the bridge had been built back in the 1950's and still had over three hundred thousand vehicles cross it every month. It was beautiful.

As they got closer, Tom glanced over to ask her if she wanted to be the one to drive across and she quickly shook her head negatively.

"I'm not sure I can, Tom," she confessed.

She'd never been afraid to cross bridges, but this one was different. And she'd heard stories of people who had thought they could drive across it only to find they couldn't and ended up stranded out there in the midst of all the traffic until somebody could get to their car and drive for them. The Mackinac Bridge Authority actually provided drivers for those folks who wouldn't or couldn't drive across. Sandy wasn't sure if she was one of those people or not, but she didn't want to find out.

As they drove across the five-mile long suspension bridge, Sandy grinned over at Tom and pointed out the window across the blue water.

"Isn't that Mackinac Island over there?"

He nodded. "Yup. We should go there someday. You have to take a ferry to get there from the mainland, and they don't allow any cars. Everyone either rides bicycles or walks. You'd love it, Sandy."

Sandy stared out the window, wishing she could see the island better. "I've heard about it for years, but never had the chance to go there. Maybe someday...."

✞✞✞✞

Tom watched Sandy's face glow with excitement as they reached the northern side of the Mackinac Bridge and headed across the Upper Peninsula of Michigan. She had another bridge to cross, and he hoped she did as well on the next one as she had on this one. He couldn't believe she had lived in this beautiful state most of her life and never been this far north. She regaled him with stories of her family trips to Traverse City and Ludington but told him she had never been across 'the bridge' before.

"How can you have lived in this state most of your life and never been to the U.P.?"

She grinned at him from the passenger seat. "I don't know. Guess I never found the time. It's like a lot of things. Life got in the way."

Tom nodded in understanding and thought more about their interrupted discussion back at her house. He had originally hoped this trip would give them time to talk. Specifically, he was looking for a time to complete the conversation they'd started in her kitchen. But Sandy was wound so tight due to the upcoming meeting with Darcy's family, he decided what he had to say to her was going to have to wait. When they did finish their talk, he wanted her undivided attention.

She continued to bubble over as they drove across the somewhat desolate Upper Peninsula of Michigan. Other than pine trees, railroad tracks, telephone poles, and a few small towns, there wasn't much to see. Then they finally arrived at Sault Ste. Marie and it was time to cross the International Bridge into Canada. They didn't need their passports to cross but would need them to re-enter the U.S.

They stopped at a small restaurant about an hour out of Sudbury for lunch, and Sandy put a call through to Thom Wilson to get final directions to his house located in a suburb of the city. He had told them he had recently retired from his position as an English professor at a nearby college so would be at home, awaiting their arrival.

After they left the restaurant, Tom drove the final leg of the journey, following the directions the GPS gave them. Sandy had programmed Thom's address in so they would have an easier time finding the place. They drove down tree-lined streets filled with modern homes, and then turned and went a few more blocks into what was obviously more of a historic district. Here were homes of distinction, sitting back from the road on large lots with manicured lawns and grounds.

The GPS gave them directions to a house on the left, a beautiful red brick colonial with white shutters and a huge wooden front door off a sweeping covered front porch. Tom pulled the car into the driveway and turned the key to shut off the engine.

Sandy took a deep breath and looked over at him with a deer in the headlights look in her green eyes.

He chuckled. "Well, Sassy Sandy. What are we waiting for? We're finally here."

Tom was rewarded with her laughter and was relieved when her face relaxed into a smile.

"Yes we are!" she announced and hurriedly opened the car door and got out. She opened the back door of her car and grabbed a bag he knew held her laptop, along with the precious diary and some other papers and photos. He saw her take a deep breath as if she were readying herself for battle.

He was so proud of her, he thought he would bust.

✞✞✞✞

Sandy dismissed Tom's offer to carry her laptop bag and instead hefted the strap over her shoulder. She started up the brick sidewalk in the direction of the front door of the house, knowing Tom was right behind her. Inhaling deeply to try and steady her shaky nerves, she pushed the doorbell button located on the right side of the large wooden door. She looked over to see Tom's eyes on her face, and she gave him a quick smile to ensure he knew she was okay. Nervous, excited, expectant, yes. But she was okay.

Seconds later the door opened. Standing on the other side was an African-American man who looked to be in his late sixties; tall and muscular, his short-cropped, curly black hair was just starting to turn gray. His eyes looked first at Sandy, then turned to Tom before coming back to rest on Sandy.

"Mr. Wilson," Sandy said. "I'm Sandy Martin. We spoke on the phone earlier. And this is my friend, Tom Brannigan."

Thom Wilson motioned for them to come in the house, and then shook hands with each of them. "It's nice to meet you both. Please come on in where we can talk."

He led them through a large two-story foyer and down a short hallway that ended in an ample-sized living area which was open to a beautiful kitchen. This was obviously the most lived in room of the house with comfortable couches, overstuffed chairs, and ottomans placed strategically in front of an ornately mantled fireplace.

Sandy let out a little gasp at the view from the windows along the back wall. Floor to ceiling windows looked out over a sweeping backyard with an in-ground pool and stunning gardens.

"Mr. Wilson, you have a beautiful home," she heard Tom say, and Sandy pulled her eyes away from the view to concentrate once more on their host.

She and Tom took the offered seats on one of the couches while Thom sat down in a nearby chair. About then a beautiful African-American woman came from the direction of the kitchen carrying a tray filled with glasses and what looked to be a pitcher of iced tea. Thom quickly stood to help her place it on the table between them.

"Please, let me introduce you to my wife, Carrie Wilson."

Sandy and Tom both stood and shook the woman's hand as she greeted them both with a gentle smile.

"Thom is so excited to see what you've brought," she said as she poured them each a glass of the cold liquid. She looked over at her husband with what Sandy could only describe in her own mind as adoration. "He hardly slept a wink last night."

Sandy chuckled. "Me neither."

She reached down and unzipped the laptop bag at her feet. "Mr. Wilson, if I may, I have a story to tell you. Then you can ask whatever questions you may have; but please, let me say what I came to say first."

She saw Thom and his wife exchange quick glances before they both turned back to look at her. Sandy knew they were confused and more than likely, concerned about why she and Tom had come to their house and what they had brought with them, but she knew once they found out the truth, it would all be worth the worry.

"Of course, Ms. Martin; please proceed," Mr. Wilson said.

Sandy took a deep breath and started to tell of how she came to own her grandmother's former house in Michigan, and how she had hired Tom to do some remodeling. When she came to the point where she described finding the secret room behind the hidden door in the laundry room closet, she knew both Mr. and Mrs. Wilson were hooked as neither spoke another word but kept their eyes glued to her. Then she reached the part of the story where she told about them finding the hidden diary, and she heard a little gasp from Mrs. Wilson.

She reached into her bag and pulled out an envelope full of photographs she had brought with them.

"Here are photos of the room," she said as she pulled a few photos out of the stack and handed them to Mr. Wilson.

Sandy told about reading the diary and discovering it had been written by a runaway slave—a young teenage girl by the name of Darcy, and how they had eventually been able to ascertain she had come from a plantation near Charleston, South Carolina. As she reached across the table to hand Mr. Wilson the stack of photos she had taken at the plantation in South Carolina, she noticed his hand was shaking. She hoped she and Tom wouldn't upset him by the news they were about to give him. Sandy waited until both of the Wilsons had time to look through the photos of Camilla House

Plantation, including those of the house and surrounding gardens and the slave quarters.

"This is where she came from?" Mr. Wilson finally asked, his voice sounding shaky to Sandy's ears.

She looked over at Tom quickly. Perhaps the Wilsons hadn't known anything about his ancestor's past. Sandy wanted to share all the information she had with him as he was Darcy's family, but she certainly didn't want to hurt him in any way.

"Yes," she finally said. "We believe Camilla House Plantation is where Darcy Brown was born and lived the first fifteen years of her life."

She saw the older man hand the photos to his wife, then take a deep breath and turn his dark brown eyes back on her.

"Please continue with your story, Ms. Martin."

Sandy nodded and then smiled gently. "Please call me Sandy, Mr. Wilson," she said.

She was rewarded with a smile from both him and his wife. "And we are Thom and Carrie, please."

Sandy smiled at them in thanks and then reached back into the bag for the reason for it all.

The diary.

As she pulled it out of her bag, then out of the plastic bag she had kept it sealed in, she knew Thom's and Carrie's eyes were locked on it.

"Is that what it looks like?" she heard Thom say, his deep voice sounding loud in the quiet room.

She nodded. "It's Darcy's diary. Tom and I found it in the hidden basement room." She stood up and reached across the table to hand it to Thom, who accepted it into his hands almost reverently.

Sandy sat back down on the couch, then reached back into her bag and pulled out a file folder. "And here are copies of all the pages of the diary I was able to scan." She handed those to Thom's wife. "I'm afraid some of the pages of the diary are in such bad shape, I couldn't get a scan of them. But those I could, I scanned into my computer photo software and touched them up enough, so they're legible." She pointed at the file folder, which Thom's wife was carefully opening. "I also typed up transcripts of what the pages of the diary have to say. They might be easier to read than the actual pages."

She fell silent as both Thom and Carrie took their turns glancing through the pages in the folder. Tom reached across the couch and took hold of her hand as they sat side by side, waiting. His hand felt warm and comforting to her, and the tears that were threatening to fall seemed to dissolve with him there beside her. She could have done this alone, but it meant so much more having him beside her.

After a few minutes, Thom looked up from the folder. "Sandy...Tom...I can't tell how much this means to me."

Sandy noticed his wife reached over to pat his hand when he couldn't continue to speak.

Then Carrie cleared her throat and spoke. "Thom researched his family history; got back as far as Darcy and Eli, and knew they were born in the United States. But, of course, there was no way to know where—or how to find any other information beyond the first census. It's not easy to trace those who were slaves."

She wiped a tear out of her eye. "But you...you started at the other end of the spectrum and came forward in time until you found us. Thank you. Thank you so much!"

Before Sandy realized what was happening, both of the Wilsons had crossed the room and pulled both her and Tom into big hugs—smiling and shaking their hands in thanks.

The Wilsons invited Tom and Sandy to stay for lunch, which was a delicious chef's salad prepared by Carrie. Sandy helped out in the kitchen, and the two of them shared bits and pieces of their lives while Carrie made the salads and Sandy got the table ready. The men sat in the family room area, and Sandy could hear their deep voices as they discussed baseball and hunting.

When the luncheon was ready, they all gathered around the table and held hands, and Thom asked a blessing on the food. When he brought up Tom's and Sandy's journey to find them, she felt Tom's hand gently squeeze hers.

"Thank you so much Heavenly Father for sending these two young people to us. Bless them for all their work in searching for my family history which led them to us. We thank you for them, Lord—and ask special blessings on them."

The talk was animated during the meal while Thom regaled them with tales of his years of teaching college English. The stories took Sandy back to her own collegiate days, and she and Tom laughed along with their hosts at the antics that young people, no matter where they were, always seemed willing to try.

After lunch, Carrie insisted on cleaning up the dishes alone while Sandy and Tom spent a little more time visiting with Thom. Sandy pulled out her laptop and loaded a couple of videos she had shot with her camera. The one of the tree 'singing' and 'whispering' in the wind almost choked her up, and she was thankful she'd thought to take videos of the laundry room closet, the hidden door, and the basement room where Darcy had been stowed so she could show them to the Thom. He continued to express his gratitude over and over at being able to see the actual spot where his great-great-grandmother had hidden during her escape.

A little later Sandy let out a sigh. It was time for Tom and her to move on, but she was so grateful she'd had this opportunity to share what they had found with Darcy's family. Before they left, she handed Thom a DVD with both videos on it and gave both him and Carrie hugs.

As Tom and Sandy followed Thom toward the door to leave, Thom turned to them. "Would you want to see where Darcy and Eli are buried?"

Sandy gasped and looked over at Tom. "Can we? Would it take us too long to get there?"

Thom turned back toward another room which turned out to be his office. He came back shortly with a map and a pen, showing Tom how to easily travel to the small cemetery east of Essex, Ontario.

"It will take you about eight hours to get there so you may want to stay the night somewhere along the way," Thom added. "But it will take less time to get back to southern Michigan this way as you can cross back into the U.S. at Detroit."

Sandy was ecstatic when Tom agreed with the plan to go home that way. She had never dreamed they'd have the opportunity to actually visit Darcy's grave, so this was an added bonus.

They spent the night in rooms in a small inn east of Sudbury and then headed out after an early breakfast. Tom and Sandy stopped once for a quick lunch, and again at a flower shop right outside of Essex to buy flowers to place on Darcy's grave.

When they finally arrived in Essex, it was to discover a small, timeworn cemetery, surrounded by woods but neatly maintained. Thom had told them exactly where to find Darcy's and Eli's tombstones, so they had no difficulty locating them. The stones were upright flat sandstones, the names and dates faded by over a hundred years of winds and weather. Eli's was in such bad shape you almost couldn't read it, but Sandy was able to run her fingers lightly across the front and tell what Darcy's said.

Darcy Wilson, Beloved wife of Elijah. 1843-1899

Sandy did a quick calculation in her head. Darcy had lived to be 56 years old—a relatively long life in those days. She placed the bouquet of flowers in front of Darcy's stone and stood there, staring at the words on the tombstone and wondering if Darcy had a good life after her escape. Sandy had to believe she had.

Beloved wife...

In those two words was the story of Darcy's days on earth. She had been loved, and Sandy was so thankful to know it.

Sandy felt Tom's presence next to her and his hand came out to take hold of hers as if sensing she needed to feel the touch of another human right then. She was trying to hold back her tears. After months of searching for the truth about Darcy and her story, she should be joyful. She'd accomplished her goal and found Darcy's family and returned the diary to its rightful owners. There wasn't anything to cry about—other than she couldn't help but wonder about those two little words.

Beloved wife.

Those two words held the significance of Darcy's life, and it made Sandy wonder. Would she ever know how it felt to be someone's beloved wife? She felt the light squeeze of the hand of the man beside her and turned her teary eyes on his ruggedly handsome face.

Well if nothing else, at least she had a friend.

✞✞✞✞

It was four-thirty when Tom turned Sandy's car down the familiar road leading to her house. It had been a long trip in a few short days, and he was sure she was exhausted and ready to be home.

He was tired too, but he had greatly enjoyed having Sandy all to himself. Even though during the long drives they hadn't talked much about anything important, it had meant so much to him to know she had wanted him to go with her. He wouldn't have missed this trip for anything. To see the look on her face when she had delivered Darcy's diary to her great-great-grandson had been priceless.

Now they had come back to Bradford Mills and their real lives, and he had to decide what he was going to do about telling Sandy the truth of his feelings. He had put it off for days due to the trip. He had thought a couple of times about trying to talk to her on the road as they'd both been distracted by the traffic. This was something he wanted to give his full attention to when he talked with her. Now they were home again, there were no more reasons for stalling.

Tom pulled the car into her driveway, noticing right away the old fallen pine tree had been entirely cut up and taken away. He heard Sandy's gasp as she looked upon her now clean—and very empty looking—front yard.

"Oh, my!" she whispered.

They sat in the car for a moment and looked at what now sat in place of the old pine tree. Then Tom opened his car door at the same time Sandy exited her side. Together they walked over to the spot where the pine tree had once stood.

"Beverly and the Historical Society must have done it," she said quietly. "I had no idea they were planning to do this!"

Standing in place of the tree was a large flat slab of the trunk, turned outward, with a plaque installed on the heavily varnished surface of the tree. Tom slowly read it out loud.

"'At this spot, a historic tree stood for over a hundred and fifty years. It was used as a beacon for the Underground Railroad to lead those searching for freedom from slavery.'"

He heard Sandy sniff a little and had to wipe a few tears from the corners of his own eyes—especially when he realized what else Beverly had done.

Planted nearby was a little tree with another small plaque placed on the ground in front of it.

This weeping cherry is planted in memory of those who made it to freedom—and especially those who did not.

"Oh Tom," Sandy finally squeaked out. "I had no idea Beverly had this planned."

Tom reached out and was pleasantly surprised when Sandy willingly came to stand within the circle of his arms, reaching around his waist with her arms in a hug. They stood that way for a time, and Tom was hoping Sandy wasn't scared away by what he was sure was his rapidly beating heartbeat.

He could have held her that way for the rest of his life.

Eventually, though, she sniffed and pulled away. "Well, time to unload the car."

She walked away from him, and he dutifully followed to help get her bags into the house and put his in the back of his waiting pickup truck. He dropped the last piece of her luggage on the kitchen floor and tried to come up with something to say to delay his departure. He wasn't ready to say goodbye and end this precious time they'd had together.

He watched Sandy puttering around the kitchen, looking lonely and forlorn. What was she going to obsess about now, he wondered? Now she'd found Darcy's family and delivered the diary, what would be her next mission?

"I need to make sure Beverly Titus and the Historical Society have copies of everything I gave to Thom, don't you think?"

He smiled at her gently. "I'm sure they will greatly appreciate it. Are you going to send copies to that place in South Carolina too?"

His heart started thudding again as she turned her big eyes on him.

"Oh, yes. I almost forgot about Camilla House Plantation. I promised Matthew I would send him copies of all of it too."

Tom clenched his jaw, feeling jealousy rear its ugly head. Matthew, huh? Whoever this Matthew guy was, he hoped he stayed in South Carolina for a long time.

"Well," he began to say it was time for him to head home but was interrupted.

"Stay for dinner, Tom. Please?"

He looked at her glowing face pleading with him, and he was a goner.

"You know I can't turn down a homemade meal, Sandy," he quipped, putting a grin on his face.

He was rewarded with her beautiful smile spreading across her face and the twinkle returning to her emerald green eyes.

✟✟✟✟

Sandy finally exhaled when Tom agreed to stay for dinner. She wasn't ready for him to leave—not yet. After these past days together—away from the rest of the world where it was only the two of them—she wasn't ready for it to be over and go back to life as normal.

Somehow she still needed to come up with the courage to apologize to him for judging him—wrongly, as it turned out. She had procrastinated long enough. If, after she spilled her guts to him, he decided he didn't want to be her friend anymore—well then, she guessed she had it coming. She hadn't been much of a friend.

While Tom put the plates and silverware on the table, she quickly threw together a dinner consisting of ham and cheese omelets, with extra cheese on his. She enjoyed seeing him make his way around her kitchen, and it tickled her to realize he'd spent enough time at her house he knew which drawer held the silverware and what cupboard door to open to find the glasses.

He didn't even need to ask.

The small talk while they ate revolved around their trip to Canada and what they had found. Sandy had taken lots of photos while they were there. She had pictures of Thom and Carrie receiving the diary and documents and had also taken a photo of Darcy's tombstone—her final resting place. Now she had to pull all the information together to complete the article she knew Mr. Drayton was expecting.

But first, she had to pay her dues.

While Tom finished up the last few bites of his evening meal, she sat silently and waited, her hands nervously tearing apart the paper napkin resting in her lap. As soon as he finished eating, she would tell him.

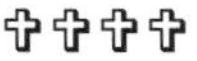

"Hmmm," Tom moaned as he pushed his now empty plate away from him. "That was a great omelet, Sandy Martin. It was just what I needed after a long trip."

He looked across the table to watch her sitting quietly and pushing the remains of her dinner around on the plate. Something was obviously bothering her. Before he had a chance to say anything further though, he saw her place her hands flat on the table and look up at him.

"I know we've already talked a little about when you went to Louisiana, but I have a confession to make to you Tom, and I owe you an apology."

That wasn't what he expected. "Why? I'm the one who left town without telling you."

She shook her head, her red, curly hair bouncing across her shoulders and around her face. "You didn't owe me any explanations, Tom. What you did, or where you went, was none of my business. No, I'm talking about something else."

She stopped talking for a second and chewed on her lower lip. Tom's eyes were so focused on those lips he almost missed what she said next.

"I'm embarrassed to admit it, but I thought you and my cousin Kate had something going on."

He was sure his mouth fell open at her words. "What? Why would you say that?"

"Well...." she stammered. "You spend all your time with Robbie, and I thought maybe you might even be his father..."

Tom stared at her in shock. She had thought him capable of doing something like that? What kind of man did she think he was? No wonder she had pushed him away.

"I know now I was wrong," she quickly added. "Kate told me you were Robbie's Big Brother and nothing was going on between the two of you, and there never had been...." Her voice faded away again as those beautiful eyes pleaded with him for understanding. "It really was none of my business."

Tom sighed and stood up. He saw her head go up and her eyes turn into huge saucers. Was she afraid of him?

Then he realized he probably appeared angry with her and she thought he was going to walk out. When she had first started her explanation, he had briefly wondered if he should just leave. Maybe he should be furious with her for believing the worst of him. Why hadn't she come to him and asked him the necessary questions, rather than assuming the worst? But then, there had been a time when he had been the very man she was describing, so why should he be surprised. So she'd made a poor judgment call. So she'd thought less of him than he would prefer. Based on his former life, could he blame her? His pride had taken a huge hit, but it didn't change his feelings where she was concerned. If he had his way, he'd spend the rest of his life proving to her she'd been wrong about him.

He gave his head a little shake and slowly walked around the table and pulled out the chair next to hers, his eyes never leaving her face. As he moved closer to her, he saw the tension leave her face. He reached over and gently pulled her hands off the table top to hold in his.

"There has never been, and there never will be anything between Kate and me," he stated, trying to keep his voice calm and clear.

He clenched his jaw in nervousness. Now came the most difficult part of the conversation for him. This was what he had put off during the last few days while they made their sojourn to Canada. What would he do if she rejected him? He wasn't sure he'd survive it.

Tom swallowed hard and took a deep breath. "That's because I am in love with someone else, Sandy." Her eyes grew large again, but at least she didn't pull her hands out of his.

"I ran away to Louisiana because I thought she didn't want to have anything to do with me, but," he paused a second and let go of her right hand to reach up and touch her cheek with his fingertips. "I never stopped loving her."

He saw Sandy swallow, her eyes never leaving his face. Did she understand what he was telling her? Was he being clear enough? He needed to make absolutely sure she understood.

"It's you, Sandy. It's always been you. God brought you into my life years ago, and I've never been able to forget you. Now He's brought you back into my life, and I've discovered I can't live without you."

She still hadn't said anything, and he was starting to worry he'd bared his heart and was now about to have it shattered. What would he do if she didn't feel the same way about him?

"Me?" he finally heard her squeak out. She cleared her throat and reached out to touch his lips with the fingertips of her free hand. "You are in love with me?"

He felt all the love for her he'd kept bottled up inside spill over. "Yes, I am." He chuckled. "Is that a problem, 'cause if it is, I'll go back to Louisiana and never bother you again."

The shocked look came back to her eyes, and she pulled her other hand free from his to grab his face with both her hands.

"Oh no, you don't, mister."

She brought her lips to his, and the sweetness of them was almost his undoing. His heart was so filled with love for her, he thought it might burst. He grinned at her when they finally broke apart.

"Does this mean you might like me a little?"

Sandy laughed the beautiful little laugh of hers and poked him in the chest. "You silly man. I'm in love with you. Can't you tell? Why else would I be dying of jealousy?"

Tom grinned, feeling as if he'd just run a marathon and won. She loved him after all. God was good! He inhaled a breath and took a huge sigh of relief.

"Well then, I want to ask you on a date. We need to take some time to get to know each other a little better before we make any real commitments." He brushed her cheek with the knuckles of his right hand.

"I want you to be sure, Sandy, and we haven't dated or anything...I don't want to rush things...."

He was surprised when she laughed.

"Well, I'm certainly not against dating for a while, Tom—but you do remember, don't you? It won't be our first date."

Tom had to laugh at the cheeky grin on her face. "Okay, all right. Well then, I want to officially ask you on our second date."

She reached out and brought his face to hers for another kiss. When they finally pulled away from each other, she whispered, "I'd be happy to go anywhere with you, Tom Brannigan."

EPILOGUE

It was a perfect late July day in northern Michigan, with a cooling breeze blowing in from the lake to make the heat of the summer day comfortable. Sandy relaxed in an Adirondack chair on the grounds of The Grand Hotel on Mackinac Island, gazing toward Lake Michigan and The Mighty Mackinac Bridge. She let out a sigh of contentment and smiled. Mackinac Island had always been on her list of places she'd wanted to visit, but she had never thought she'd get to. She couldn't believe she was actually here.

Suddenly a shadow blocked her view, and she looked up to see a familiar silhouette blocking the sun. He leaned down to give her a lingering kiss, then moved to sit in the chair next to her, reaching across the open space between the two chairs to hold her hand.

"So, what do you think, Mrs. Brannigan? Was this what you had in mind for a honeymoon?"

Sandy chuckled. "I love it, Tom. You couldn't have chosen a more beautiful place!"

She rubbed her thumb across his knuckles and let her mind wander as she once again leaned back in the chair to relax. Tom and she had been almost inseparable after returning from their trip to Canada and the dinner conversation that had changed their relationship. As Tom had requested, they had dated—gone to dinner, movies, church functions, had picnics; they had basically spent all their time together every opportunity they got. She had been afraid at first he might get tired of being with her all the time, but he never had.

Neither had he asked the question for which she was waiting.

So, Sandy had kept busy. She had donated the information and photos she had about Darcy's story to the Bradford Mills Historical Society. The Society had created a wall for information about the local Underground Railroad and had incorporated all the information about Darcy, including another slab of the trunk of the old pine tree Beverly Titus had saved for that purpose.

Sandy had also mailed a huge packet of information to Matthew Pierce in South Carolina for inclusion in the Camilla House Plantation museum. She knew he had asked her to deliver the information in person, but she wasn't interested in making the trip back. She had seen the plantation once, and that was only to get a feel for Darcy's birthplace and the place she had run away from. There was nothing there to draw her back for another visit.

The Thanksgiving holiday had come and gone with Sandy spending it with Tom and his Mom, Katie and Robbie, and several people from the church, including Pastor Armstrong and his wife, Trudy. Then Christmas had arrived, and she had taken special joy in setting up her decorated Christmas tree in the bay window of her house—the same location her grandma had used all those years ago. Sandy had received a beautiful sweater and necklace from Tom, and she had bought him a level and the newest best-selling mystery novel. She had secretly hoped for a ring box under the tree but was trying her best to be patient, knowing the timing of their relationship was in God's hands—as was their entire lives.

Finally, when she was beginning to fear it was never going to happen, Tom had popped the big question New Year's Eve after a special candlelight service at the church. And of course, she had said yes.

Suddenly they were thrown into the madness of planning a wedding. Even though Tom had assured her she didn't have to, she had wanted a small wedding with only a few friends and family attending. They had a large reception following the ceremony with what she was sure was the entire town of Bradford Mills attending. God had truly blessed them both with wonderful friends, and it had been a joyous occasion.

And now here they were in this idyllic setting, watching the sun drop lower in the horizon.

Three days from now they would go back to the reality of their lives in Bradford Mills. For now at least, Sandy still had the job at the library, and Tom's calendar was filled with a lineup of jobs for his construction business. But ever since their return from Canada, Sandy had been thinking about a special project, and had even started working on it.

She took a deep breath. "Tom, I'm considering writing a book—a historical novel—based on the story of Darcy Brown. I've had it on my mind ever since we got back from Canada...."

The firm squeeze of his hand was confirmation he was listening.

"What a great idea, Sandy!

Sandy gave him a smile. "I initially thought about writing it as a non-fiction book telling Darcy's story, but I don't want to do anything to disturb Thom's privacy, so I thought a Christian fiction novel sounded better. What do you think?"

She felt him squeeze her hand again. "I'm sure anything you decide will be great. You're the writer, and you'll have to tell the story God gives you to tell." He paused for a moment. "Do you have any idea what you'll name it?"

Sandy gazed out over the blue waters of Lake Michigan on a late summer's eve and smiled as an image of a tall pine tree came to her mind.

"I'm thinking of calling it, "The Whispering Sentinel."

THE END

SANDY'S CHILI SAUCE/SALSA

(Note: this is a sweet, mild relish)

12 Ripe Tomatoes, Large (peeled)
2 White onions
2 Green peppers
1/2 Tablespoon cinnamon
1/4 teaspoon ground cloves
1/4 teaspoon allspice
1/2 cup white granulated sugar
3/4 pint vinegar
1 - 6 oz. can tomato paste

Chop the vegetables and add to the vinegar, sugar and spices in a large pan.
Cook for three hours, covered, stirring occasionally.
Then place in sterilized canning jars and seal.

Yield: Approximately 6 pints

Hint: The easiest way to peel the tomatoes is to place them in a sink of very hot water for a moment before peeling them. The hot water makes it much easier to pull off the peel.

Find out more about the Author on the following page!

**Thank you so much for reading my book.
If you've enjoyed it,
please check out my other books at Amazon.com:**

"True Cover" - Book I

"True Cover-Book 2-Bluecreek Ranch"

*"The Dove and The Raven -
A Christian Historical Romance"*

"Endless Season"
A contemporary Christian Romance

You can also check out my Facebook page at:
www.facebook.com/ruthkyser.author

and Barnes & Noble at:
http://www.barnesandnoble.com/c/ruth-kyser

and my blog "A Few of My Thoughts" at:
http://ruthkyser.wordpress.com/

or my Twitter page at: @kyser_r

Or you can email me at:
ruth.kyser@gmail.com

I greatly enjoy hearing from my readers!

Made in the USA
Columbia, SC
15 March 2018